"Do you have a badge?" she asked him.

"I never bring it when I work undercover."

Autumn had no reason not to believe him. He'd just saved her. "What now?"

"I'm going to get you to your room safely."

Was that all? Did she hope there'd be more? The elevator stopped and they stepped out. She realized she'd never see him again after this.

"I could come in for a little while," he said.

Why did strange new men appeal to her so much? Strange new *masculine* men. Good-looking men. This was a dangerous habit....

His green eyes never left hers when they entered the room.

"I bet you're a really good agent."

"Among other things," he murmured as he leaned in to kiss her.

She closed her eyes to sweet sensation while a faint inner voice cautioned, *Don't do it*.

She didn't listen.

Dear Reader,

For this story, I wanted a strong, sexy, mysterious hero. He had to be tough, a little bit of a lawbreaker and a loner. But principled. Meet Raith De Matteis. His flaws are all wrapped around his relationship with his estranged father. It's an emotional reunion—one I won't give away here!

The second oldest daughter of a famous movie producer, Autumn Ivy's brave independence is just what Raith needs. She pushes him with his father and helps him grow as a man. A good thing, too, since the secret she's keeping will change his life forever.

Welcome to the third story of the Ivy Avenger's miniseries, where two independent hearts learn that solitude won't keep the press away—or their love.

Jennifer Morey

ONE SECRET NIGHT

—

Jennifer Morey

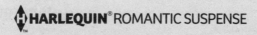
HARLEQUIN® ROMANTIC SUSPENSE

Recycling programs
for this product may
not exist in your area.

ISBN-13: 978-0-373-27887-9

ONE SECRET NIGHT

Copyright © 2014 by Jennifer Morey

Printed in U.S.A.

www.Harlequin.com

JENNIFER MOREY

A two-time 2009 RITA® Award nominee and a Golden Quill winner for Best First Book for *The Secret Soldier*, Jennifer Morey writes contemporary romance and romantic suspense. Project manager *par jour*, she works for the space systems segment of a satellite imagery and information company. She lives in sunny Denver, Colorado. She can be reached through her website, www.jennifermorey.com, and on Facebook.

For Allie, my new baby girl, a beautiful, sweet, five-year-old rescued Australian Shepherd. She's discovered how much fun being a dog can be and no longer shies away from the strange, boxy thing that I type with and always put on my lap.

Chapter 1

One of Hollywood's favorite heartbreakers had just spent the day being an ordinary tourist in distressed-denim jeans. Being normal rejuvenated Autumn Ivy. Here, she was no longer a spectacle. Here, she could escape the ridiculous extravaganza over the last man to fall prey to her flirtation. All of that had fallen away with the sights of Iceland's spectacular southern coastline.

Autumn entered the hotel, almost regretting the day had come to an end.

The guide had taken her and the other tourists in the group through villages, Skaftafell National Park and the Skogafoss waterfall. Most memorable was the boat ride in the Jokulsarlon glacial lagoon. The boat could also drive on land. She'd taken pictures of icebergs covered in volcanic ash floating out to sea and gorges and valleys of the enormous Vatnajokull glacier. Everything about this day had been perfect. Everything except the jeans.

Slinging her purse from left shoulder to right hip, her waterproof hiking boots touched soundlessly on the tiled floor as she headed for the elevators. Her long, light red hair swung in a tight ponytail. It was around seven and she'd stopped for dinner on the way back to the hotel. She couldn't wait to soak in the Jacuzzi in her room and put on a pretty nightgown. Maybe she'd do her nails.

A man with a shaved head waited at the elevators. His gray eyes followed her movements as she stopped a few feet from him to wait. He'd already pressed the button. Thin and over six feet tall, he looked to be in his late thirties. The way he kept watching her made her uneasy. It was almost ten at night and there weren't many people in the lobby.

Another man approached. This one drew her eye much more notably. A couple of inches taller than the shaved-head man, his body was sculpted with muscle. Autumn feasted on the sight of him. Dressed all in black, from his sturdy leather boots and cargo pants to the long-sleeved Under Armour shirt with a quarter zip, he had black hair that was far above his shoulders but thick. His green eyes glowed like lanterns and zeroed in on her. Dark stubble added to his manly appearance. So did the way he moved, smooth and sure. The platform of his chest and bulging arms oozed testosterone, but the bulge of his crotch stirred her curiosity most.

Although man enough to add to her heartbreaker reputation, she'd rather stay out of the limelight awhile longer. The elevator doors opened and Autumn debated whether she should wait for the next one. The shaved-head man stepped inside, and the other man followed. The two eyed each other and then waited for her. The shaved-head man pressed the button that would keep the door open, and the man in black didn't seem to like that. Autumn shook off the weird feeling she had and stepped into the elevator.

The man in black pressed the top floor, which also happened to be hcrs. The other man pressed the button for the sixth floor.

Standing nearest the elevator doors, Autumn glanced back to her right at the man with the shaved head. His gaze shifted from the other man to her. She glanced back to her left. The man in black looked right at her.

She faced forward, watching the floor lights as the elevator slowed to a stop at the sixth floor. The doors began to slide open.

The shaved-head man stepped forward, but instead of getting out of the elevator, he hooked his arm around Autumn's waist, pinning her arms and locking her against him. She sucked in a startled breath. Was that a knife he had at her throat? While she struggled not to panic, he turned with her and backed out of the elevator. The man in black had drawn a gun from somewhere in his clothes. How had he concealed it? Autumn met the stranger's green eyes and felt him assess her. She focused on his cool demeanor and kept fear from robbing her of clear thought.

"Why are you following me?" the man who held her asked, stopping out in the hall.

"Let her go and I won't have to kill you," came the other man's unruffled response.

Autumn looked down the hall without moving her head. It was empty. The stranger took a step forward and the man behind her adjusted his hold. She unzipped her purse at the same time. If she could get to her Mace...

"Don't come any closer," the shaved-head man said.

"Let her go."

The stranger wasn't going to negotiate. There was something ominous about him. Deadly.

"Wait a minute…I *know* you," the shaved-head man said.

"Let her go or die."

They knew each other? Autumn sensed the man behind her assess the bigger one and see that he was not afraid. She believed he would kill the one with the knife to her throat. Her captor must have picked up on the same signals. The hand with the knife faltered as though he was considering leaving her and running.

He glanced down the hall. In his brief distraction, the other man fired a silenced shot. But instead of shooting to kill, he shot lower. Her captor yelled and his grasp on her loosened as he stumbled. Autumn shoved the knife away from her and twisted free to run down the hall.

As she looked back, she tripped and fell, tumbling over the commercial-grade carpeting. Sitting on her rear, hands braced behind her, she watched the shaved-head man stagger into the stairwell and the man in black follow.

Autumn considered making a run for her room. A sense of obligation stopped her. The stranger had saved her and she couldn't leave without making sure he was all right. Dangerous curiosity played into her motivation, as well. Why had he gone after the shaved-head man and how did the two know each other?

Climbing to her feet, she adjusted her purse and hurried to the stairwell door. Inside, she saw the man in black kick the other down a flight of stairs and then jog down after him. On that landing, the shaved-head man blocked the first two of the stranger's strikes and then missed the next few well-placed blows. The man in black moved fluidly, blocking the smaller man's attempted kick and then jumping up and pushing off the wall with his feet. Airborne, he swung his leg and clocked the other man on the side of the head before flipping his body back to the floor. The other man fell against the metal railing, retaliating with an unsteady swipe of the knife. The man in black had to leap back to avoid being sliced.

That's when Autumn realized he'd tucked his gun into the back waist of his pants. He didn't intend to kill the man. He kicked the other man's arm before he had a chance to stab him. The knife flew into the air and fell to the cement floor. The smaller man charged, ramming the man in black. The two crashed against the wall. The man in black rammed his knee to the other man's sternum. A punch sent the man back a step. The smaller man had managed to come away with the man in black's gun. But he kicked that man's wrist again and the gun went the way of the knife. Before the smaller man could recover, the man in black drove his hand into his throat. Stumbling backward, the smaller man choked and gurgled, putting his hand to his neck. Falling against the opposite wall, he stared at the man in black and then slumped to the floor, where he went motionless.

Had the man in black just killed him?

Autumn gripped the cold metal railing.

Bending to pick up his gun, the man in black tucked it back into his pants, where she now noticed there was a holster that his shirt covered. Then he went to the man's body and began searching his clothes, all very methodical and cold. Finding a cell phone, he stuffed that into his front pant pocket and then looked up at her before climbing the stairs.

He was a man practiced at what he'd just done. Kill a man with one hand…

Things like this never happened to her. They happened

to her siblings Arizona and Lincoln. Not her. Shopping happened to her. Nail salons. Trips to new and exotic places.

The stranger stopped before her. "We have to get out of here."

She came out of her stupor. "Wh-what?" Did he mean to run away?

He took her hand in his and led her up to the next floor.

"We have to call the police," she said.

"No police."

Were they going to leave the body there for someone to find? She began to resist, tugging her hand. She'd go contact the police. The fact that he had no intention of doing so made her suspect he had a criminal element to him.

"Let me go," she demanded.

At the door leading out of the stairwell, he stopped and put his hands on her shoulders. "That man was wanted by the FBI. I tracked him here and was supposed to arrest him."

But he hadn't had the chance. The man had taken her hostage. It was only when the other man had gone after his gun that he'd had to use deadly force.

"You're FBI?" She began to feel marginally better. "What did he do?"

"He's a well-known assassin."

"An…" He killed people? "He said he knew you."

"His name is Tabor Creighton. I've been looking for him for a while now."

This was too strange and unreal. Should she trust this man? What he'd told her so far seemed plausible and yet she hesitated. "How do you know each other?"

He cocked his head in growing impatience.

"Tell me or we part ways right now and I'm calling security." She dug out her phone for her purse.

Before she could lift it all the way out, he put his hand on her wrist. She looked up.

"One of the people he murdered was a woman who was rescued from the Middle East."

What did he mean, rescued? "Why did he murder her?" Was it just her or was he reluctant to talk about this?

"She met and married an Arab man in the United States, who then convinced her to move with him to his homeland. She had two kids with him and finally couldn't take his mistreatment any longer. She was killed less than a month after her rescue. Her children are being raised by her parents now."

"Oh…" she breathed with the awfulness of that, looking down the stairs. The assassin was out of sight, but she imagined him there. How terrible for some unwitting person to stumble upon all that gore. "Okay, he's a bad person, but we can't just leave him lying there."

After a moment of considering her, he said, "I was going to get you out of here first." Then he took out a phone and made a call. "Yes. Hello. I was just visiting someone in a room here and heard a gunshot. It sounded like it came from the stairwell." With that, and the faint sound of the clerk asking him questions, he disconnected and put his phone away.

"Let's go." He held out his hand.

She didn't take it. Folding her arms, she stuck out her right foot. "Why aren't we calling the police? And why did you hang up on that person like that?"

"This is Iceland." He opened the stairwell door. "Come with me."

She just stood there, all too aware of a dead man in the stairwell below and not sure about this stranger yet. "I don't like this. It's sneaky and immoral." Did he have something to hide?

Still holding the door open, he said, "I'll tell the SAC what happened and he'll deal with the politics. Please don't make me deal with the politics. I didn't think he was going to take a hostage."

"What's a sack?" She lowered her arms and moved toward the door.

"Special Agent in Charge. My boss."

Still uncertain but believing him, she went into the hallway. "Won't the security cameras show us fighting that man?"

He walked down the hall beside her. "I disabled the system before I went after him."

At the elevator, he pressed the up button while she gaped at him.

"Why did you do that?" she asked when he didn't volunteer any explanation.

"I have to protect my identity."

As an FBI agent? Her attention drifted to his muscular arms and chest, biceps stretching the material of the black shirt. When she looked up and saw him notice, she jerked her head forward. How bizarre. A man was just killed and she was attracted to his killer. She couldn't deny she had a weakness for hot men, but should she be concerned?

"Do you have a badge?" she asked.

"I never bring it when I work undercover," he said.

He was working undercover. She tried not to be awed by that. But it did explain a lot...*if* he'd told the truth. She didn't really have a reason not to believe him. Still, there was something off about him. And then not. It would be different if he had been the one with the knife to her throat. Instead, he'd been the one who'd saved her. An FBI agent.

The elevator doors slid open and they stepped inside. He pressed her floor.

"What's your name?" he asked.

She scoffed. "What's *yours?*"

He grinned. "Russ Markham. I'd show you my passport, but I left it in the rental."

"Is that your *real* name?" Folding her arms again, she watched the numbers climb on the elevator.

"It's what my passport says."

In other words, it was probably his cover name. Should she be bothered by that? Strangely, she wasn't. He wasn't lying to her. "Autumn Ivy."

The way his gaze roamed all over her for a brief moment revealed his pleasure that she'd let down her guard.

She dropped her arms. "What now?"

"I'm going to make sure you get to your room safely."

Was that all? Did she hope there would be more? The elevator stopped at the top floor and she stepped out ahead of him.

"What brings you to Iceland?" he asked, now walking beside her.

"A job. I'm a translator. A commercial contractor needed me to talk to the local workers. I only have another week to go."

"You speak Icelandic?"

"And a few other languages, yes."

His brow rose. "You must be smart."

"No, I just like to travel." She stopped at her suite door. "I've never been to Iceland."

"So you learn the language of everywhere you want to go?"

"Not everywhere. Sometimes I just visit places, but I'm not the kind of girl who can handle a lot of downtime. I like to stay busy. Stability, routine—not for me."

That was why she hadn't settled down yet. Being settled equaled stability and routine.

A long moment passed during which he just looked at her with high regard. "An adventurer, are you?"

"Yes, I suppose I am." That was one word to describe it. Insatiably curious, and craver of new discoveries was more accurate.

"Not afraid of much, either," he said. "You handled yourself pretty well back there."

She shrugged off the compliment. She had been afraid. "Nothing to fear but fear itself, right?" That was survival.

He seemed to like her response. "Right."

More time rolled by as they just stood there looking at each other.

"Are you staying at this hotel?" she asked, shamelessly flirting.

"No." He glanced at her still-closed hotel room door.

It suddenly occurred to her that she'd never see him again after this.

Another long moment passed where they said nothing and communicated only with their eyes.

"I could come in for a little while…" he finally said.

She watched his mouth as he said that and while caution reared up inside her, a natural, insistent response kept it from taking over. She didn't know him. Should she let a stranger into her room? He worked for the FBI. And she wasn't getting any eerie vibes from him. She could sense a person's overall goodness and he came across as relatively harmless.

Not one to shy away from impulse and chances, she said, "All right."

She dug out her room key from her purse and opened the suite door.

Wood flooring and modern furnishings welcomed them. Dim light came from a lamp on a table next to a taupe-colored sofa with red-and-white pillows. The windows all along the far wall were dark now.

Russ wandered over there. Autumn joined him, seeing flashing lights in the parking lot below. She wanted to ignore the reminder of what had brought them to this moment.

"When will you call your SAC?" she asked him.

"In the morning. He doesn't like to be bothered at night."

She supposed that was reasonable. The assassin was dead and local authorities were on the scene. But was he using delay tactics? How would she know if he called his SAC? And did it matter if she did? Maybe she was still shaken up over what had happened.

Turning away from the window, she asked, "Something to drink?"

"Whatever you're having."

At the small bar area, she began to uncork a bottle of red wine she'd asked to be brought to her room. Maybe this would help her sleep tonight.

Russ appeared beside her, making her jump. He was so quiet. Reaching for the bottle opener, his hand touched hers as he took it from her. Seared by acute awareness, she inched away and waited for him to open the bottle and pour two glasses. Why did strange new men appeal to her so much? Strange, new, *masculine* men. Good-looking men. Maybe this was dangerous behavior. Maybe she deserved what the media said about her and her dating habits.

She often justified herself with the explanation that

she wasn't ready to settle down, but what if there was more to her taste for men like Russ?

He handed her a glass of wine and she held it while he took a sip from his and observed her with those gorgeous green eyes.

"Where do you live?" she asked.

"Lander, Wyoming."

"Hmm." She nodded. "Do you like it there?" Mundane conversation defused some of the puzzling chemistry mixing between them.

"Yes. It's quiet and remote."

Agents like him probably preferred their solitude. Or was there a different reason he preferred quiet and remote?

"You?" he asked.

"Dallas, Texas. And sometimes Colorado. I just bought a new place in Denver." She scanned the room of the suite. "But I travel a lot." And that's the way she liked it.

"You must be doing well in your career. Two houses." Since he was keeping secrets from her, she'd keep one of her own. "Yes, I am." He didn't need to know who her father was. The great Jackson Ivy, famous movie producer. He was the reason many of her relationships didn't last. Either the men she met already knew who her father was, or as soon as they found out, the game changed and she became desirable for that rather than her charming personality and good looks.

"Do you have family in Wyoming?" she asked.

"No." He didn't say more, taking his glass and walking over to the sofa.

Autumn found that curious. Following him, she asked, "Not a big family?"

Bending for the remote, he held the glass in the other

as he turned on the television. "I have a dad in Phoenix and a brother in San Diego. He has a family of his own. I don't see them much."

Watching him surf channels, she wondered if he needed the distraction. She moved closer, a warm part of her drawing her to do so. "Because of your work?"

Finding a sports channel, he put the remote down and straightened to face her, taking in her close proximity before he finally answered. "I haven't spoken to my dad since I was seventeen." She caught a brief flash of emotion in his eyes before he continued. "My brother left the house when I was fourteen. He's four years older than me. My mother died a few months before he left."

"Oh." She almost regretted asking. Although he explained his family so matter-of-factly, he had to have some negative baggage over losing his mother at the age of fourteen. "I'm sorry…about your mother."

"It was a long time ago."

"How old are you now?"

"Forty. Your turn." He took a big sip, clearly finished discussing his family.

Okaaay…

"I have a *big* family." She felt the megawatt smile spreading on her face as she thought of them all. "Seven brothers and sisters. Parents are still married. We're spread all over the States. I'm second oldest, and I'm thirty-nine." They were so close in age.

He lifted his gaze from her smiling mouth. "And not married."

Sparks showered through her. "No. Are you?"

He laughed once. "No."

"You say that as though it was a joke."

Now he sobered. "I've never met anyone independent enough to put up with me."

She was independent. Fiercely so. She had the reputation to prove it. Taming the wild attraction racing through her, Autumn stepped around him and sat on the sofa. He put his glass down on a side table and sat beside her.

"Is adventure what made you decide to become an FBI agent?" she asked, needing to keep the topic casual.

"That was part of it."

"What was the other part?" He intrigued her so much. She couldn't pinpoint why. His mystery. His masculinity. Both…

"It seemed better than going into politics."

He didn't strike her as the political type, not the conventional kind anyway. "You were going to get into politics?"

"I studied international relations in college."

Mmm…a college man…rugged *and* educated. "Did you aspire to be president?"

"Of course. Political issues interested me."

In his youth, he'd thought anything was possible, but as he grew older, something had changed his mind. "So, why didn't you follow that path?"

"I realized politicians only care about their own special interests. Nothing moves where it should in the time that it should. They have their perks and holidays and no one really takes any real risks to make a true difference. They get in the way of progress rather than move it forward."

He felt strongly on the matter. She liked a man with an opinion.

"Are you a Republican or a Democrat?" she asked in a flirtatious tone.

"I'm a nonconformist," he answered in kind.

"Rebel?"

He grinned, really sexy. "All the way."

She leaned toward him, loving his candor. "I bet you're a really good agent."

Leaning closer to her, he murmured, "Among other things."

When he kissed her, she closed her eyes, surrendering to sweet sensation while a faint inner voice cautioned, *Don't do it.*

Chapter 2

Caution had never been one of Autumn's strongest traits. Caution deprived her of excitement. And this man excited her.

After kissing for several minutes, Autumn stood and backed up, giving him a come-hither look he couldn't mistake.

Russ got up and she walked backward all the way to the suite bedroom. When she came to the bed, she stopped and began to undress.

"Take your clothes off, agent man," she said.

He complied, both of them not looking away until the last of their clothes lay in piles on the floor. He aroused her further with the caress of his gaze all over her nakedness. She did the same but took less time. When he finished and took a step toward her, she pulled the covers back and got onto the bed.

Lying back on the cool sheets, she reveled in the sight

of Russ climbing over her. She reached for him, touching rigid muscles, running her hands down his beautiful body and then curling her hand around his impressive hardness. If she wasn't so taken by him, she'd be ashamed of her wantonness.

"I don't normally do this," she confessed.

He lowered himself onto her and pressed his mouth to hers.

"I usually get to know a man first." And then left them.

"Me, too." He kept kissing her, but she wasn't ready yet.

"Except the last one." She almost lost her train of thought as he kissed her deeper. "I didn't know him, either."

Now Russ lifted his head and looked down at her as she continued.

"I broke up with him before coming to Iceland."

"Maybe this isn't such a good idea." He started to roll off of her.

"No." She tightened her arm around his back. "No." He felt so good on her. Knox was a one-time thing. This... this felt different. With Knox, it had been sexual. With Russ, there was something else. A connection.

"I just need you to know that I don't usually do this."

"I heard you the first time."

His was patient, ready for whatever she decided. And his gravelly voice turned her on.

"I'm ready now," she murmured, in pure response to his voice.

"Are you sure?" he asked.

"Yes." Oh, yes. "This is different than the last one."

With heat in his eyes, he kissed her. Softly but briefly.

"This is different than anyone," he said, his voice doing intimate things to her.

He couldn't have chosen a better response. He felt it, too. What tomorrow brought, neither could speculate, but the reward of being together right now outweighed stopping and going their separate ways.

"Let's see how sure you are." He kissed her again, a sensuous caress that went on for endless moments.

When she groaned against his mouth and tilted her head to seek more of him, he lifted his head, depriving her of what she craved. Entwining his fingers into her hair, he kissed her hard. He moved on her, rubbing his hardness against her, searching for and finding her sensitive spot.

Autumn ran her hands over his toned butt, up his rippling back, to his shoulders.

He raised up, his gaze roaming over her naked breasts and lower. His mouth slightly parted, passion burned from him and heated hers. Sitting up on his knees, he lifted her with him. She straddled him. With her hands holding his face, she kissed him while he raised her up once more, and then brought her down on his erection. Putting her hands on his shoulders, she helped guide him into her. When she sat with him inside of her, she gasped for air, riding him and letting her head fall back in sheer ecstasy. She was going to come, grinding her hips over him.

He grunted, telling her he was just as close.

Laying her back on the mattress, he entered her again and thrust urgently back and forth. When she reached for him, he took her hands and pinned them on each side of her head, intent only on pleasure. She tipped her hips to take more of him and won another grunt. She won something for herself, too. With each stroke, the pleasure built to a crescendo. She was barely aware that she was screaming as she came, a deep and wrenching yell that was all-consuming.

He lay still on her and they both had to spend some time catching their breath. Autumn also tried to make sense of how this could feel so intense. Why him? Was it his mystery? She couldn't allow that to matter. She'd have no regrets in the morning. She'd vow to take this glorious memory with her, whether she ever saw him again or not.

Sometime later that night, Autumn woke, still beside him but no longer touching. She propped her head up on her hand, elbow on the mattress, and watched him sleep. After that first time, they'd dozed off for an hour or so, and then he'd made love to her again. Slower, longer and with his eyes looking into hers. She'd never experienced anything like it. A disturbing connection. She was so drawn to him.

Troubled over how she felt, she stood from the bed and went into the other room for a bottle of water. As she drank, she noticed Russ's cell phone on the coffee table. He'd left the assassin's phone in his pant pocket. This one he'd removed from the pocket of his Under Armour shirt.

Walking there, she stopped and listened. Russ hadn't stirred. She picked up the phone and navigated to the new text message.

Not the way we planned, but the problem is solved. Thanks. Let's talk when you can.

There was no name, only a number. Russ's SAC? Or had he lied about that? He'd said he would call his boss in the morning. Had he lied about that? Why would he lie?

There were no other contacts in the phone, and any calls and texts Russ had sent or received had been deleted, even the one to the hotel front desk. It was a clean phone, deliberately kept that way.

A little disturbed by that, she put the phone down and dug out a pen from her purse. The man was probably Russ's boss, who might have contacted him before Russ had planned, but she couldn't shake the feeling that there was something about this text that wasn't right. She'd jot down the number. If she never needed it, then good.

Writing the number down on a hotel notepad, she tore the page off, opened her purse and put it into her wallet. Then she took the bottle of water back into the bedroom. Russ was working undercover, so a clean phone wasn't all that unusual, she reminded herself. As she climbed back into bed, he began to stir. His sleepy eyes opened as she curled onto her side.

God, he was gorgeous.

Reaching up, he slid his hand behind her head and pulled her down for a kiss. Again? Feeling her body respond, she didn't resist, forgetting all about the text message.

He rolled her onto her back and kissed her while he slid into her for the third time that night. He aroused her into a steaming eddy in a matter of seconds. He thrust with gradual force, bringing her to a mind-erasing orgasm.

She floated back down to earth while he finished with a long groan. Then he lay on his side behind her, holding her close as they once again fell asleep, Autumn to fitful dreams of tearful goodbyes.

Autumn stretched along with a long breath as she slowly woke. Sunlight streamed into the room. And then her cheery mood settled. She flattened her hand over the other side of the bed. Empty.

Empty?

She lifted her head. Russ was gone. She looked around the room. Not there. The bathroom door was open. Not there. She flung the covers off and walked to the bedroom door, still naked. The suite was quiet. Too quiet.

Had he gone to get them breakfast or coffee? Why not call room service?

A knock on the door sent her searching for a robe. She donned a white terry-cloth one from the bathroom and went to open the door. A hotel staff member stood there holding a vase full of red roses, about two dozen of them.

"A gentleman asked us to deliver these to you," the man said.

She took the vase. "Thank you. Just a minute." She put the vase down on the entry table and opened her purse for some money. She tipped him then let the door swing shut. A small card was tucked in an envelope fastened to a plastic holder. She slipped it free and removed the card.

Sorry I had to leave so early. I will never forget last night.

He'd signed it *R*.

She looked at the beautiful red roses. He couldn't face her and say goodbye? Didn't he intend that they see each other again? Hadn't she known, deep down, that they wouldn't? Her gaze fell on her purse and she recalled writing the cell number down. The only number in Russ's phone...

Stepping up to the checkout counter at a Lander, Wyoming, hardware store, Raith De Matteis set down the new router he'd found. While he waited for someone to help him, his mind wandered to a beautiful redhead with sensual eyes. Ever since leaving Iceland, he couldn't stop thinking about Autumn. He wished he could have done more than leave her flowers. At least the initial he'd signed on the card hadn't been a lie.

He looked around for George and saw him wave as he approached.

"Got another project?" George started the register. He and his wife ran the hardware store and kept a couple of teenagers busy stocking inventory a few times a week.

"Shelves." He needed a project. Nothing had turned up from Tabor Creighton's cell phone, and the bodyguard he'd assigned to protect Kai had reported nothing unusual. There was little he could do with Creighton dead and no other leads to follow. He'd searched every database he could find to dig up information on Creighton. There wasn't much. He hadn't expected much. An assassin of Creighton's caliber was no amateur when it came to anonymity.

"Didn't you just make those last year?"

"That was for my bedroom. This is for the living room."

George smiled fondly. "Between jobs?"

"It appears that way."

George never questioned him about his job. He must have caught on that Raith couldn't talk about it.

"Brew Festival is this weekend," George said. "You should stop by."

Usually, it was George's wife who tried to get him out of the house. Most knew Raith, but didn't really *know* him. He kept to himself whenever he was home, and that wasn't often or for long periods of time.

"I might." He paid for the router. "Thanks, George."

"We'll save you a seat in the main tent. They're serving ribs at five tomorrow."

That meant he'd better show up. "All right. See you then."

He left to George's pleased chuckle.

George and Frieda invited him to their house for dinner a lot. He accepted most of the time, but only because they never asked him about his business. They had at first but must have gotten the hint that it wasn't something he could openly discuss. He appreciated that they accepted him despite his secrets. Frieda thought he should find himself a nice woman and start a family. George just liked to talk shop with him and watch an occasional game. He spent Christmas and Thanksgiving with them. Sometimes he thought they felt sorry for him. He was such a loner. But what they didn't understand was that he preferred to live that way.

George and Frieda were special, though. He could never say no to them. They'd lost their only son to leukemia when the boy was just fifteen. Raith wasn't comfortable with filling that void in their lives, but he knew that in some ways, he did. Their son would be about the same age.

"Good afternoon, Mr. De Matteis."

Raith turned to see the owner of a gift shop stop sweeping in front of the door to greet him.

"Dory."

"Will we see you at the festival tomorrow?"

"George is saving me a seat for the barbecue." Why had he chosen a small town to live in? He'd blend in more in a big city.

He drove home and it was long enough to bring his thoughts back to Autumn. That night with her had been burned into his mind. And not only the phenomenal sex. Her. He'd never, ever met any woman like her.

He'd almost called her when he returned home. She didn't know it but he'd looked on her phone and gotten her number. She'd still been asleep that morning. Taking her number was the only thing that had stopped him from climbing back in bed with her.

What harm would there be in seeing her for a while? He hadn't told her the truth about himself. Not all of it. That was one giant reason. She hadn't completely trusted him or his story. If she had, she wouldn't have been compelled to look at his phone. The text message from Kai had already been opened. Autumn had read it. He'd discovered that after looking up her cell number. Both of them had checked each other's phone. He suspected her motive was more out of suspicion, however. That he'd slept through her checking his so revealed a lot about the state of his head that night. He'd been so taken into the seduction that he'd been complacent. She didn't have his real name, but if she tried to get it from the number, she'd learn he wasn't an FBI agent. And worse, she'd expose herself to Raith's investigation. Tabor Creighton might be dead, but whoever had hired him was still an unknown and a danger.

But what had really doused his temptation was the internet search he'd done. It hadn't been difficult to learn more about her. Autumn Ivy was Jackson Ivy's daughter. He'd laughed when he'd first read that. Of all the things that would keep them apart, he hadn't imagined that one. Seeing Autumn was impossible. No way in hell could he risk that kind of publicity. Especially since she generated a fair amount of it all on her own...breaking all those men's hearts. Raith had read all about the actor, Deangelo Cassa-something, and the detective, Knox.

Funny, the woman he'd spent a night with was nothing like the one who's face was plastered all over the Hollywood tabloids. He hadn't laughed when he'd read about her dating escapades. Her relationship with the detective should have been normal. Why had she broken it off with him? Clearly, the woman was not one to commit or settle down. While that bothered him, he could hardly fault her. He was no different.

As he drove off the long, winding dirt road and onto his driveway, he saw a car parked in front of the closed gate. The gate was the most visible security feature he'd installed. That was enough to get the town talking, and every Halloween, some kids came by to throw toilet paper on it. He knew who they were—the cameras recorded every toss. But he let them have their fun.

Recognizing the car and the man sitting in the driver's seat, Raith pressed the remote clipped to his sun visor. The fact that he was here didn't bode well, because it meant Autumn had gotten curious. Too curious.

Mayo Chambers drove ahead of him to the gravel parking area in front of Raith's six-thousand-square-foot snecked ashlar, gray-stone house. Three spires stood like sentinels. White-trimmed windows and the porch added a fresh touch, but didn't diminish the old, isolated feel of the place. The same kids who'd T.P.'d his gate had probably started the rumor that his house was haunted. It did have a bit of gothic revival flare.

He got out of his Dodge Ram truck and his boots crunched over the dry gravel.

"Raith." Mayo extended his hand.

Raith shook it, not looking forward to what news he'd bring.

It had been a little over a week since he'd left Iceland, and Autumn lying partially covered in bed, hair fanned out over the pillow, most of one breast exposed, so beautiful he'd nearly stayed a few more days.

"Just as you asked, I've been tailing the Ivy woman," Mayo said.

An ex-CIA operative, he'd gone private and did a lot of this type of surveillance for Raith. Although, it had never been this personal before.

"I take it she got interested in me," Raith said.

Mayo didn't crack a smile at Raith's humor. "She left Reykjavik when you said she would, but she contacted her brother, Lincoln Ivy, and asked him to run a cell number." He showed Raith a piece of paper with a familiar number on it. "He's a bounty hunter."

Raith didn't take the paper. "Did he find anything yet?"

"No, but you should expect him to trace the number, and the Ivy woman will know who this number belongs to."

Wonderful. "All right. I'll take it from here. Why don't you come inside and I'll pay you what I owe."

"You don't want me to find out whose cell number this is?"

"I already know whose it is." He walked toward the front entrance.

Inside the entry, Raith hung his light jacket on an old-fashioned coatrack beside the door. A short, wide hallway ran along the stairway wall. At the end of the hallway, double doors made of thick wood beneath arched trim required a code to unlock them. Flanked by two dark blue wingback chairs, a dainty table along the stairway wall held a vase of fresh flowers, his personal assistant's touch. The stairs had a cheery strip of white carpet running up the middle and a black metal railing. They curved up to another pair of double doors with a coded entry.

Raith led Mayo to his office, strategically located to the right of the entry at the foot of the stairs. His assistant had done the decorating in here, too. He'd painted the walls a pale yellow and stained the trim a medium brown. The bulky wooden desk had a Tuscan chestnut finish with burnished edges and antique brass cup pulls. Raith went around the desk and unlocked the top right desk drawer to retrieve a cash box. Flipping through the money, he counted out what he owed Mayo.

"Do you mind me asking why you had me tail that woman?" Mayo asked.

Putting the box back into the drawer, Raith looked up. "She got in the way of a job."

"How so?"

He closed and locked the drawer and then straightened. "In a way that wasn't planned."

Mayo nodded and then grinned. "She's very attractive."

Raith avoided reacting to that. Mayo had obviously drawn his own conclusion about Autumn and him.

"What are you going to do?" Mayo asked.

"Stop her from getting any more curious than she is right now."

"Are you going to…"

Kill her? Raith laughed briefly. "No. Does she look like someone I could kill?"

Mayo laughed in return, but it was more of a relieved one. "No."

Raith had a deadly reputation that included fierce protectiveness over his identity. But Autumn was different. His jobs didn't involve women he took a romantic interest in. She was a first in that regard.

"How did she get that cell number?" Mayo asked.

"She looked at my phone while I was sleeping." Raith moved around his desk and handed Mayo a wad of cash.

Mayo took it, meeting Raith's eyes, getting his meaning. "You slept through that?"

"Hard to fathom, isn't it?"

"For you? Yeah." Mayo chuckled. "Must have been some night."

No, just some woman. An incredible woman. And now he had to stop her from getting herself killed.

"I'll call you if I need you for anything else." Raith went to the office door and saw his personal assistant standing just outside the office, under the guise of awaiting a request, no doubt. Desi Hildebrandt frequently put himself nearby so he could overhear discussions. He especially liked the ones that resembled what he'd heard just now.

"Good luck with Autumn," Mayo said, and then left through the front door.

Raith turned to Desi, who stood straight and tall in perfectly pressed black slacks and a light blue dress shirt. He always dressed up for the job, even though Raith had told him a couple dozen times he didn't have to.

Desi lifted his hand, palm up, as he often did when he was about to broach a touchy subject with Raith. "Your trip to Iceland wasn't all business."

His soft, almost-lilting tone grated on Raith's patience, but only because he'd broached such a personal subject. Desi's homosexuality had taken some adjustment, but he respected his assistant's dedication and, most of all, his trustworthiness.

He started toward the stairs. "I need you to arrange a flight to Denver."

"Your friend said the woman is attractive." Desi followed him up the stairs.

Raith didn't engage.

"Are you going to see her again?" Desi asked.

"My flight?"

"Right away, sir. We can talk about this later."

"Stop calling me sir." Raith stopped at the top of the stairs and faced Desi. "Will you also call George and tell him I can't make it to the barbecue tomorrow night?"

"It would be nice if you gave him a reason."

Raith turned toward the locked doors. "I have to work."

"It's not work if you're going for the woman you met. What's her name?"

Raith entered the security code into the keypad next to the doors. "Then tell him whatever you like." He would, anyway. It had taken him a while to figure out that it was his personal assistant who'd sparked George and Frieda's interest in him. They'd started by asking questions whenever Desi had to go into town for Raith. As with many here, they'd wondered who the new guy was who'd moved into the gothic mansion. Raith didn't consider it a mansion, but it was big and, he supposed, imposing. Desi had struck up a friendship with George and Frieda and that had developed into regular status reports about Raith. Sometimes the way they all cared about him drove him nuts. Like now.

Desi trailed him into the main living room. Floor-to-ceiling windows toward the front offered a view of Lander. Toward the back, a sliding door and wall of windows overlooked a balcony and the Tetons in the distance.

"I'll prepare a room for the woman," Desi said. And when Raith turned to him, he added, "Just in case."

How had his personal assistant drawn such a conclusion? Why did he think Raith would bring Autumn here? Never mind. He didn't need to know. Desi had great insight into people. He was afraid of the insight he had over his night with Autumn.

His cell phone rang. Taking it out of his front shirt pocket, he saw the number and ignored the call. As he stuffed the phone back in his pocket, he noticed Desi watching.

"Your father again?" he asked.

"I like you, Desi. Which is why I'd really hate to have to let you go." He hadn't spoken with his father since he left home when he was seventeen, and he wasn't going to start now.

With a disappointed look, Desi headed for one of the four guest rooms in the house. He knew Raith would never fire him. And Raith would never admit that Desi was like family to him. So were George and Frieda.

Raith left the living room and passed the dining area and parlor to reach the secure doors leading to his office—his real office. Inside the long and spacious room, he went to the large L-shaped desk where all of his computers hummed and blinked. Opening his secure email, he saw there were none from a contact he had in the FBI.

That meant more waiting. Just as well. He'd be delayed dealing with Autumn, anyway.

A week after she gave Lincoln the number associated with the text she'd read on Raith's phone, Autumn sat with her sister Savanna on Lincoln's sofa. His living room had a lot more feminine touches since Arizona had moved in. Much more decorative and colorful. She was away on one of her adventure outings, and Savanna had stopped by for a brief visit with Lincoln. Slightly taller than Autumn, Savanna had darker hair, with only a hint of red, and the most stunning blue eyes. Caribbean-blue and just as clear.

Lincoln was still on the phone with their mother, who'd recently had a run-in with the paparazzi and now it was all over the news how she'd taken one of the photographer's cameras and bashed it on the pavement in front of a conference center where she was holding a charity event. Lincoln was trying to calm her down.

"What do you mean he held a knife to your throat?" Savanna asked, appalled.

Autumn was in the process of explaining why Lincoln had asked her to come here to talk. "I almost didn't get on the elevator. But Russ saved me from him."

"The man who was after him? Russ — is that what you said his name was?"

"Yes."

"How did he save you?"

"Well…first he shot the man in the leg, and then they fought and Russ ended up…killing him."

Savanna's eyes widened. "Really?"

"He's an FBI agent and was going to arrest him, but he was forced to kill him instead"

"You sound like you're defending him."

Autumn stopped herself from fidgeting in her discomfort. Was it that obvious how much her night with Russ had affected her?

"Why was he going to arrest the man?" Savanna asked.

"He's a hit man or something. Wanted by the FBI." She tried to sound nonchalant but suspected she failed.

Savanna angled her head, eyeing her closely. "What happened after he killed the man?"

"We…" How could she explain that? *We went to my room and had sex* seemed so…right out of a movie.

"Well…he refused to talk to the police and so we talked awhile and then…"

"Why did he refuse to talk to the police?"

"He was working undercover." That explained why he hadn't called the police…sort of.

"And then what?" Savanna pressed.

"We…well…we…went to my room for a while."

"To hide?"

Autumn hesitated. "No…yes…maybe." Had that been his intention?

Savanna's head angled more. "Did you sleep with him?"

Autumn tried not to appear sheepish, but Savanna's head snapped straighter and her mouth dropped open.

"You slept with him?" Savanna made a disgusted sound. "Autumn, you have to stop doing that! You're getting to be a real floozy."

Autumn never flushed but she began to now. "No. This was different than with Knox." Knox had been exciting up until he'd taken too much of an interest in her dad, and she hadn't been interested in him as a person. Not beyond his profession as a detective.

As Savanna continued to observe her, her mouth closed and her face softened. "You like him."

Autumn couldn't deny it.

"You *really* like him."

"I wouldn't—"

"I've never seen you this way before."

"Savanna," Autumn protested.

"Is he going to call you?"

Lincoln hung up the phone and came to stand before them. "If he does, you shouldn't answer."

Autumn had given him the cell number she'd gotten

from Russ's phone. What had her brother discovered? "Who did the text come from?"

"What text?" Savanna asked.

"Russ left before I woke up," Autumn said. "But, in the middle of the night, I looked at his phone."

"And there was a text from someone?" Savanna asked, still confused.

"A 'things didn't go as we planned but problem solved' text," Lincoln said. "It was from a guy named Kai Whittaker. He's a defense contractor. A *major* defense contractor. Their specialty is night-vision equipment."

"Is he legitimate?" Autumn asked.

"Yeah, but that isn't what has me worried." Lincoln sat next to Autumn and leaned forward with his forearms on his knees. "I looked up Russ Markham and found five of them in the United States. None of them work for the FBI."

"I told you that isn't his real name, Lincoln."

"He was working undercover," Savanna chimed in.

"I talked to a friend of mine at the Bureau. He confirmed Tabor Creighton was wanted by the FBI, but there were no cover ops in Iceland. No agents were sent there."

"But if he was undercover…"

"He's not an agent, Autumn. He lied to you about that."

Autumn could only stare at her brother.

"I'm sorry. No one at the Bureau knew Creighton was in Reykjavik. Kai Whittaker hired Russ to go after him. Russ isn't official. He's black ops and private. He has to be. Creighton being a known assassin, we can only assume he was going to kill Kai. Why? I'd rather not know, and you shouldn't, either." He put his hand on Autumn's shoulder. "You have to forget this guy, Autumn. Whoever he is, he's no good for you."

Disappointment shattered her. She'd never felt this

way before. Why should a man she'd only known for one night affect her this much?

Savanna rubbed her back.

"Okay," Autumn said, nodding, and adjusting to this new knowledge. "Yeah. It's good I found out now." She smiled at her brother. "Thanks for checking, Lincoln."

"Anything for my sisters." He winked at Savanna. "At least I don't have to worry about you."

Savanna smiled in a way that disputed his declaration. "Actually...I met someone."

The news perked Autumn up. "Did you? When? Where?" Savanna seeing someone was significant. The family had begun to wonder if she'd ever give anyone else a chance again.

"He's a lawyer for one of the biggest firms in Denver. We met at a supermarket in front of the deli counter. He was getting lunch and I was picking up an order Mom had for the Evergreen house."

"That's fantastic, Savanna." Finally, a man who could take care of himself and not rely on Ivy fame.

All the while, disappointment over what Lincoln had revealed about Russ gave way to nagging curiosity. Why had someone like Kai Whittaker been in contact with Russ about a known assassin? And why had Russ gone after the assassin if he didn't in fact work for the FBI?

Chapter 3

Two weeks later, Autumn's hand trembled as she held the pregnancy test she'd just taken. It was positive.

Positive?

Oh, God. It was *positive!*

She panted for air and stood from the closed toilet seat, where she'd collapsed after seeing the plus sign. What was she going to do? She'd have the baby, of course, but what would she do about Russ? That wasn't even his real name. She didn't even know the name of her baby's father!

She was one of *those* women. *Floozy.* Her sister was right!

"Oh, God." She hyperventilated some more. She put the test on the counter then walked out of the bathroom and held on to the railing as she descended the stairs on wobbly legs.

"Oh, God, oh, God, oh, God…I'm not ready for a

baby." She was supposed to go to Germany on another translation contract next week. Single motherhood didn't scare her, but having a baby did. She didn't need a man to raise a child. It was the drastic change that bothered her. She'd be responsible for a life and her own would be over. Nothing would ever be the same. She'd have to give up her independence. No more flying to other countries on a whim. Not for a while, anyway.

In the kitchen, she leaned with her hands on the kitchen island, bending over, light-headed with a racing heart.

Maybe her mother could help her. Or Savanna. Or Lincoln.

No. None of them could help her. No one could. Moreover, she didn't want anyone to help her. She didn't want anyone to know she'd gotten pregnant from a one-night stand.

How could she have allowed this to happen? She'd stopped taking her birth control pills after Knox, having feebly vowed to stay away from men for a while. But it had only been a few days before her trip when she'd stopped. She'd thought she was safe.

Guess not.

Straightening, she stared out the window, unable to stop her thoughts from drifting to that night. To *him*. Unbelievable that they'd made a baby together. Of all the luck. And then…it was a miracle. What were the odds of this happening to anyone? To her?

She had to find out who he was.

Even if he chose to have nothing to do with her and the baby, he had the right to know about it and she had to know his real name.

Turning, she made her way through the living room and went down the hall to her home office. Sitting at the computer, she typed in Kai Whittaker's name into a search engine. Moments later, she had the website to the defense contractor company, DT Corporation, and the main number. DT stood for Defense Technologies.

Without hesitation, she grabbed her phone and called the company.

"DT Corporation."

"Yes…uh…would you please transfer me to Mr. Kai Whittaker?"

"One moment."

The line switched to another woman. "Kai Whittaker's office."

Autumn repeated her request.

"Is he expecting your call?"

"No." Standing, she began to pace the office. "He doesn't know me, but it's important."

"May I have your name and number and what this is about?"

Yeah, right. "I need to speak with him now." She turned and walked back across the office.

"I'm sorry, but—"

"Tell him it's about Tabor Creighton. He'll talk to me."

"One moment."

Autumn stopped walking. Several seconds later, she had Kai on the line. "Who is this?"

"Mr. Whittaker, my name is Autumn Ivy. I was in Iceland when Mr. Creighton was killed. I met the man who killed him."

There was a long silence before Kai said, "We need to meet in person."

"Why?"

"I don't have to meet you, lady. We talk about this in person or we don't talk at all."

What was he afraid of? Being heard? She experienced

a moment of hesitation and dismissed it. "I'm in Dallas, but I can fly to Houston. How about tomorrow afternoon?"

He told her a time and place.

Sitting outside at a chain coffee shop, Autumn checked her cell phone for the time. Kai was fifteen minutes late. Cars passed along the busy Houston, Texas, street. Across that, there was a shopping mall. She'd already stopped there on her way here and bought a new outfit, one she wouldn't be able to wear pretty soon. Her mood sank lower as she noticed a billboard advertising her dad's latest sci-fi film. She hoped Kai didn't recognize her.

"Ms. Ivy?"

She turned to look behind her and saw a man approach. Another hung back as he reached the table. He took the seat beside her.

"Thank you for meeting me." She looked at the man again. "Who is that?"

"Security." The waitress was walking over to them. "Would you like anything?"

She shook her head. It was water and decaffeinated drinks for her now.

Kai ordered coffee and waited for the waitress to leave. "Now. Why did you call me and what is it you want?"

"I need to contact the man who killed Tabor Creighton," she said.

"Why do you need to contact him?" he asked as though it was an absurd question.

"It's a…a personal matter."

"Personal." Kai leaned back, looking directly at her. "You obviously don't know how dangerous it was for you to call me, much less meet me."

"But you said—"

"What did you expect me to do, have this conversation over the phone?" he snapped. "You bring up names like Tabor Creighton, and I don't have much of a choice."

Autumn had to find a way to convince him to talk to her. "Look, Mr. Whittaker, I didn't ask to be held with a knife to my throat, and I certainly didn't ask to cross paths with the man who saved me."

With cold, calculating eyes, he studied her. "Who have you told about this?"

He didn't bat an eye over her mention of the knife to her throat. He must know that she'd been there when Russ killed Creighton. She began to feel uneasy. How did he know? When had he spoken with Russ, and why would Russ talk about her?

"No one," she lied. She'd told Lincoln and Savanna. "Please, Mr. Whittaker, I need to contact the man who killed Tabor Creighton. He said his name was Russ, but I know that isn't his real name."

"I can't tell you anything about him. I only met you here today so that I could warn you to stay away. Don't contact me again, and don't try to contact this man you're so curious about. And above all, tell no one what you saw in Iceland. You have no idea the danger you've put yourself in by coming here."

"Why? The assassin is dead. You yourself said the problem was solved in your text." And that raised other questions she had. "Why was the assassin a problem for you? Was he going to kill you?"

His coffee arrived and he didn't answer her.

When the waitress left, she asked, "Was Russ helping you? Is he still?" If Creighton was going to kill him, someone had hired him to do so.

He looked at her for a long moment. "No one else can." Sipping his coffee, he put the cup down.

What did he mean no one else could? "Who is he?" She received another long look.

"Why was an assassin going to kill you?" she asked. Still, he only looked at her.

"That's why you hired Russ, isn't it? What does he do? Why go to him and not the police?"

Abruptly, he leaned toward her. "Listen to me carefully. He may have saved you, but I didn't go to him because he had a conscience. My advice to you is to forget whatever private matter you have to discuss with him."

Oh, dear. Had she gotten herself knocked up by a ruthless killer? But he'd been the one to kill an assassin. Was he also an assassin?

"How do you know him?" she asked.

Taking another sip of his coffee, he reached for his wallet inside his jacket. "This meeting is over." He dropped a ten-dollar bill on the table. "Go home. Forget you came here. And don't ever come back or contact me again."

"Wait." She put her hand on his arm before he could stand. "I just need to talk to him. A phone number is all I need." She met his unsympathetic gaze. "Please."

"Something personal, hmm? Dying is personal. Is whatever you need to talk to him about worth that?"

She was beginning to wonder. Kai wasn't going to tell her anything, anyway. She'd have this baby and never know who its father was. Averting her head, she stared at the mall across the street, more upset than she'd been in years. The sting of tears astonished her.

She pushed back her chair. "Thank you for meeting me. I won't contact you again." She stood.

Kai put his hand on her arm. "I'll tell him you're trying to reach him. That's the best I can do."

Maybe that would be enough. With a single nod, she left, not believing she'd ever hear from Russ, or whatever his name was.

Autumn was still fighting tears when she reached her rental car. Throwing her purse onto the passenger seat, she started the engine and sat there for a while. Well, there was nothing she could do if Kai decided not to talk to Russ, or if Russ decided not to contact her. She'd tried. That's all that mattered. Now she'd have to face single motherhood.

Motherhood...

She gripped the steering wheel tighter as she drove into the street. Few things intimidated or frightened her, but the thought of raising a living being all by herself came pretty close. It wasn't that she doubted her capability. It was the living being part. Taking on the giant responsibility. Would she be good at it or would she yearn for her old life back? Maybe it was the lack of choice that daunted her. Like being Jackson Ivy's daughter.

Her flight wasn't scheduled to leave until morning. She'd have the whole night to think about all of this. What torture.

A car appeared beside her on the four-lane road. She slowed down, not liking it when other drivers went the same speed as her and blocked all the traffic behind them. When the other car slowed with her, she sped up. The other car did, too.

Annoyed, she looked over and saw a man pointing a gun at her. He had a mustache and wore a baseball hat and bulky jacket. At first, she was startled, but then, galvanized into action, she slammed on the brakes just as a bullet shattered the driver's window. The other car slowed with her and the car behind rear-ended him. Autumn wasted no time. She floored it and raced past the accident.

Glancing at the side mirror, she saw the gunman coming after her, and the car that had rear-ended him starting to chase.

The gunman changed lanes and raced up behind her.

She fought her fear and concentrated on driving. Veering around a car, she changed lanes to get around another.

The other two cars followed. What was the third car doing? Why was the driver following? Was he trying to help? The third car rear-ended the gunman's again, this time harder. It was deliberate. Had the driver seen the shooting?

The gunman nearly lost control, swerving onto the shoulder and then correcting. Autumn pulled to the side of the road, ducking as the other car passed, expecting bullets. But none came. The shooter had decided to flee. As the third car raced past her, she recognized Russ in the driver's seat.

How had he known she was here?

She wasn't going to wait around for him to come back and tell her. He was the reason that man had shot at her. She should have never come here, never gone to see Kai Whittaker. Doing so had drawn her back into whatever trouble Russ had stirred up by killing that shooter in Reykjavik. She'd put her life and the life of her unborn baby in danger by coming here. The sooner she got away, the better.

For a second she considered calling the police to report what had just happened, and then quickly decided against that idea. Kai had warned her of the risk in meeting with him and now someone had just shot at her. She needed no further convincing. The faster she got out of this situation the better, and hopefully no one would try to find her. Hopefully the driver who'd shot at her would forget about her, and hopefully she never saw Russ again.

She'd be safe at her parents' California mansion. Safe from Russ and all of this trouble.

Sick to her stomach, Autumn put the gear into Drive and took the nearest exit off the highway. This baby was a secret now. At least from the father.

Raith swore all the way to Autumn's hotel. Once he was inside, he kept swearing in his head. Damn her. Why did she have to come here? He'd flown to Dallas after Mayo had come to see him, and after a week assuring himself that she wouldn't try to contact Kai, he'd returned home. But watching her had cost him. He'd daydreamed about going to her door and taking her to the nearest bed. Even after he'd left, she'd haunted him.

Now he was in Houston, on his way to really see her again. Sexual tension and frustration over the fact that he felt that way had him more than a little uptight. She'd gone to see Kai. That was the only reason he was here. Not to have sex. Make love. It would be making love now. It had been making love after the first time. The first time qualified as sex. Anything after that had felt like more.

At her room door, he knocked. Hard.

She didn't answer, but he heard her television.

He pounded on the door. "I know you're in there. Let me in."

Still nothing.

"It's Raith." Catching himself, he corrected, "I mean, Russ. You know me as Russ." He looked up and down the hall. Empty. "My real name is Raith De Matteis."

He waited.

At last she opened the door, the security latch stopping it at two inches.

Wide, dark green eyes stared at him, long, fine red hair falling all over her shoulders. Wearing an off-white knit tunic with knee-high lace-up boots, her C-cup breasts pushed out and her waist dipped in. Around five-six, slender and dressed in another one of her feminine outfits that was very different than the jeans he'd seen her in, she was so beautiful it staggered him.

"Let me in before someone sees me," he said.

"I don't care if anyone sees you."

He believed her, and she charmed him for it. "Let me in. You're the one who came here looking for me."

A long pause stretched between the other side of the door and the sliver of sexy woman he could see through the opening. "How do you know that?"

"Kai called me right after you left the coffee shop."

"You were already there."

"He called me after you contacted him at DT Corporation and then called me again after you met. He was freaking out that you knew about him and his connection to me. I had to explain how you did." He'd left out the part about him going into her hotel room, though.

Her eyes shifted back and forth between his as she considered what he'd said. "You two are good friends."

"No, not friends. Let me in."

She stared at him awhile longer before closing the door and releasing the security latch. He stepped inside, not comfortable at all with being in another hotel room with her. Another nice suite.

"Why are you looking for me?" he asked.

In response, she just cocked her head, without words telling him to shove it.

Apparently, she'd changed her mind about talking to him. He went to the kitchenette and found a bottle of water in the fridge. Holding it up at her, he waited for her to shake her head before closing the refrigerator and going over to the sofa. Sitting with a long sigh, he put his foot up on the ottoman and drank a few gulps.

"Get thirsty after you kill people?"

So that's why she no longer felt like talking. Lowering the bottle of water, he saw her standing to the side of the ottoman. "Only when you're around."

"You killed the driver of that car?" she asked, appalled.

"No. He got away." His frustration over that came out in his tone. He'd made no progress since Reykjavik. To come so close to capturing Creighton's conspirator rankled him.

She looked at him as though recalling that he'd killed the man in Reykjavik. Judging. She probably regretted coming here. Another man had threatened her life because of him. He must not be painted in a favorable light in her mind.

Putting the bottle of water down, he got up and stood in front of her. "I wasn't the one who tried to kill you." No, in fact, this was the second time he'd saved her life. He watched her register that and then grow distracted by his logic. She had trouble thinking of him as a good guy. He felt inclined to prove her wrong.

Falling into a study of her beautiful face, vivid memories of the last time they were together followed.

Autumn caught herself first and blinked a few times. Then she turned away and walked to the windows overlooking Houston.

"Why would anyone try to kill me?" she asked.

"Someone must have found out about you. What did you say to Kai when you called?"

"That I knew about Creighton…and the man who killed him."

"Well, there you have it. It's obvious why someone started shooting at you." The person who'd hired Creighton had likely panicked and decided not to take a chance that Autumn would discover his identity. Either that, or he'd heard what Autumn had said to Kai, which meant Kai was being bugged.

She turned and he caught her unappreciative look in response to his sarcasm. "Tell me the truth about Tabor Creighton."

He stared at her a moment and then relented. "Kai contacted me after Creighton tried to kill him at his home in Houston. He was in his garage, had just gotten out of his car when Creighton drove by and took a few shots at him. Luckily, he missed, and Kai's security cameras captured Creighton's image. That's how I was able to track him down."

"In Reykjavik."

"Yes."

Autumn walked from one end of the window, turned and walked back to where she'd stood before. "So… whoever hired Creighton is watching Kai."

"Yes."

She walked the length of the window again, stopping at the end and facing him. "Do you think whoever shot at me today is the one who hired Creighton?"

"Yes."

"Then…why not shoot Kai? Why go after me when he could get the job done?"

He joined her at the window. "Kai was in a public place and he has a bodyguard. I'm sure given the chance, he'd try to kill him again."

"You could expose him. Has he tried to go after you?"

It wasn't only her that threatened today's shooter. "He'd try to kill me, too, if he had the chance."

He watched her process that. The reason the shooter didn't have a chance was that Raith was good at what he did. The shooter was probably scared and was at the point where he'd do anything to avoid getting caught taking a contract out on Kai's head.

"Why didn't Kai go to the police? Why go to you for help?"

"The police were involved. Still are."

"But he doesn't think they'll be able to catch the man who hired Creighton?"

"No. Not in time." He was already complaining about how long it was taking Raith, as it was. With Creighton dead, there was no one Raith could seek out for information, and he'd been unable to find anyone close to him who might know something.

"He told me you were the only one who could help him."

He had nothing to say in response to that. He had a lot of experience at what he did. Whether it was rescuing Americans from foreign prisons or kidnappers, or taking down killers. He was a black market cop, one without a badge.

"What did you need to talk to me about?"

She glanced at him before leaving the window and going to stand by the sofa again, putting distance between them. "I was going to ask you why you left without saying goodbye. I guess I have my answer now. You weren't telling the truth."

"You weren't exactly honest, either...*Ivy?*" More angst went into his tone than he intended.

"It's not my fault you didn't recognize the name."

Was she put off that he hadn't? He followed her over to the seating area, leaving a few feet to separate them.

Distance might be prudent. "Should I have recognized one of your boyfriends, too?"

Her eyes narrowed and one of her hands went to her hip. "Now you're being mean."

This felt like an argument between lovers, but Raith couldn't stop himself. "I can see why the actor didn't last, but what was wrong with the detective?"

She almost blanched as her arm lowered, her eyes no longer narrow with anger. "Why do you care?"

He did sound as if he cared. Did he? Yes, but to what degree? Ever since he'd met her he'd been mystified by her effect on him. When he'd discovered who she was, the disappointment had been crushing. He had no business being disappointed.

"You should have stayed home and away from here," he said.

"I have a flight home tomorrow. I think you should leave now," she said. "I won't bother you anymore."

"I'm afraid I can't let you do that. Kai is still alive and whoever wants him dead went after you. That means two things. Kai needs to debug himself, and you know too much."

"I don't know anything. Least of all about *you*."

That made her mad. He heard it in her voice and saw it in the fire of her eyes. "You know about Creighton."

"So do you."

"Yes, but no one knows who I am." They had to be well aware that someone was helping Kai, and by now maybe even that he was someone to fear. All the more reason to protect Autumn. She was a witness to an attempted contract killing.

Raith would have liked nothing more than to leave her and finish this investigation alone, but she was defenseless without him.

His phone rang. Seeing his FBI contact's number, he answered.

"I've got something for you," the agent said. "All this time we've been looking for Tabor Creighton and we should have been looking for Leaman Marshall. He was operating under a false name. I discovered that when I found a death certificate on Creighton and checked it out. He's been using that name for so long we had no reason to suspect it wasn't his birth name. Marshall lived in Houston. I can't spend any more time on this than I have, but you should have no trouble locating his family. Creighton had none still living, which made him a perfect cover for Marshall."

"You have an address on Marshall?"

The agent gave it to him and then said, "The only reason I help you at all is because I think you're an okay guy. But I've got cases."

"Understood." Raith thanked the agent and disconnected.

"Be careful."

In other words, don't do anything illegal and don't get caught. "I always am."

Except with Autumn. And now he had to take her with him to his home, where he had a secure network set up and access to the resources he needed to locate anyone close to Leaman. He never took women there. This was a first.

Chapter 4

Kai Whittaker pulled into the four-car garage, checking the rearview mirror again. The bodyguard Raith had assigned to him parked right behind him outside. As instructed, he waited for the man to get out and come to him. When all was clear, Kai was free to get out of his own damn car. Having a big, expressionless brute tag along with him day and night had its annoyances, but it was better than being dead.

He'd talked to Raith on the way home for status on his investigation. Not much progress had been made. Kai couldn't push him the way he could push his employees. He claimed to be having difficulty locating anyone who knew Tabor Creighton, but Kai wondered if the distraction of Autumn Ivy had slowed his progress.

Inside, Thor checked for abnormalities while Kai put down his computer case and keys. Thor wasn't his real name, just a small source of private entertainment for Kai.

"You're home at a decent time."

Seeing his wife approach, his day improved. Ten years younger than his fifty-two, she looked twenty-nine. Blond-haired, blue-eyed, she still had her beautiful shape after two kids. The silky gold pantsuit dipped low enough to show off her ample chest.

He leaned in for a kiss as she put herself against him. "You're better than a tall, cool drink."

She smiled at his compliment. "I love you, too."

Thor returned to the living room, looking like a hulking star of a bad TV crime show, not rode hard enough and not having seen enough terrible things to be a believable character. He'd hover until they went to bed. Maybe he was simply out of place in a suit and in Kai and India's five-thousand-square-foot home in downtown Houston. They had this house here and a second one outside the city limits that was on a lot more land. He and India usually went there on weekends. It was bigger than this house and much more secluded.

India moved back from him, seeing his gaze go from the guard to her.

"You know we need him," she said.

"Yes."

"Have you talked to that man lately? Raith or whatever his name is? He sure doesn't believe in status reports, does he?"

No. Raith ran by his own rules. "I called him on the way home." Kai stepped farther into the living room. With high ceilings and a piano beside a huge, gray Italian sectional made with hand-tied coils, it was homey but elegant.

"Something smells good."

"Beef bourguignon." She followed him to the kitchen. "You had to call him?"

He opened the refrigerator and took out a bottle of sparkling water.

"Is he working on your case at all?" India had two glasses ready on the kitchen island. He poured without answering. She wasn't all that impressed with Raith.

"Yes."

"How do you know if he never calls you?"

"He said he'd call after he found the person who hired Tabor."

India leaned against the kitchen island and angled her head. "He should be here protecting you, Kai."

"That's what Thor is for."

"Thor?"

He grinned. "I made that up." When she didn't share his humor, he said, "Raith is good at what he does, India." He picked up the glasses and went around the island corner to hand her one.

"How can you be so sure?"

He'd gone over all of this with her before. Raith's secretiveness didn't reassure her much. "A close colleague of mine recommended him. He was kidnapped and held for ransom by members of the People's Revolutionary Army in Argentina. Raith rescued him. He does that sort of thing for a living."

India still didn't look convinced.

"He's got a respectable reputation. There are people in the military and law enforcement who know about him and don't touch him. They know he stands on principle, that he fights on their side even though he works in the shadows. He's unencumbered by protocols or laws. He can move in and accomplish a job before anyone has time to react." Kai put his glass down on the counter after taking a sip.

"What about that woman who witnessed Raith kill Tabor?" India asked. "Why was she asking for Raith's contact information?"

"Maybe she likes him." He grinned again.

When a smile began to push up the corners of her mouth, Kai stepped forward and slipped his arms around her. She put her glass down and looped her arms over his shoulders.

"Don't worry, my love." He planted a kiss on her mouth. "I wouldn't have hired Raith if I didn't think he was capable of handling this."

She brushed her thumb over his cheek. "You trust him?"

Kai didn't trust anyone. "He'll do what we need him to do. That's enough."

She leaned back. "What if he doesn't find the man who tried to kill you? What are we going to do then?"

India was still shaken over the shooting. She was afraid to be at home alone now, and afraid to let him go to work. He didn't like her being that way.

"He'll find the man."

India studied him the way she always did when she thought there was more going on than he was saying. They'd been married almost twenty years now. He'd met her when she was just nineteen and he twenty-nine and well on his way to launching a successful career. Falling in love with her had been unplanned and exciting. Their love was real and lasting. He considered himself a lucky man to have found a woman who matched him so well. But some things she could never know.

"You're worried," she said.

"Of course I am. Someone is trying to kill me."

"No." She shook her head and stepped back, slipping out of his arms. "There's something else. What is it, Kai?"

He moved a step closer, putting his hands on her arms. "Nothing. Just some business issues." At least that wasn't a lie. Not entirely...

Chapter 5

Raith's house surprised Autumn. Passing through a towering, impenetrable iron gate, the driveway wound across open land toward the castlelike structure. The stone blocks were light in color, but the turrets and its aged appearance cast a dark shadow.

"Your house looks like it could be in a horror movie," she quipped. Feeling Raith's drilling look, she got out of the car and waited for him to get her luggage before walking with him toward the front entry. "It's beautiful in such a creepy way."

"Thanks. I like it, too."

She stopped herself from laughing at his humor. It was a lot like hers.

The entry was long and narrow with white marble floors. Stairs with a strip of white carpet and an ornate, mahogany-topped black iron railing ran along the right side, curving to the landing above. Other than a chandelier hanging in the middle of the entry, there were no other furnishings or lights. The single window next to the front doors provided dim light. To her right and at the base of the stairway, two doors were open to an office. There was a keypad on the wall next to them, so the option to lock them was available.

"Was this a prison before you bought it or did you just turn it into one?" she asked.

Raith rolled her luggage to the bottom of the stairs.

One of the doors in the entry opened and a slim man with short, straight brown hair in a light pink dress shirt and gray slacks appeared. He walked with smooth, graceful strides and his arms swung at his sides.

"This must be your friend from Iceland," he said, reaching both hands to take one of hers in greeting. "I'm Desi Hildebrandt, Raith's personal assistant. Anything you need during your stay will be my pleasure to accommodate."

"Thank you."

"Don't overdo it, Desi," Raith said.

He put his hands together in front of him. "I knew you'd bring her home."

Autumn smiled, finding an instant friend in the man. But how had he known Raith would bring her here? He must know about their night, but Autumn couldn't picture Raith confiding in him.

"Show her to her room, would you?"

Dismissed. Autumn glared a little at Raith as Desi lifted her single bag. "Right this way."

She followed him up the stairs, looking back to see Raith go into his office and shut the door, the sound of the automatic lock sliding into place a clear message. *Leave me alone!*

"Don't worry about him," Desi said, reaching the top

of the stairs. "He growls like a bear, but inside, he's only the stuffed kind."

Autumn laughed. "How long have you worked for him?"

"Fifteen years. We moved here five years ago after his business took off."

"What business is that?"

Desi turned to the door and entered a code. "The number to get in is one, two, three, four." The door unlocked and he looked back as he pushed it open. "I changed it for you to make it easy to remember. It's the same code downstairs, but there's another staircase you can use in here."

The personal assistant was loyal to his boss. She was impressed. Maybe Raith had a soft side, after all.

"Raith will ask me to change it after you leave." He rolled her luggage through the door, glancing back again. "If you ever do."

She wasn't sure how to take that remark. And its importance faded as she followed Desi down a wide hallway with red mosaic carpeting and four white stone arches spaced out evenly down the length of the room. Passing windows on the right, she saw that the back of the home was U-shaped, and below was an outdoor pool surrounded by shrubs and flowers. The Tetons towered in the distance.

Opposite the windows was a library, the doors open and welcoming. She caught a glimpse of arching windows framed in white and floor-to-ceiling shelves filled with books before Desi led her onward. Halfway down the hall, a wide, red-carpeted staircase led down to the main level. Next, she passed a large main bathroom and a bedroom with a dark wood canopy bed. The hall ended and turned to the right. Five open doors were spaced far apart. Desi stopped at the first one.

"I chose this room for you. If you'd rather have another, let me know." Desi stood aside so she could enter the bedroom.

A dainty four-poster bed with a white comforter and yellow, sage and brown pillows had a bench at its foot. A yellow rug spread out from the bed over the off-white carpet. On each side, big windows overlooked the pool. To the right were two chairs with a lamp on a table between, and to the left was a bathroom.

"There is a closet through the bathroom," Desi said.

There were no dressers in the bedroom, only a television on a table that matched the design of the bed and bench.

She turned back to Desi with a smile. "This is lovely."

He smiled back and began to leave.

"Wait."

He stopped.

"How did you know we met in Iceland?" she asked.

"I overheard him talking to an associate," he said.

"An associate?"

"An ex-CIA operative he asked to watch over you once he realized you looked at his cell phone," Desi said.

Ex-CIA? How did Raith know someone like that? This must not be information he wasn't allowed to share. And she wasn't surprised Raith had known she'd looked at his phone.

"Raith watches over everyone he cares about," he said.

Having no reply to that, she waited until Desi gave her a bow of his head and left. But his revelation gave her mixed feelings. Kai had hired him because someone had tried to kill him. That suggested Raith had at least a bit of a heroic streak in him. But was that enough to trust him with sharing her news? Autumn wasn't convinced.

The next morning, Autumn used the stairs she'd passed on the way to the bedroom last night. On the main level, she found herself in a hallway similar to the one above, except this one opened to the right into a spacious living room. One of the turrets arched the line of windows in front. High above, modern chandeliers hung from a thick beam running the length of the room.

She heard activity in the kitchen and went there. Desi was busy preparing something, some sort of breakfast casserole.

He glanced back at her. "Make yourself at home. Raith will be out in a few minutes."

"Where is he?"

"In his office."

Again? "What's he doing in there?"

Desi resumed whisking an egg mixture in a bowl. "I stopped asking him those questions a long time ago."

She walked to the kitchen island that divided the living room from the kitchen. "You don't know what he does for a living?"

"Oh, I have an idea. But I've found it's best not to ask questions." He glanced at her again. "I'm sure it's nothing too terrible."

Too terrible?

"He's a good man, that's the important thing."

Autumn wondered if that was the case all the time. "You cook for him?"

"Clean, cook. Shop. Whatever he needs me to do. He asked me to prepare meals while you're here." He stopped whisking and looked back at her again. "He said to make them good." He winked and resumed his work.

Where did all his romantic ideas come from? "You care about him."

"As I've said, Raith is a good man."

Beginning to feel awkward, Autumn turned toward the dining area. Through an archway to the right, there was a small entry and a double door—the one that led to the front door. Past the dining room, another archway led to what appeared to be a parlor. Intrigued, she wandered there, feeling Desi eye her.

The parlor was charming, with a piano positioned in a turret, sheer white drapes swooping over four tall windows. A Victorian sofa and two butter-yellow chairs sat before a gas fireplace. Behind the sofa, there was plenty of room to walk along a floor-to-ceiling bookshelf.

Another archway led to a vestibule with three doorways. The one to the left was glass and revealed a portion of an indoor pool. The one to the right had a keypad next to it. Autumn tested the handle to the one ahead and discovered a huge garage. Going to the third door, she entered the code Desi had given her into the keypad. The door didn't open. But as she pulled her hand free and was about to return to the kitchen, it opened and Raith stood there.

Beyond him, she caught a glimpse of a large U-shaped desk with several computer monitors and a living area with a kitchenette. He shut the door behind him.

"What's in there?" she asked.

"Security system and my office."

"I thought your office was off the front entry."

"This connects to that."

A secret office?

"This part is off-limits to everyone but me."

She found that both peculiar and believable. "Why? Are you hiding dead bodies in there?"

His face didn't even crack a wrinkle of humor, and humor is what would get her through this. Pregnant. By him, this mysterious, black ops man.

"Your personal assistant won't even say what it is you do," she said.

He cocked his head, possibly a little incredulous over her audacity.

"People hire you when their lives are in danger." She'd seen that much. "How do you drum up business? Advertising must be tough. Are you incorporated?"

"LLC."

"You pay taxes?"

He chuckled. "Yes."

"What do you put down as your professional title?"

"Private investigator."

Was he really a P.I.? "Can you be a P.I. without some kind of license?"

"I'm legal, if that's what you're wondering."

"What kind of cases do you take?"

"The word-of-mouth kind." He walked past her.

She followed him through the parlor. "But not the kind that involves the cops." He didn't respond.

"Are you an assassin?"

In the kitchen, Desi handed a glass of orange juice to Raith, who took it and turned, his eyes hard and on her while he drank. Desi handed her a glass, too, and when she took it, he went back to work on breakfast. He sure was in tune with his boss.

When Raith lowered the orange juice, he didn't back down from her eyes.

"Are you?" she asked, despite his attempt to intimidate her to stop grilling him.

"If someone shoots at me, I'm going to shoot back."

"No one's ever paid you to kill someone?"

His eyes remained unexpressive. Shrewd. Cold, even. A chill prickled her skin. What things had this man seen and experienced to make him this way? What had led him down this path?

Behind him, Desi sneaked a look at them after checking the breakfast casserole he had in the oven. He may not ask about Raith's profession, but must know something.

Raith's cell phone began ringing. He removed it from the holder on his belt and checked the caller ID. An instant later, the indifference in his eyes flared into resentment. Putting the phone back into the holder, he looked at Desi.

"You're going to have to answer it eventually," Desi said, pausing during the task of rinsing out a bowl.

Raith continued to look at him.

"He's going to keep calling until you do."

"Who?" Autumn asked.

When Raith didn't answer, Desi said, "His father."

"Why aren't you talking to your father?" He'd said he hadn't talked to him in years. Why was he ignoring his father's attempts to do so now? She couldn't imagine not talking to hers. Her mother wouldn't stand for it, first of all. Family meant everything to her.

"What's the point?" Raith asked.

The bite in his tone told her that somewhere inside of him he did want to talk to his dad. He just hadn't admitted it to himself yet.

"He's obviously trying to reach out to you," Desi said. "Maybe he's trying to make amends, have a son in his life for real this time."

"I'm not going to pick up where we left off. He had his chance."

Autumn sat on one of the stools before the island. "How many times has he tried to call?"

"A lot," Desi said, and went on despite the glower from Raith. "Almost every day for about a month now."

"He must need to get a hold of you," she said to Raith.

Raith looked at her. "Leaman Marshall has a sister in Houston. I need to go meet with her, and I can't leave you here."

"What?"

"Be ready to fly back there in the morning," he said. "I made flight reservations for 10:00 a.m."

He'd explained that he'd learned Tabor Creighton's real name. "You've been busy in your top-secret office."

Raith ignored her and turned to Desi. "Would you bring me some of that when it's ready?" He gestured toward the oven.

"Of course," Desi said.

With one more hard glance at Autumn, Raith headed back toward the secure door to his hidden office.

When she heard the door latch and lock, she looked at Desi. "What's the story with him and his father? He told me he hasn't spoken to him since he was seventeen and that his mother died when he was fourteen."

"He told you that?"

"Yes." Why was that so significant?

"He never talks about his mother. Never. Not to anyone." Desi studied her as though she held some kind of magical power.

"It seemed like a difficult subject for him."

Desi moved with a slow, knowing blink to the island and put his hands on the edge. "Difficult is an understatement. Raith's mother got sick with a severe case of pneumonia. That's how she died. His father was an alcoholic and didn't take care of Raith very well. He wasn't there for him at all."

"He also mentioned that his older brother left a few months after his mother died."

Desi nodded. "Raith becomes angry when I say it, but he has terrible abandonment issues."

Autumn could see how grief and the lack of love from his father could drive a wedge between them, but would it be enough to shut his father out for the rest of his life?

"His mother died shortly after she discovered his father was having an affair with one of her close friends," Desi said. "He blames his father for her death."

She'd died of pneumonia. Her resistance must have been down, or she'd had other issues going on to lower her immunity.

"Did his mother drink?"

"Raith has never called her an alcoholic, but I suspect she did drink more than he likes to reveal. And I also suspect Raith's father was having affairs long before the one she finally confronted him with."

"What happened when she confronted him?"

"He denied it and she didn't press him any further."

And bottling up all that emotion had led to her death, according to Raith. "That's so sad."

"Yes. For Raith's mother and for him."

The next morning, Autumn was unusually quiet as Desi drove them to the airport. She looked out the window as if she was deep in thought. A couple of times he'd watched Desi in the rearview mirror. How much had he told her? Nothing about his work. Raith trusted him with his life in that regard, but when it came to personal matters and matchmaking, Desi couldn't resist intervention.

When Desi drove to a stop in front of the passenger drop-off area, Raith got out and retrieved his and Autumn's luggage, which were both carry-ons.

Wearing black-and-white leopard-print stockings that drew the eye to her slender hips and thighs, frivolous black high heels and a flowing black shirt that stopped just below her waist, she took the handle of her bag. When he'd first seen her this morning he'd had to stop himself from choking on coffee. "I hope you packed more sensible clothes."

She looked down at herself. "What's wrong with this?"

"Great for indoor activities, but not much help if you have to run for your life."

Her head jerked back a fraction. "I'm going to have to run for my life?"

He didn't answer. She knew what he was talking about. She was just being sarcastic.

"I'll call you with the return-flight information," he said to Desi. He and Autumn had open-ended tickets.

Desi nodded. "Have a safe trip."

Autumn waved with a smile and walked with Raith into the terminal.

"Has your dad tried to call you again?" Autumn asked.

What was it about his dad that had her contemplating so much? "No."

"Desi told me about your mother. I'm sorry you had to lose her that way."

Unloved by her husband. Depressed. Unfulfilled. But loving the man who made her so unhappy. "Part of life."

They moved forward in the security line.

"I mean, losing a mother would be hard on any kid. But not having your father's support at a time like that? I…I just… I can't imagine."

He wished she'd stop. Why was she delving into this, anyway? Why were his mother's death and his estranged relationship with his father so important to her?

"Does your brother keep in contact with your dad?" she asked.

"I don't know. I doubt it."

"Maybe if you talked to him it would help."

He looked over at her. She was pretty tall compared to his six-three. Most women he ended up with were shorter. He'd never been with anyone with red hair before. Autumn's was a soft red and shimmered in the light. Her beauty defused some of his angst that she had to bring this up.

"Why are you so concerned?" he asked.

Facing forward in the line, she shrugged. "It's sad and…so different from the way I grew up."

"With normal parents? Didn't you have challenges being a famous movie producer's daughter?"

"Well, yeah, but my parents love each other. And they were always there for us—as much as they could be having eight kids."

"You're lucky, but I don't have any regrets about not being in contact with my father. It doesn't matter why he's trying to contact me after all these years. I don't care why. And I don't care about him. He is dead as far as I'm concerned."

As they approached the security checkpoint, he saw her doubt. She didn't believe that he didn't care.

A small part of him did care, but he wasn't fooled when it came to his father. Nothing he had to say would change the damage he'd done. It wouldn't bring Raith's mother back, and it wouldn't make the way his father had treated her and his kids forgivable. Raith would never forgive his father.

On the way to the gate, Autumn fell into another period of consternation. Her somberness didn't seem to match her sympathy for his years in a broken home.

"Is something wrong?" he asked.

Her head snapped up and over, and her green eyes met his briefly. "No."

As he walked beside her and observed her profile, he grew certain her answer wasn't an honest one.

Chapter 6

Kamira Marshall lived in an apartment building with tan-wood lap siding. Not the grandest in Houston but not the worst, either. Autumn was still uneasy over her changing perception of Raith. Compassion had offered some insight into the reasons he'd chosen such an atypical career, but was she prepared to tell him about her pregnancy? Doing so would link her to him if he intended to be part of the child's life, whether they ended up together or not. Having a baby with him made her feel trapped. He debatably had a moral heart. He had a controversial, violent profession. He was essentially a gun-for-hire. Not the ideal father figure. And then there was the whole issue of how she felt about settling down. She had an urge to run. Get away from him and any possibility of tying her down.

A tiny internal voice whispered, *What if he would make a good father? What if he settled down with her and shared the responsibility of raising a child? What if it worked out for them?* A secret spot inside of her tickled with hope. But that spot had to be tamed into submission. Her sometimes-public life opposed his secret one. If he wasn't willing to make drastic changes, letting her heart rule her head was dangerous.

Autumn had always prided herself on being open-minded. It went along with her sense of adventure and spontaneity. She'd never expected to meet a man like Raith. She couldn't afford to be open-minded with him. He would have to turn his life upside down the way hers was going to be turned upside down as soon as the baby was born, and she didn't see him doing that.

Kamira opened her apartment door, which had an entry to the outside. An average-size woman with light brown hair and eyes, she had blotchy skin and was dressed in jeans and a football T-shirt with an unbuttoned shirt over that.

"Kamira Marshall?" Raith asked.

"Yes?" she said warily.

"We're here to ask you some questions about your brother, Leaman Marshall."

"Who are you?"

"I'm Raith De Matteis and this is my girlfriend, Autumn. We're here trying to locate an associate of Leaman's."

Autumn expected him to lie, but he didn't, well, not really. While she stiffened with the shock of Raith calling her his girlfriend, Kamira eyed them both before saying, "My brother is dead."

"We're aware of that. We still think you may be able to help us."

"What associate are you looking for?"

"That's part of the problem. We don't have a name."

After several long seconds of contemplation, she said, "I don't have anything to do with his trouble. I'm sorry, I can't help you." She was about to close the door, when Raith put his hand on it and stopped her.

"We're aware that your brother was a contract killer," Raith announced.

Autumn wondered how that would make her more comfortable. Would she protect him?

"Why are you looking for this associate?" Kamira asked. "Are you cops?"

"No. We're helping the man who was almost killed. We're looking for the person who hired him."

Kamira blinked a few times as though the subject of her brother upset her, and not only because he was dead. What other associate could there be than someone who'd contracted for his services? Her disappointment was evident. Much of her grief must center around her brother's poor choices.

"Please. We just have a few questions," Raith said.

"I don't see what good that will do if he's dead."

"We're talking to everyone who knew him."

She hesitated but seemed to consider relenting. "Did my brother shoot someone?"

"He made an attempt and missed."

"He missed?"

"Yes, fortunately."

Kamira contemplated them a moment more. Then, rather than invite them inside, she stepped out onto the concrete sidewalk in front of her door.

"What do you need to know?"

"When was the last time you saw him?" Raith asked.

"About two months ago."

Fairly recent. "Were the two of you close?" Autumn asked.

Kamira shrugged. "We had each other growing up. Messed-up parents, you know?" She reached into the pocket of the button-up shirt she wore and took out a pack of cigarettes. After lighting one and taking a puff, she blew out a stream of smoke and said, "He wasn't the type to make it home for the holidays, and I don't think he ever saw any women long-term. He traveled a lot. Hardly ever home, but when he was, he came here for visits regularly. He spent time with his best friend, too."

Autumn was amazed at how freely Kamira spoke. She didn't condone her brother's lifestyle, but she must have loved him despite all of that.

"Who is that?" Raith asked.

"Garvin Reeves. He runs a gun shop and shooting range here. They've been friends for years. Met in school. Leaman was always so reclusive. A loner. And he was always getting arrested when he was younger. Garvin looked up to him."

That didn't say much for Garvin's character if he looked up to someone like that.

"What about when he was an adult?" Raith asked.

Kamira shrugged again, taking another drag off her cigarette. "He stopped getting arrested. I think he got good at skirting the law. He never talked about what he did and I didn't ask about it. I never liked his obsession with guns. He got that from Garvin. I suspected he was into some pretty serious crime and always thought it would be only a matter of time before the law caught up to him." She eyed them both as she took another drag. "Sorry, I'm afraid I can't help you much."

"Why didn't you talk about what he did for a living?" Autumn asked.

"It disturbed me. I worried about him. I didn't need to worry more with more details. He was a criminal. I guess

I expected to lose him eventually. Having some distance from him helped his death be a little more bearable." She looked across the parking lot again. "I often wonder if he hadn't been bullied as a kid if he'd have ended up where he did. If he hadn't been bullied, I doubt he'd have gone into the military. He was always into science and math. Maybe he'd have gone to college to be an engineer or something. Something different."

"We're very sorry for your loss," Autumn said.

Turning to her, Kamira continued with her ruminating. "Leaman was a good person. Few people had the privilege of seeing that. He just had bad parents and a hard time in school socially. Some people can't overcome. He was one of them. His way of coping was rebelling."

Kamira knew him the way no one else had. She knew the boy. But perhaps she only thought she knew the man. A killer.

"What happened to your parents?" Raith asked.

Waving her hand, Kamira fanned out the trail of smoke from her cigarette. "Who the hell knows. My dad was a drunk and left when I was five and my mom was a crackhead. She's probably dead by now. They both probably are. Who cares?"

"Do you have any kids?"

She shook her head. "I'm not married."

"Were you ever married?"

"No. Are you investigating me, too?" She sucked on her cigarette.

Raith smiled and Autumn wondered if that was strategic to make her relax. "No."

He was only trying to find out if there was anyone else he could talk to.

"You said Leaman got into guns because of Garvin," Raith said.

She raised her eyes in annoyance. "Yeah. He and Garvin got into trouble together when they were kids. Then Garvin started making a living selling guns."

"Illegally?"

She nodded. "Not one hundred percent. More on the side and through his gun shop. Garvin's not a guy to piss off."

"He's got some impressive clientele?" Raith continued with his line of questioning.

"I never ask. Like I said before, Leaman and I didn't discuss his business. But he did once say he got a lot of his business through Garvin." Kamira didn't seem happy about that. "At least in the beginning."

"And then Leaman earned a reputation," Raith said.

She nodded again. "He started to make a lot of money. I mean, *a lot.* As in hundreds of thousands per job. He sent me money every month. Things are going to get harder for me now. He never came out and said he killed people. But once he did say that rich people hired him to take care of their problems."

And she'd translated that correctly by guessing that meant he was hired to kill.

"Do you know who killed him?" Kamira asked.

"No," Raith said. "He was good at hiding. He knew someone was after him. He said something went wrong during his last job." She got that faraway look again. "Whoever killed him must be somebody as dangerous as him."

Autumn glanced over at Raith. That someone was him. Assassin. Killer. Was that really what Raith was all about? She sensed not and that didn't settle well with her.

"I would imagine." Raith put his hand on Autumn's arm, indicating it was time for them to go. "Thanks for talking to us."

"Just as dangerous, huh?" Autumn said when they reached the parking lot.

He said nothing, only seemed to try to determine the source of her disgruntlement. Or maybe he already knew and couldn't reassure her.

Raith drove with Autumn to Garvin Reeves's gun shop and shooting range. Inside the flat-roofed, single-story warehouse, the front was partitioned off and filled with glass gun cases that ran along three sides and one down the middle. A double door in the back must lead to the shooting range. Posters advertising ammunition and the latest rifles on the market hung on the walls. Two windows in front and one on the side had old, cheap white blinds that were kept shut but allowed light in through broken panels.

A clerk helped a customer to their right. Another saw them from where he stood in the back near the doors.

"Can I help you?" that clerk asked, putting his hands on the edge of the counter. A skinny man and not very tall, he had dark circles under his brown eyes and chapped lips.

Raith walked toward the man, Autumn following. "We're looking for Garvin Reeves. Is he here?"

"Who's asking?" The clerk pushed off the counter.

Raith caught the clerk's guardedness. Garvin's workers were trained to be on the lookout for cops.

"Raith De Matteis. This is my girlfriend, Autumn."

Autumn turned to look at him. This was the second time he'd introduced her as his girlfriend. Did she like playing the role of his girlfriend or did it offend her?

"Wait here." The clerk disappeared through a door. The sound of gunshots grew louder until the door swung shut again.

Autumn leaned closer to Raith and whispered, "Why aren't we using false names?"

"We don't need to," he whispered back.

"Why not?"

"It doesn't matter if these people know who we are."

Before she could ask why, a man emerged from the back. Close to six feet tall, Garvin was more muscular than the clerk and had almond-shaped blue eyes that leveled on him, hard and shrewd.

"Mr. De Matteis." Garvin said his name as though he were a long-lost acquaintance.

"Garvin Reeves?"

"Yes."

"We're here to talk to you about Leaman Marshall. His sister, Kamira, said you were good friends."

"You talked to Kamira?"

"We just came from her apartment."

He looked from him to Autumn and back again. "Are you some kind of investigator or something?"

"I'm a private investigator," Raith answered. He didn't see much to gain by lying.

"A private investigator, huh?" He looked at Autumn again. "And this is your girlfriend?"

"Yes." Did he wonder why he'd brought her?

He turned to Autumn. "You look familiar."

"We're here to talk to you about Leaman," Raith said. "He was hired by someone to kill Kai Whittaker."

Garvin turned to Raith, still pondering whether he'd seen Autumn before. "Who?"

"Kai Whittaker. CEO of DT Corporation."

"Leaman never mentioned anyone by that name," Garvin said, and it may or may not be the truth.

"Did you sell Leaman any guns?" No professional killer would own a registered gun.

Garvin shook his head, but in a cynical way, almost mocking. He folded his arms. He was definitely lying.

"I wonder how much inventory is missing from your records," Raith said.

"Is that a threat?"

A man like him wouldn't respond well to threats. "No. I just find it hard to believe that you wouldn't help out a friend." He insinuated that the kind of help offered would be illegal.

"Leaman never talked to me about any of his jobs." He grinned. "Real sorry about that."

Raith hadn't expected Garvin to talk.

"He did tell me about you, though," Garvin said. He lowered his arms and leaned on the counter, bringing himself closer to Raith in a menacing way. "He said you wouldn't leave him alone and that you were the reason he went to Reykjavik."

"I've been looking for him for quite some time." Raith didn't have to explain to Garvin his history with Leaman. Even with the horrible things his friend had done, Garvin would victimize him.

"You should have kept your nose out of his business."

"He should have kept his out of mine."

Beside him, Autumn looked from Garvin to him. Not much ruffled Raith, and this man certainly didn't. He must sound that way to Autumn right now.

"Did you kill him?" Garvin asked.

"I thought Leaman never talked to you about his jobs."

"He talked to me about you. But you probably already knew that, right? Otherwise, why come in here and show yourself, much less use your real name?" He let a few beats pass. "Did you kill him?"

Raith didn't justify that with an answer. He wasn't

going to lie, and he wasn't going to volunteer the information. But Garvin drew his own conclusion.

Anger pinched the bridge of Garvin's nose and darkened his eyes. "I should kill you right now."

"You could try."

"You think you're invincible, but you're not. Your day will come. When your guard is down, your day will come."

"Judging from everything I've heard about Leaman, I'd say he got what he deserved. If I were you, I'd be careful not to follow the same path."

Garvin looked past them and gave a single nod.

Two big men approached, flanking Raith and Autumn.

"Have a nice day, Mr. De Matteis," Garvin said. Then he looked at Autumn. "My regrets for not meeting you under different circumstances."

Autumn didn't respond, only turned with Raith. He put his arm around her, ushering her ahead of him.

Outside, the door slammed shut and he and Autumn walked to the car.

"Now what are we going to do?"

"Find another way to get information out of him."

Parking right in front of Garvin's tri-level in a 1970s neighborhood, Raith noted the evidence that his business wasn't doing very well. Garvin may sell guns illegally, but he wasn't making significant income from doing so. That suggested that he may be keeping it to a minimum and perhaps, at least to some extent, he had respect for the law. Or feared it, which really was the same thing. Maybe now that Leaman was dead and no longer able to influence him, he'd live a legitimate life.

"What are we doing?" Autumn asked.

"We're going to see if Garvin is hiding anything in

his house." He climbed out of the car, fleetingly catching Autumn's confused look.

When she walked beside him on the dying grass of the front lawn, he said, "Stay close to me."

"Isn't this dangerous?" she asked. "And *illegal?*"

"I won't let anything happen to you."

"What about the illegal part?"

The decided edge to her tone and her brisk pace revealed her antipathy. What had her so uptight? The illegality of breaking and entering did have cause for concern, but the emotion he sensed in her clued him in to more. Her reaction had to stem from more than the situation she had been unwittingly drawn into. It was more personal than that.

"Would you prefer to wait in the car?" he asked.

"No," she snapped.

He stopped, looking around to make sure no one took special notice of them. "If you have a problem with this…"

"I don't."

"Then what's wrong?"

"Nothing." She started walking briskly again.

He caught up to her. "Is it Garvin?"

"Is what Garvin?"

"Did going to talk to him bother you?" She'd looked at him funny when he'd subtly threatened the man.

"No. Just drop it."

"Sorry, you just seem a little moody all of a sudden."

They walked around the side of the house. Autumn didn't respond, but he could see and feel her emotions churning.

At Garvin's back door, he glanced at Autumn before he pulled out his special tool and had the garage open in less than a minute. It had an old, worn lock.

"Not your first break-in, huh?" Autumn sneered.

"I'm not the bad guy in all of this, Autumn."

She eyed him as though that was debatable.

He stepped into the garage. The inner door was unlocked. He led Autumn through a messy kitchen with chipped butcher-block counters, gold appliances and fake oak linoleum floor. The small living room had badly stained off-white carpeting and a worn blue cloth couch and chair framing a square coffee table littered with trash and evidence of drug use.

"Remember to stay close to me," he said to Autumn.

"Where else would I go?" she asked. "I'd like to still be breathing after this is all over."

That stopped him. He faced her. "All right, tell me what's got you so upset. Is it because I called you my girlfriend?"

"No."

He heard the half-truth in her voice. "Why does that upset you? Because you aren't?"

"You lie and shoot a gun for a living."

Should he be the one offended now? "So you resent being portrayed as my girlfriend."

"No."

Now he heard the truth and softened. But there was still something missing, something she wasn't saying, and wouldn't say.

"It's just…I've never had a boyfriend like you before. One who…breaks the law."

"And that's what upsets you?" That's all?

"Yes."

Raith didn't see himself as crooked. But he did see how that would bother her—if she were actually his girlfriend.

"I've thought about getting out of this and doing something different," he said.

Her face brightened. "You have?"

"I can't travel the world and shoot people my whole life. I'd like to retire someday."

"When is someday?"

"I could retire now if I decided to." Why did his getting out of his current profession appeal to her so much?

That warmed her even more, he saw. "You'd be bored."

"Exactly why I haven't done it yet."

"You could find something else to do. What do you enjoy?"

"Do-it-yourself projects. And I do like working in criminal justice."

"So maybe a twist on that." She smiled.

He looked down her body in a flowing yellow top that flared over the waist of dark blue leggings. She'd hung her small beaded purse securely from her shoulder, gripping the strap, a bulky yellow-and-blue bracelet matching her earrings and necklace.

"Yeah. Maybe."

A thump on the window made her jump. It was only a bird that had flown into the glass.

"Are you armed?" Autumn asked.

He grinned at the innocent question that would require he protect her. Lifting his short-sleeved button-up shirt, he showed her the holster.

She put her hands on his chest and patted. "Good." He let her push him out of the way as she led him down a lower-level hall and entered the office.

This was probably the nicest room in the house. Although the desk looked used and abused, the computer was shiny and new. So was the leather office chair. Somebody spent hours working here, and Raith was pretty sure it wasn't for the shooting range.

Autumn began sifting through papers and files stuffing a bookshelf while Raith sat at the desk. He dug through drawers and found a key in one that opened a metal lockbox. In that was a small notebook with a page of what appeared to be passwords. He tried them all until one unlocked the computer. After hacking into it, he navigated to the email program. While he searched for anything unusual, he listened for sounds of Garvin's return home.

A few moments later, Autumn finished with the bookshelf and moved on to a trash can.

Raith found an email from someone named Nash Ralston. It read, Sorry to hear about Leaman.

He committed the name to memory and searched the other emails. There were several advertisements and purchase confirmations but no other acquaintances. He checked the Deleted folder. That was kept clean. It was empty.

Chapter 7

Autumn sat beside Raith in an internet café as he searched for information on Nash Ralston. It hadn't taken long to learn who he was. Chief executive officer of NV Advanced Corporation, a government contractor similar to the one Kai Whittaker ran.

"That can't be a coincidence," Autumn said. Doing all of this investigative work took her mind off her mood swing earlier. Nash Ralston knew Garvin, whose close friend was Leaman Marshall. Both Kai and Nash were CEOs of night-vision equipment companies. The two had to be acquainted on at least a professional level.

"Do you think Ralston hired Leaman through Garvin?" she asked.

"It's possible. Why don't we go talk to Kai." Raith closed his session on the computer.

"What about Nash?"

"Later. Let's see what Kai has to say." He took Autumn's hand and left the café with her. Outside, he made a call.

"Mayo. It's Raith. I need you to look into someone for me. See what you can dig up on a Nash Ralston. He runs a government contracting outfit in Houston called NV Advanced Corporation."

When he hung up, she got into the car with him. "Who was that?"

"Mayo Chambers. He's ex-CIA."

The one Desi had told her about. "You're supposed to be a P.I. Why don't you do your own checking?"

"Because I'd have to use one of my contacts in law enforcement and they can't be tipped off to who I'm looking into until I know more about this Ralston character."

"You have contacts in law enforcement?"

"A few."

"Are they crooked?"

He grunted a laugh. "No."

That almost made him seem legitimate. Autumn turned toward the window rather than torment herself with his handsome profile. Seeming legitimate wasn't the same as being legitimate. He took the law into his own hands. Even if he worked on the side of good, he was still breaking the law. She struggled with that for a while as she stayed silent.

After a few minutes of driving, Raith asked, "What's wrong?"

This was the second time he'd asked, and both times she'd been upset over her pregnancy—specifically with him being the father. Was he beginning to suspect something?

"I was just thinking that I'd love to go to shopping in Milan."

He glanced at her as he drove. "No translating?"

"No. Just to go. To get away." Although she'd made up the idea to cover up what she'd really been thinking, a trip to Milan really did appeal to her right now.

"Is that what you're going to do when this is over?"

"Maybe. I have another translating job coming up in Europe. I could combine the two and make it an extra-long trip." The thought of that soothed her. There would be no guns. No media. And no lawless renegades.

"It's an escape for you."

As Raith pulled into a parking lot and found a spot, she searched his face. What did he mean?

"You travel because it gets you away from whatever you're avoiding here."

"What's wrong with that? I like no media around."

"I can appreciate that, but is it only the media?"

"No. I love to travel." What was he fishing for?

"I can see that. You also love learning new languages. But it all started with an escape."

She wasn't sure of the significance of that, but it did make her think of her days in high school, when all she'd tried to do was get away from there. Even the private schools were painful. She'd put on a good face. No one would have guessed she hated being recognized and treated differently than the other kids. Being Jackson Ivy's child made her and her siblings automatically popular. She'd always felt as though she couldn't be herself, as though being herself wouldn't make her popular. She'd had to act the part.

"That might have a little to do with it," she finally admitted. "The first trip I took by myself was during my senior year in high school." She smiled with the memory. "It felt so good to get away. I could just be me and enjoy living."

"You couldn't be yourself in high school?"

"Hello…Jackson Ivy's daughter. It was the same for all of us." She rested her elbow on the door frame and chewed on a thumbnail. She'd never thought of herself as insecure, but maybe she had been in high school.

"Why does that mean you couldn't be yourself?"

Lowering her hand, she turned toward him, wondering why he'd asked. "Because they all expected someone popular."

"You'd be popular regardless of how you acted. You could have been yourself. Why weren't you?"

She continued to stare at him, startled that she didn't have an answer. She'd never thought of it that way. "I suppose because it was my dad they were all in awe of. I was Jackson Ivy's daughter, not Autumn Ivy, the girl who loved languages. How boring is that?"

"When you travel you can be yourself."

Out of the camera's eye. "That's part of it. I'm not the rich socialite the media portrays me as. I'm not a celebrity. I'm rarely recognized when I travel. I'm just a translator or a tourist. Me."

As he held her gaze from across the car, she could see him deducing things he kept to himself. He was a man who never put on a face for anybody. He was himself all the time, whether he appeared to others as hero or killer. He was a man who never compromised himself.

She admired that about him. Envied him, even. And in the next instant, she also realized that maybe the real reason why she never committed to anyone. Why she was a lone wolf…like him but not like him.

As soon as men made her feel as though she had to put on a face, she ran away to foreign countries.

That was fine by her. It might be an escape, as Raith said, but if a man made her feel as if she had to fake who she was to be with him, she'd rather be an entertainment headline and travel to far-off places than erase herself.

Raith didn't make her feel erased. Ever since meeting him, she hadn't faked anything. There went her mood again.

"Come on, let's go," he said gently, as though guessing her thoughts.

How had he gotten so smart? By being a survivor? A rebel one...

Autumn walked with him toward NV Advanced Corporation.

Raith held one of the glass doors open for her, and then asked the security guard to inform Kai they were here. Seconds later, they were given visitor badges and escorted by Kai's assistant to the top floor.

Led to a glass-walled office that took up an entire corner of the floor, Raith greeted the man guarding the door before they were allowed into the office. Kai's bodyguard. A big man, he stretched the black suit he wore as he stood with meaty hands clasped in front of him.

Kai remained seated behind his desk. "Raith. I wasn't expecting you."

Raith stopped on the other side of his desk, behind two black leather chairs. Autumn stood beside him.

"I see you got in touch with Raith," Kai said to her.

She glanced at Raith. Clearly he hadn't updated his client in a few days. She didn't expect him to reveal any personal details.

"I'm a little surprised to see you," Kai added, still looking at her.

"Someone followed her after you met her," Raith said. "They shot at her."

Kai's brow rose and he leaned forward in his chair,

obviously taken aback. He glanced at Autumn, knowing why she'd been shot at. His look conveyed a recollection of what he'd told her, how dangerous it had been to reach out to him. Autumn lifted her chin and met his eyes. She didn't need an I-told-you-so.

At last he said to Raith, "Why didn't you tell me? Did you see who the shooter was?"

"I didn't recognize the man, and the plates were from a stolen car that was later recovered. The police have no leads as to the identity of the thief."

When had he ferreted out that information? Autumn eyed him and concluded he must have done that when he'd ensconced himself in his secure office.

"You didn't think that was important to tell me?" Kai asked. He was obviously a CEO who was not accustomed to being left out of the loop.

"I'm telling you now."

With a disapproving frown, Kai leaned back against his big leather chair. "How did he get away?"

"It was too public to risk a forced interrogation."

"Is that what you came here to tell me? Why did you wait so long?"

"Since I had nothing to report, I didn't think it warranted your concern. We're here because we've had some breaks in the investigation."

"I'm flattered that you decided to finally share."

"How well do you know Nash Ralston?" Raith asked, dismissing Kai's sarcasm.

Autumn realized he hadn't contacted Kai until he had to. An investigation could unearth unexpected things. Did he not trust Kai? More likely he didn't trust anyone.

A few stunned seconds passed before Kai said, "He's a business associate. We're in the same business. Our companies compete for contracts. Why are you asking me about him? I don't see how he's connected to whomever shot at me."

"So you're not friends?" Raith asked Kai.

"No, not friends, but not enemies, either. Are you suggesting Ralston may have been the one to hire Creighton?"

"I'm not suggesting anything. I found his name in Garvin Reeves's email files. He expressed sympathy over Creighton's death, who, incidentally, is not Tabor Creighton. His name is Leaman Marshall. He and Garvin were close friends."

Kai leaned back and rubbed his chin, his elbow on the armrest. "And Garvin and Ralston are friends?"

"So it would seem."

"Have you spoken with Nash?"

"Not yet."

Lowering his hand, Kai contemplated what he'd learned so far. "I can see why you're pursuing this. Nash could have found Mr. Marshall through his friend Garvin. The only question is does Nash really have motive?"

"That's why we're here."

"Nash is a business associate."

"A competitor," Autumn said. "You compete for big government contracts. Night-vision equipment."

"I find it a stretch that Nash would go to such extremes. Why would he? To get more contracts for his company? I doubt he's that desperate to keep his job… or lose it if he's caught."

He had a valid point.

"What about the email?" Autumn asked, anyway. "There's an obvious link between Ralston and Marshall."

Kai turned to Raith. "You said the email was between Nash and Garvin."

"It was. Expressing sympathy over Leaman Marshall's death. That implies Ralston at least knew of Marshall."

Kai considered that for a long moment, longer than Autumn thought reasonable. He seemed to be holding something back, and trying to steer this discussion away from Ralston as a suspect in his attempted shooting. "All right. It's possible he contacted Marshall without going through Garvin."

"Do you know Garvin?" Raith asked.

Kai grunted cynically. "No. Why do you think I would?"

"You don't seem willing to accept the possibility," Raith said.

"I just can't imagine Nash hiring someone to kill me. What have I ever done to him except beat him to a few prime contracts?"

Autumn looked over at Raith. He'd caught Kai's use of the word *beat*.

"Do you beat him a lot?"

"I beat everyone a lot. It's because of me that DT Corporation is the leading supplier of night-vision equipment to the U.S. government."

Would that be enough to drive Ralston to such extreme measures? Or was there something else that Kai wasn't saying? Something that *would* be enough to drive Ralston to extreme measures. Like murder.

Chapter 8

A stop at NV Advanced Corporation proved to be a waste of time. Ralston was away on business travel and wouldn't be in the office until the next day. Back at the hotel, Autumn didn't feel like ordering room service. Raith didn't protest, so they'd gone down to the nicest restaurant in the hotel.

With a tealight burning in the middle of the table, it had begun to feel like a date.

"No wine?" Raith asked.

Would he have joined her if she'd have ordered some? Or was he curious for another reason?

"This is romantic enough. Anymore and we might be in trouble." That should divert his inquiring mind.

He smiled just a bit. His emotions never came into his face much. He kept them under control. He reminded her of a detective on one of those investigative reality shows. Not much animation came into their faces, although she sometimes could tell they made an effort. That's what happened when a person saw too much death.

"Is that your way of stopping yourself from feeling too much for a rebel like me?" he asked.

"Shouldn't you be doing the same with a heartbreaker like me?" Two could play that game...

His smile grew but only marginally. "Would you break my heart?"

"Milan is awfully appealing right now." She smiled back at him.

He chuckled. "Yeah, but what would happen when you got back? Would you stay away? Would you be able to?"

That he'd even asked such a flirtatious question went against her perception of his character. And then she realized he was talking about the chemistry they'd generated in Iceland, hot enough to melt a glacier.

"I suppose we'll have to wait and see."

"An adventure to look forward to."

The waiter arrived and Autumn took longer than she should have needed to order. Raith suffered no awkwardness. In fact, he seemed to enjoy flustering her.

What was he doing? Did he hope to seduce her again? Seduce her and then leave her the way he had in Iceland? That wouldn't bother her if she wasn't pregnant.

The rest of dinner passed with idle talk and many long looks. Autumn still hadn't cooled by the time they left and rode the elevator to the top floor. She dreaded being in the suite alone with him, and then anticipated it at the same time. Raith slept on the sofa bed in the seating area and she slept in the bedroom, but it may as well be one giant king-size bed in a huge, wall-free room.

Just as they entered the suite, Raith's cell rang.

Glad for the reprieve, Autumn went to stand by the

window to gather her wits, looking out at the city lights to wait for Raith to answer the call. He never did.

Turning, she saw him putting his phone on the table beside the pullout bed.

"Your father again?" she asked.

He sent her a brooding look.

A clear enough answer. He was sure dogged about ignoring his father. "He's calling you a lot."

Raith picked up the remote and turned on the television. End of discussion.

She walked over to him, ready to do some serious probing. Her own cell rang and she stopped next to a chair. Seeing it was her sister Savanna, she answered.

"Where are you?" Savanna demanded.

"In Houston."

"No one knows where you are. Why haven't you answered your phone?"

She'd only answered Savanna's call because Savanna already knew about Raith. Her mother didn't, and she didn't feel like explaining.

"I've been busy." She met Raith's eyes. He hadn't turned on the television to watch it, only for something to take his mind off his father, apparently.

"Not that busy. What's going on with you, Autumn? Is it that guy?"

"What guy?"

Raith leaned back, no longer brooding. She was a better distraction than the television now.

"You know what guy. The one Lincoln doesn't like."

Autumn couldn't respond.

"What are you doing, Autumn?"

"I'll be home soon."

"Call Mom. She's worried to death about you."

"No. Will you call her? Tell her I'm fine. I'm just on another trip. The media is all over me because of Knox."

One of Raith's eyebrows rose higher than the other.

Her sister scoffed. "You're a terrible liar. Call Mom."

Autumn sighed. "All right. I'll call her." There was no avoiding it.

"Now."

"All right," Autumn snapped.

"If you don't, I'm going to call you back. Over and over again."

"I'll call her. Geez."

After disconnecting that call, Autumn sat on the chair near the sofa. She stared down at her phone for a while.

Relaxed against the sofa, a slight grin formed on his sexy mouth. He was enjoying this. She almost went into the bedroom to do this, when her cell rang again.

Mom.

Savanna had no doubt texted her or something and she couldn't wait.

Autumn connected the call. "Hi, Mom."

"Autumn Ivy, I'm so relieved to hear your voice. Why haven't you answered my calls?"

She looked over at Raith, dreading the inevitable. Her mother had strong family values and never took kindly to her children going into radio silence. "I'm fine, Mom. I'm not twelve anymore."

"You know I need to hear from all of my babies on a regular basis. Wondering where you are and how you are when you're not in contact with anyone is terrible. How can you do that to your own mother?"

"Sorry." Autumn smiled. "I've just been busy." Chasing assassins and conspirators to murder...

"Lincoln told me about that man you met in Iceland. Is that who you're with?"

They were going to find out eventually, anyway. Having a baby couldn't be kept secret forever.

"Yes."

"Then I'm going to worry even more about you. Lincoln said he lied to you about what he did for a living. He's since done some more checking and discovered he's a private investigator."

"He is."

"Lincoln doesn't believe that. He said if you're with him that you shouldn't be. He's trouble, Autumn."

"He's not bad, Mom."

A long silence ensued and Autumn didn't look at Raith to see his reaction to what she'd just said. Finally her mother said, "Bring him to the house so I can meet him."

What? "Mother—"

"Bring him here so we can meet him."

"I can't. Not now, Mother."

"Autumn, this is not up for negotiation. If this man is no good for you and you're saying otherwise, I need to see for myself. We're having a cocktail party this weekend. Saturday night. You be here for it or I swear I'll have your father step in and send someone to get you."

She'd do it, too. "Mother, I'm serious. I can't get away right now."

"Why not? What kind of trouble has this man gotten you into that you can't come to a cocktail party at your mother's?"

"You want me to bring him to *California?*" This weekend? Impossible. Raith would never go for it. Not only would a cocktail party at the Ivy mansion attract heavy media, he was in the middle of catching whoever hired Leaman.

"Yes."

When Autumn didn't respond, her mother said, "I mean it, Autumn, I'll talk to your father."

"Oh, I don't doubt you would. All right. We'll be there." Or she'd be there. She couldn't vouch for Raith.

She disconnected and met his no-longer amused look.

"I have to go to my parents' this weekend."

"You can't go anywhere until it's safe."

He had never been to her parents' mansion. Security there was as tight as the White House's. "Well, then, you're going to have to go with me."

Raith leaned forward, forearms on his knees. "Go *with you?*"

"Yes."

"To your parents' house."

"I-it's more of a…a mansion, but yes." Just imagining him there stressed her out. He'd be so out of his element. Then again…maybe that was exactly what he needed. Shake him a little.

He stared at her. "Can't it wait?"

"I wish it could, but no. There is no such thing as waiting when it comes to my mother. Her dinner parties are very important to her. Her kids are even more important. She needs to see for herself that you're someone to be trusted with one of her precious daughters."

"Why? We aren't really a couple."

"Then I'll just go, and I'll stay there until you find whoever hired the shooter."

Raith stared at her. "I didn't mean…"

"It's okay. I understand."

"No, you don't. We aren't really a couple but we do have something going on."

Did he think that? Did they have something going on right now? "Then I should feel okay with bringing you home to meet my parents." And she didn't. Especially since she was pregnant by said man. "And you should be able to attend dinner parties."

"Not the ones held at a famous movie producer's mansion."

Suddenly the reality of how different his life was from hers weighed on her more than she could bear. As a person, he shared many similarities with her, but his livelihood wrecked all of that. He could never stand by her side with cameras flashing. It didn't matter if she didn't like the cameras, they'd always be flashing. And he'd always be hiding.

What would she do when she could no longer hide her pregnancy?

She could say it was Knox's.

A choking sensation inundated her so strongly that she had to stand and go to the window. Hugging her arms, she began to feel scared. Her life was in a free fall. She had no control anymore. She couldn't catch a flight to Milan or anywhere, and she couldn't escape the fact that in less than a year, she'd have a baby to take care of, a baby she would have difficulty explaining. And in the meantime, she'd have to keep everything a secret.

It was the secrecy that bothered her. She'd felt the same in high school. She'd hidden her true self and let perception become reality. But that had cost her happiness. She couldn't live that way. She'd have to tell the truth about her baby's father. She'd either do that or live a lie.

Raith's hand on her arm startled her. Her whole body jolted.

"Something's bothering you," he said.

Dropping her arms, she turned. "I have to go see my parents. I can't put it off. I've been out of touch for a long time." Maybe the break from him would be good. But if she did go, it would be a permanent break. That made her look away.

"Is it really that important to you?"

Getting away from him? No. And yes. Seeing her parents, her mother? Yes, more so if he accompanied her.

After observing her awhile, he sighed and she could feel his tension. "All right, then I'll have to go with you."

She felt somewhat hurt that he'd go out of obligation rather than a desire to be with her, and then silly for caring. "Maybe it's best if I went alone."

"No. Not alone. I'll go."

Great, now she'd have to introduce him to her parents. They'd assume they were a couple. It would be different if he actually *wanted* to go. Dejected, Autumn started to walk away.

"Autumn."

Stopping, she tipped her head back.

"Something else is bothering you," he said.

Her heart thudded in earnest against her chest as she faced him. Had he guessed? "It's just my parents. The timing for the party. That's all."

He walked to her and she could tell he wasn't buying that. Damn, he could be a real P.I.

"It's nothing," she said.

He studied her for a while and then seemed to decide not to press her. Maybe because he suspected it had something to do with them. He was avoiding the issue as much as she was, only her avoidance involved more than the way she was beginning to feel for Raith.

Walking up to the front entrance of NV Advanced, Raith had difficulty staying focused on the unannounced meeting with Nash Ralston. The way Autumn refused to tell him what was on her mind plagued him. This heat between them sizzled, and the sizzle kept getting hotter. Her breasts bounced and her heels clicked on the concrete sidewalk, slender ankles, calves and generous portion of thighs teasing his senses.

Inside the lobby of the corporation, Raith took in all the green-and-black images of soldiers and the equipment they used, silhouettes showcasing the night-vision technology the company designed and developed. The lobby was busy today. People sat in three seating areas, with potted trees making the space less cold and sterile. A large group of military people waited to be checked in with security. A big meeting must be taking place.

Across the lobby and to the left of the front desk, Raith spotted someone he had not expected to see here. Kai Whittaker spoke to another man, both in suits and ties. He recognized the other man as Nash Ralston from the pictures he'd seen in his online search.

Taking Autumn's hand, he tugged her so that she faced him. He put his arm around her waist and watched the men over her head.

"Kai Whittaker is here," he told her.

She looked up at him, and he loved that she didn't try to turn and see the man. "Why do you think he's here?"

"He came to meet with Ralston."

"That can't be a coincidence."

They'd just been to Kai's office yesterday. The two seemed to be having an intense conversation. They had probably met in Ralston's office to discuss whatever had brought Kai here. Had he come to confront Ralston on his own? Why would he do that? In public like this Kai was safe. But why tip his hat, reveal that he suspected Ralston had hired someone to kill him? He was paying Raith to take care of this. It seemed odd that Kai would come here, especially without telling Raith. What other secrets did Kai harbor?

Kai turned from Ralston and walked toward the exit. Ralston watched his retreat, mouth tight and eyes radiating anger.

Raith waited until Kai left the building and then led Autumn toward Ralston, who had turned and approached a secure door.

Raith maneuvered through the crowd of military personnel. "Mr. Ralston."

Nash Ralston stopped and turned, looking from Raith to Autumn in question.

"We need a word with you."

"Who are you?"

"Raith De Matteis and Autumn Ivy." He took out the fake FBI badge he carried with him. He decided a little bit of a lie was best right now. "We followed Kai Whittaker here. We're investigating him in connection to a case we're working."

"You're investigating Kai Whittaker?" Ralston asked. "What for?"

"We can't discuss the details of the investigation. We'd like to ask you some questions."

Ralston eyed them both for several long seconds. Then he turned to the reception desk. "I need these two badged. Now."

Raith and Autumn checked in with the security officer and were given visitor badges. Then Ralston led them through the door. They rode an elevator to the second level and walked down a long hallway that opened to cubicles surrounded by offices that took up all of the window space.

Ralston's corner office was enormous and had a view of the city. There was a glass desk and black leather chairs both behind it and in front of it. The room contained a conference table that could seat fourteen, while a black leather sofa with a coffee table and two more chairs offered seating for less formal gatherings. A white bookshelf against the nearby wall was the only homey touch. Nash took them there. Autumn sat beside Raith on the sofa and Nash took a chair across from them.

"How well do you know Mr. Whittaker?" Raith asked.

"I've known him for years through business."

"Would you consider it a friendly relationship?"

"He runs NV Advanced's number one competitor. We get along."

The way he spoke, especially the sarcasm in his tone, hinted of a tolerant relationship at best. His demeanor in the lobby, however, indicated the relationship was more complicated than he let on.

"What did he come here to talk to you about today?" Raith asked.

Ralston took a moment while he ascertained what they had seen. "Does he know you were following him?"

"No."

Still, he hesitated. "He came here on a business-related matter."

Ralston was clearly not willing to give a direct response. "What matter was that?"

"It's classified."

Raith didn't believe that. "You didn't seem very happy when he left."

"I'm never glad to see Kai. He can be bullheaded about having his way." Ralston glanced at Autumn. "Do you always let your partner do all the talking?"

"I'm a new agent," Autumn said, crossing one of her sexy legs.

Ralston's attention was drawn there. Then he looked

at Raith with a lopsided grin. "Hard to believe she's a federal agent. She belongs on the arm of a wealthy man."

Ralston obviously preferred trophies over satisfying relationships. Raith caught Autumn's narrow gaze as he talked as though she weren't there.

"You're married?" Raith asked.

"For eighteen years." He said it as though it was a burden.

Raith waited for Ralston to catch on to why he had asked. It was a subtle barb. Ralston had insulted Autumn and he didn't like it. Ralston sent a quick, unconcerned glance at Autumn and then turned to Raith.

"Why is it significant that Kai came to see me?"

"What kind of business deal are you working on with Kai?" Raith asked.

"I'm not working on any deal with him. We have no contracts in place between the companies. He asked about a specific project of ours."

"What project?"

Ralston raised his brow in mock reproach. "Like I told you, it's classified."

"But you discussed it with Kai? How did he know about it?"

"He's working on a similar project at his company."

"How did he know about yours?" Raith asked.

"Kai has his ways, I suppose."

What ways did Ralston think he had? Raith didn't believe anything Nash said except that Kai had come asking about a specific project. *That,* he'd buy.

"Is there anything you can tell me about Kai?" he asked. "What do you know about him? As a business associate, you must be acquainted somewhat."

Nash leaned back in his chair and put his forefinger

alongside his mouth as he studied Raith. "He's a ruth-less son of a bitch."

Raith found it interesting that Ralston had chosen that as his first observation. "In getting government contracts?"

"In everything. He'll do anything to stay ahead of the competition."

"Would he kill anyone?"

His brow raised again. "Do you suspect him of mur-der?"

Raith couldn't tell if Ralston would like to hear that Kai had committed some heinous crime for which he was about to pay the ultimate price. He was, however, sure that Kai had brought the subject up during his visit.

"What about you, Mr. Ralston? What would you do to stay ahead of the competition?" Raith had asked to see what kind of reaction he'd get.

Ralston breathed a derisive laugh. "Not kill anyone. Kai, on the other hand? I wouldn't put it past him."

Ralston thought Kai was capable of killing someone. Was he only saying that because Kai was an adversary or was there some merit to it?

"I read about the shooting at Kai's home," Ralston said. "The news said it appeared random. Was it?"

"Someone put a contract on his head. What do you suppose he's done to earn that?" Raith watched Nash closely.

"Someone contracted to have Kai killed?" He laughed genuinely, lowering his hand. "I suppose I shouldn't be surprised."

Or as glad as he seemed.

"Why do you say that?" Autumn asked.

Ralston moved his gaze to her, roaming it over her as though anything she said was a prop to her physical appearance. "As I've said, Kai is a ruthless son of a bitch. I can understand why someone would want him dead. He's not much of a likable guy."

"Do you want him dead?" Raith asked.

"Let's just say that if I heard in the news he'd been killed, I wouldn't attend the funeral. If you're asking me if I'm capable of murder, the answer is no."

"You could hire someone to do it for you," Autumn said. She must have picked up on Nash's condescension, because her tone was sharp.

"I'd still have to be capable of murder," Ralston said.

"Who would want Kai dead?" Raith asked.

Ralston met Raith's eyes for several seconds. "Any number of people. Employees or ex-employees. Have you spoken with anyone else in the industry?"

"No."

"Then I suggest you start there."

"He bullies other CEOs of weapons manufacturers?" Autumn asked.

This time when Ralston looked at her, it wasn't to appreciate her female assets. "I wouldn't know."

Autumn cocked her head shrewdly. "There can't be that many others like NV Advanced and DT, not for night-vision equipment."

"Then I'm sorry I've been of no help to your investigation." He shifted his attention to Raith. "But I do wish you luck."

He'd love to see Kai go down in a fiery ball of destruction, but he couldn't—or wouldn't—reveal the true purpose of his and Kai's meeting. It may have included questions about Kai's shooting, but there had been more discussed.

Raith decided to switch tactics. "Garvin Reeves is a good friend of yours, isn't he?"

Ralston sat straighter in his chair. It was obvious he hadn't expected him to bring up Garvin. "I wouldn't say good. We're acquainted. Why?"

They were finished here. Without answering Ralston's question, Raith stood and reached for Autumn's hand. She gave it to him and he helped her to her feet. She always looked as if she needed it in the heels she wore.

"Thank you for your time." Raith started for the door, keeping Autumn's hand in his.

Ralston followed them. "Why are you asking me about Garvin?"

"You use his shooting range." Raith answered. If Ralston was guilty, he knew Leaman was Garvin's close friend. And now he'd understand that Raith was on to him.

"What does that have to do with why Kai came to see me today?"

"Well, Mr. Ralston, that's what you haven't told me."

A long stare passed between them. Clearly, Ralston was nervous about the connection to Garvin.

"You'll need an escort to the front," Ralston said.

Raith stopped with Autumn and looked back at Ralston.

"Paisley," he said to his assistant in an annoyed tone. "Take these two to the front and make sure they turn in their visitor badges."

The slender woman with long blond hair jumped to attention. Standing and moving with quick, jerky steps to move out from behind her desk outside her boss's office, Raith got the distinct impression that she was terrified of her boss.

"Right away, sir."

Raith put his hand on Autumn's lower back so she'd precede him. Apparently, Kai wasn't the only ruthless son of a bitch in this business. Was he ruthless enough to hire a killer to eliminate his competition? Why the sneakiness?

Chapter 9

That Friday, Autumn walked next to Raith as they left the airport and headed for passenger pickup. Her mother had a car waiting for them. Raith had been relaxed all the way there, but underneath that remained his discomfort in attending a Hollywood cocktail party.

After meeting with Nash Ralston, whom she disliked on sight, she'd listened to Raith call the ex-CIA operative Mayo and ask him to get a background check on Nash Ralston. It would take Mayo a day or two. The timing was perfect for a trip to California to keep her mother happy.

Outside, she walked with Raith and spotted the sleek black sedan parked along the curb and the driver waiting. Seeing her approach, he opened the back door.

Just then, a flurry of activity erupted. A camera went off in front of them. Paparazzi. Somehow they'd learned of their arrival. Who had informed them? Someone her mother told?

"Who's the new man, Autumn?"

"How long will this one last?"

"Where have you been hiding out lately?"

Autumn pushed away the camera that was closest to her face.

Raith grabbed the camera clicking pictures of him and yanked it out of the man's hands, throwing it to the ground.

"Hey, you're going to pay for that!"

There were three of them. One had a video camera. Autumn hooked her arm with Raith's before he could go after them all. He got inside the sedan first. She closed the door and stared through the black-tinted windows. The men continued to film and snap photos as the driver drove away.

She turned to Raith, who looked through the back window at the paparazzi. When he faced forward, he leaned his head back and closed his eyes.

"I'm sorry." She didn't know what else to say.

He opened his eyes and lifted his head, looking at her. "How did they find out we'd be here?"

"I don't know. My mother must have let it slip to someone she invited to the party."

"This is exactly what I was afraid would happen. This is exactly why you and I shouldn't be together."

He sounded so angry.

"We aren't together."

"I knew this was a bad idea."

She felt like telling him she hadn't forced him to come along, but kept quiet. The *This is exactly why you and I shouldn't be together* comment revealed plenty about his intentions regarding them.

The window separating the driver from them slid

open. "I've alerted security at the mansion," the driver said.

"Thank you," Autumn replied.

The driver closed the privacy window.

"There should have been security here at the airport."

He was upset. She was, too. By tomorrow morning there'd be a fresh wave of press covering her latest man.

When they arrived at her parents' mega-house, she saw that a throng of paparazzi had gathered at the gate. Security had forced them back and allowed the driver to easily pass through. Raith looked back to watch the gate slide shut.

"They know we're here," he said.

"It's not me they're interested in," Autumn said. "Not entirely. There are some movie stars who will be at the party tonight."

"Why didn't you tell me that?" Raith asked, sounding frustrated.

She began to lose patience with the way he was talking to her. "Hey, it's not my responsibility to keep the press off you. I have enough trouble keeping them off myself! And it's not my fault you chose a secret career."

The car stopped and she got out, heels clicking on the stone walkway leading to a private entrance to the gigantic house, an Italian villa with intricate stone trim.

At the door, he caught up to her and swung her around. Not rough but firm enough.

"We have to get out of here."

She pulled her arm free and went inside. "You can go ahead and leave. I'm staying."

"There will be press all over this place tonight."

"No, there won't. They'll only be allowed outside the gate."

He swore. "I can't believe this."

Autumn stopped and faced him, feeling hurt as well as angry. All he cared about was exposure. Protecting his identity, his job. She was never going to tell him about the baby. Not only would he never be able to be seen in public with her, his selfishness stung. If he truly cared, he'd find a way around the press.

She began to feel suffocated. Now that the media had found out about him, they'd paint their own version of their relationship. She'd be someone she wasn't again. It tainted the way she saw him. If only she could get away. Away from him. Because without him, the press would have nothing to prattle about and she could go on living her life.

"I'll stay here until you find whoever hired Leaman," she informed him. "You can call me to let me know. There's enough security here. I don't need you. The driver will take you back to the airport." With that, she turned and headed for the stairs that would take her to the room she always used when she stayed here.

Raith didn't follow, but she saw his surprised look.

"That's it?"

She stopped and looked back at Raith.

"You've decided right now that we go our separate ways?"

"Your work has nothing to do with me. It was an accident that we met. You'll be able to find the person who hired Leaman Marshall a lot easier without me."

"You sound as though you're trying to convince me."

Images of the paparazzi snapping pictures of her, a woman they knew nothing about, thickened a protective layer around her heart. Even his green eyes, full of certainty and confidence, even his big, tall body that so appealed to her senses were not enough to penetrate the icy wall. The media would not stop now that they knew of him, and his mystery would only intrigue them more.

"Goodbye, Raith." As his head cocked to one side as though challenging her, she made her way upstairs.

On her way down a long hallway, she ran into her mother. Blue-eyed and hair swept up from its usual blond bob, she wore a long, cream-colored beaded evening gown.

"You're here, finally." Her mother leaned in for a hug and then leaned back. "Are you all right?"

"Yes."

"You look upset."

"The party starts in an hour." They had cut it close traveling here. "I'll go get ready and then we can talk."

"I was beginning to wonder if you were going to make it. Thank goodness the driver called."

"Oh, Mother. I'm not a kid anymore."

"Where's the man you were with?" her mother asked rather than acknowledge her comment.

"Leaving."

"Leaving?"

"Paparazzi were waiting for us at the airport."

Her mother made a disgruntled sound. "I'm sorry. I should have planned for that."

"It's not your fault. It's not my fault, either." Even though Raith may see it differently. Or did he? The way he'd looked at her before she'd climbed the stairs made her wonder. Maybe what he needed was that confrontation with the media. Maybe it would make him take a look at where his life was going.

"He actually left?"

She nodded. What else would he do? Stay for a celebrity cocktail party? Even if the encounter with the media had done any good, she couldn't imagine he'd want to put himself through that.

Feeling a sting begin to drill through the wall of ice, she said to her mother, "I have to hurry."

She sensed her mother watching her walk down the hall a few seconds before Autumn heard the swish of her gown as she made her way to the stairs.

In her room, she found her luggage that the servants had taken up already and began to get dressed for the party. She chose a formfitting spaghetti-strap mini with shimmering clear sequins covering the low bodice and trailing into the all-black skirt. She curled her hair and put it up in a sleek updo. Wearing makeup and a sexy ensemble, she should feel better than she did. Raith was probably well on his way to Houston by now.

She walked down the curving staircase in the east wing of the fifty-five-thousand-square-foot mansion. The entire length of the lower east side was a ballroom. She was an hour late and heard music and voices as she approached. People milled around the seating area outside the ballroom. She entered through one of the open panels.

Big, beautiful chandeliers hung from high ceilings with elaborate trim. Jazz music played. Women in stunning gowns and men in tuxedos held flutes of champagne and stood in groups or sat at the white linen–covered round tables, each decorated with huge arrangements of fresh flowers.

Everyone in her family was here except for Macon, who, ever since going through rehab, preferred to avoid these types of parties. She searched for a familiar face and found two standing near the dance area. Her sister Riana wore a silky, long, low-cut black dress, along with dangling diamond earrings and matching necklace and bracelet. Brandie wore a white gown with flaring, knee-length skirt and eye-catching sapphire-and-diamond jewelry. They were about the same height and had slender frames. Brandie's light red hair and green eyes resembled Autumn's, but Riana's hair was short and thick and dark red. She had the Ivy green eyes, though.

Next, she spotted her brother Jonas with a woman, a sophisticated one. She looked nothing like his past mistakes. Maybe he was coming around after all of his divorces. His body wasn't so grotesquely muscular, either. He was leaner but still strong looking. He stood close to the woman, completely absorbed in her.

"Fashionably late?"

Autumn turned to see Savanna and a man with dark hair and brown eyes. He had his arm around Savanna's waist. What she noticed most was the sparkle in her sister's blue eyes. She really had fallen for this guy.

"Hi, Savanna."

Her sister moved away from the man to hug her. Then she turned a beaming smile to him. "This is Emmitt McPhail."

McPhail? Autumn took in more of Savanna's beaming smile and then Emmitt's less revealing one. That's when a feeling swept Autumn. Something about him didn't fit.

"I hear you're from a big law firm in Denver," she said, testing him.

A look of arrogant pride slid his mouth up at the corners. "Causting, Stoker and McPhail."

"Seriously?" Autumn laughed, unable to hold it back.

His grin grew a little more humble. "One could argue that it's good advertising."

No wonder Savanna had been hooked in. He was a real charmer. But that brief glimpse of superiority didn't impress Autumn.

He slid his arm around Savanna again, looking at her

with a similar glow as the one she saw on her sister's face. As long as Savanna was happy...

"There she is."

Autumn turned to see Arizona approach, shoulder-length blond hair shining under the chandelier light and wearing a silky red dress that flattered her shape. Her husband, Braden, was beside her.

Autumn hugged her.

"Getting into trouble?"

"Trouble got me this time."

Arizona laughed softly.

"Hello, Braden," Autumn said as Arizona's handsome dark-haired husband leaned in for a brief hug.

"What's this I hear about a new man in your life?" Arizona asked when Braden stepped back.

"There is no man."

Arizona looked at her strangely and then she and Savanna shared a look. What was that all about?

She didn't get a chance to ask. Lincoln and his wife, Sabrina, joined the group. After more hugs, they formed a circle, Emmitt and Savanna to Autumn's right, Arizona and Braden across from her, and Sabrina and Lincoln to her left.

"How's the adventure business doing?" Autumn asked Arizona.

"Busy. We hired a new manager," she answered.

"Not that busy. There's another reason we hired someone." Braden grinned down at his wife.

"Not now, Braden," Arizona protested.

"Too late," Sabrina said. "Now you have to tell."

There was no stopping Braden. "Arizona is pregnant," he said proudly.

While Arizona, Sabrina and Savanna oohed and

aahed, Autumn stood rigid with a wave of shock, reminded of her own predicament.

Seeing Arizona and Savanna take notice, Autumn quickly said, "Of all the girls in this family, you're the last one I'd have expected to have a baby."

"She's come a long way," Lincoln commented. "Congratulations."

Everyone followed suit and congratulated the expecting couple.

"As long as we're sharing," Lincoln said, putting his arm around Sabrina. "Sabrina and I are trying."

They were trying to have a baby. Autumn wished she could be anywhere but here right now. All of these kids would be close in age.

"Mother's going to be thrilled," Savanna said.

"You have a big family," her lawyerly boyfriend commented. Was he bored?

Bigger than they knew. Autumn averted her gaze, wishing the topic would change. She watched her parents talking to a director and a female movie star as though it was the most natural thing in the world. Then she spotted Deangelo Calabrese talking to a beautiful blonde with a huge boob job. His hair was slicked back and he'd worn leather instead of a tuxedo, still looking good.

"Mother invited *him?*" She grunted her offense.

"He's in Dad's new film," Savanna said. "Mom didn't think you'd care since you've gone through two other men since him."

"She hasn't gone through both of them." Lincoln gestured with his finger to a point behind Autumn.

She turned and at first saw nothing in the crowd. But then a woman moved out of the way and she found herself looking right at Raith. He stood near the wall, no drink in his hand, eyes directed straight at her.

"You got involved with him, anyway," Lincoln said.

She faced him. "Not by choice." Although it had been a choice to sleep with him.

"I couldn't believe it when Mom told me," he said.

"He's hot," Sabrina commented. When Lincoln sent her an unappreciative glance, she smiled at him, teasing.

"Definitely drool-worthy," Savanna added.

"Exactly her type," Arizona finished.

"Would you all just stop?" Autumn needed to get away from them. "Nothing's going on with us. I thought he left."

"Mom caught him in the foyer talking to a servant," Arizona said. "She was going to show him to a room where he could get ready for the party but discovered he was asking the servant to show him. He never planned to leave."

"Why did you think he left?" Savanna asked.

"Because I told him to," Autumn said. He must have told her mother that when she'd intercepted him.

"Mom also told me about the media swarming you at the airport," Arizona said.

"So, she's getting ready to bolt again." Savanna took a glass of champagne from the lawyer. "Where are you going this time?"

"I was going to stay here."

Savanna's brow lifted. "Really?"

"What happened?" Lincoln asked, demanded more like.

When Autumn didn't answer and instead sent him a questioning look, he pressed.

"You wouldn't stay here, of all places, if there wasn't a reason. You would travel somewhere. Now, what is going on?"

"I...went to find him and then someone came after me."

She watched him add it all up. She'd witnessed Raith kill an assassin. Now whoever had hired the killer had come after her. "What? Why did you find him? I thought you were going to forget him."

She would have if the life inside of her hadn't been created. "That's why I asked him to leave. That's why I was going to stay here." She'd be safe here.

Lincoln ran his hand down his face, clearly exasperated.

Autumn put her hand on his shoulder. "I'll be all right."

He lowered his hand. "Damn right you will. I'm going to see to it." He started to walk toward Raith.

Autumn curled her fingers around his arm and squeezed, stopping him. "No, Lincoln. I'll take care of it."

With all eyes putting weighty speculation on her, Autumn let go of Lincoln and then walked toward Raith.

Away from them, her focus became only Raith in a tuxedo, big and tall, thick black hair combed neatly.

"You clean up nice," she said as she came to a stop before him.

A waiter came by with a tray of champagne. He lifted two glasses and handed her one.

"No, thanks." She took the glass and put it back on the tray.

The waiter moved on. Raith watched him go and then scrutinized Autumn.

"I thought you were leaving," she said before he had a chance to question why she wasn't drinking.

"I know you did." He sipped his champagne.

"Why didn't you?"

"I found it interesting that you tried to throw me out after the media found out we'd be at the airport."

"You wanted to go."

"True." He took a step closer.

The predatory way he moved made her nervous.

"But then I realized what you were doing."

He was irresistible like this. A manly man going after his girl. "Which was…?"

"Running away. You felt smothered so you ran. And you dumped me like you do with every other man."

"I can't dump anyone who is undumpable."

"It seemed pretty easy for you."

"That's not what I meant." They weren't even seeing each other. "I doubt you stick around long enough to be dumped."

Him and his secretive job…

"I didn't feel like being dumped today." He stepped closer yet.

She sensed he was deliberately cornering her. And she understood he'd guessed why she'd run. So, this was a game to him? Had he stayed to prove a point? Why did it matter to him?

"I see your ex-boyfriend is here tonight."

Autumn glanced over at Deangelo and saw him watching her with Raith.

"He must have really liked you."

Deangelo didn't appear happy to see her. He hadn't taken it well when she'd told him she wasn't going to see him anymore. He barely acknowledged the blonde as she leaned close to say something in his ear.

"Your mother said she was disappointed to see the detective go."

Autumn turned to him. "You had quite a conversation with her."

He nodded, a half grin tugging his kissable lips. "After she asked me a lot of questions, she talked me into coming to the party."

"I thought you decided to stay on your own."

"I did."

Just not attend the party. "Did you tell her you were a P.I.?"

"Yes."

"Did you tell her about Leaman?"

"Yes."

She had to spend a few seconds grappling with her surprise. "You did?"

"It's not exactly a secret."

But a lot of what he did was. Carrying out an investigation on who had hired a gunman to kill Kai Whittaker seemed redeemable. Some of his other work likely would not seem that way. Or maybe that was a matter of interpretation. He may be a mercenary but he didn't kill unless forced and never the innocent. In fact, one could argue that he protected the innocent. Isn't that what he'd done with her?

What had made her mother talk him into going to this party? "She was worried about me. I bet she wasn't so fond of you when you first started talking. What kind of charm did you work on her to make her invite you to this?"

He laughed briefly and from deep in his chest. "She interrogated me thoroughly. It was what I had to say about you that swayed her."

She searched his handsome face. "Don't keep me in suspense."

Sliding his hand around her waist, he moved forward, forcing her to step back. In the next instant, she found herself surrounded by other couples dancing to a love song. Wasn't he a wily one? Going along with it, she danced with him.

"I said the only reason you told me to leave was the media."

"So? She knows I don't like the media."

"You don't like what they say about you. Which, and your mother agrees, is the truth."

"The truth is I'm a bimbo rich girl who gets around with the boys?"

"No," he said with a fond tone. "You run from men the media catch you with because the media makes you feel like a bimbo rich girl who gets around with the boys."

"That isn't a news flash."

"It is when you consider how you're perfectly willing to throw away the worthy men right along with the unworthy." He looked over her head to where she'd last seen Deangelo standing.

That carried a peculiar sting. "Most women would think Deangelo was a catch."

"Just because he's famous?"

She slid her arms farther around his shoulders, dancing oh-so-close to him now. "Are you suggesting you're worthy?" He was the antithesis of famous.

"I didn't like being made to feel like I was *unworthy*."

She smiled at his clever dodging of what had to be a sensitive topic.

"Do you think I'm unworthy?" he asked.

Now she was the one who had to dodge a sensitive topic. But instead of dodging, she took a chance. "No."

He moved smoothly with his arms looped comfortably around her waist, she against him and gazing up into his eyes and the mirroring warmth there. Their heated chemistry stirred to higher temperatures, mellowing the tension between them.

"Is that all you and my mother talked about? Because so far it isn't a major revelation."

"She was enlightened when I told her you ran because you felt more like yourself when you were traveling. She was especially happy to hear how much I love your adventurous spirit."

"Really? You *love* it?"

The jingle of his cell phone interrupted the moment. She knew he was expecting a call from Mayo, the ex-CIA operative.

After taking her hand and leading her away from the other dancers, he answered the call just before it went to voice mail, keeping his eyes on her as he listened.

She could tell Mayo had disappointing news by the darkening of his face. Thanking Mayo, he disconnected.

"Nothing?" she asked.

"Nash checks out. He's clean. No criminal record, not that I expected any."

But he'd expected something. "How did you find Mayo?"

"When he worked in the field for the CIA, I helped him get out of Lebanon when the government would have left him there. He resigned after that."

"How did he know to call you?"

"He didn't, but one of the diplomats who worked for the Lebanese government did. And I can't tell you anything about him or how I know him. I may need him again in the future."

She smiled, pleased that he'd told her that much. It showed that he trusted her, at least with most of what he did.

"If Nash is clean, he may not be the one who hired Leaman," Raith said. "But there's something going on there."

He meant with Kai. Both men seemed to have something to hide. What could that be, and could it be related to the contract killer? Neither man was revealing much about their relationship. They were business rivals. But there had been too much emotion involved when Kai had gone to visit Nash. Competing executives may have a legitimate reason to meet, but that visit hadn't appeared business related. It had seemed personal.

They had to get back to Houston and find out how or if any of that was related to the contract killer. As soon as the thought came, Autumn resigned herself to the decision. She'd go with Raith, but she'd go for him, not for the investigation or for fear of being hurt or killed. Raith was capable of keeping her safe and she wasn't afraid. No, she'd go with him for a far more personal reason.

She was thinking about telling him about the baby.

Chapter 10

The next afternoon, Raith waited with Autumn outside a supermarket in Houston. Nash Ralston's assistant had gone inside to do some shopping.

His cell rang, breaking the silence that had settled in the car rental. They hadn't said much on the trip here. Autumn had been waiting for him this morning, baggage packed and dressed for travel—in a fall vest over a silk blouse and skirt with a new pair of light-colored high heels and large costume jewelry that any woman could find in a mall. He was beginning to grow attached to her talent for looking great, always with a touch added to show off her adventurous personality.

Her outfit wasn't the only thing that had him preoccupied. It was the fact that she was here with him. When he'd found her waiting for him, she hadn't said anything and he hadn't questioned her. They'd just left the mansion with a better plan to maneuver into the airport undetected. She'd been standing there waiting for him, and he'd let the surge of satisfaction overtake him. She was here for him and no other reason.

He saw the caller was his dad and hesitated.

Autumn noticed.

"Answer it," she said.

He'd been softening more and more each time his father called. And something Autumn had said bothered him. What if his father had something important to tell him?

Did he care? It was easier not to.

He started to go for the button that would ignore the call when Savanna reached over and put her hand over his and squeezed.

"Answer it, Raith."

Easier to ignore, but he discovered he would not be able to. He had to find out why his dad kept calling.

Finally he relented. "Hello?"

Brief seconds of only breathing came across the line before his dad said, "Raith?"

"Yes."

"It's your…your father. Before you hang up, I need to talk to you."

His father had never tried to contact him. Ever since he left—escaped—he'd heard nothing from him. Why was he trying so hard to do so now? Raith didn't welcome the sense of dread that weighed him down. "What about?"

"It's not something I want to discuss over the phone."

Raith's defenses shot up. This wasn't a risk he was willing to take. "I can't meet you."

"Please, Raith. It's important." A moment or two passed. "I know I haven't been the model father. I know I wasn't when you were a kid. All I'm asking is to meet and talk in person."

There had to be more, another reason. Something had happened to make his father reach out. Was he broke? Was he hoping his son would support him? Help him out of a difficult time?

"Call Malcolm, he can help you," he said.

"I've already done that."

"Then why do you need me?"

"I've already spoken with Malcolm, Raith."

He'd already said that. What did he mean? Why had he spoken to Malcolm and why was that important? Had his older brother accepted some kind of an apology?

"I asked him not to talk to you before I had a chance to myself," his dad said.

Raith began to get a bad feeling. Whatever his dad needed to talk to him about might be more than reaching out to try to connect. Raith never had a connection with his dad, not a good one.

"Please," his dad said. "I need to talk to you."

Raith sighed. "All right. When?"

"I'll come to you."

"I'm in Houston."

"I thought you lived in Wyoming."

"I do. I'm here on business. I'm staying at the Four Seasons Hotel. We can meet here." Raith wasn't going to go out of his way for a father who'd treated his mother like dirt and who'd loved alcohol more than his own children. They discussed the logistics.

"All right," his father said. "I'll make the arrangements and call you with a schedule. We can set up a time then."

"All right."

"And Raith?" his dad said. "Thank you."

Raith mumbled a yeah, sure and ended the call. Then he sat in the car, looking straight ahead, cell phone still in his hand on his thigh.

"Are you all right?" Autumn asked.

He turned to her briefly and didn't respond. How could he? He couldn't sort out his own emotions right now. Part of him was angry that his dad had called and that he'd agreed to meet. Part of him felt a sense of foreboding.

"It will be all right," she said. "You'd regret not doing this, Raith. In the long run, you would regret it."

Her family was intact and happy and full of love. She had no idea.

"No, I wouldn't. I might regret meeting him, though."

Seeing the sympathy in her eyes, he turned away.

Ralston's assistant appeared from the entrance of the grocery store and headed toward her car. Good. No more talk about his dad.

He and Autumn got out of the rental and started after her.

The assistant stopped with her grocery cart next to a silver BMW X3. She looked at them as they approached and recognition made her stop and face them with a perplexed look.

"Raith De Matteis and Autumn Ivy," Raith said. "We met with your boss."

"Yes. I remember you. I'm Paisley Orman."

"How long have you worked for Mr. Ralston?" Raith asked.

"Too long." She raised her eyes in disgust and then caught herself. "Sorry. Are you a business associate of his?"

"No. We're investigating a shooting and we think maybe Mr. Ralston knows something about it. Would you mind if we asked you a few questions?"

Paisley eyed them uncertainly now. "Who are you?"

Raith only lied when he had to. "We're with the FBI.

There isn't much we can tell you about the investigation. We're just hoping you can help."

"I don't think I'll be much help. I'm Nash's assistant. He doesn't tell me anything. I'm basically his slave. He asks me to do his personal errands, like picking up his dry cleaning and setting up doctor's appointments. I have to get him his lunch all the time, too, and sometimes he makes me stay late and bring him dinner." She rolled her eyes again. "I'm not a maid."

"You're not very fond of him," Autumn said with a smile.

"It would be different if he was nice."

"He's not?"

Paisley shook her head. "He orders me around and yells at me when I don't do things exactly the way he envisions they should be done. As if it matters. Who cares if I schedule meetings in the same email as the conference room reservation? That's what he got mad at me for today. I didn't schedule the conference room separately from the attendees." Another roll of the eyes came with a grunt this time. She opened the back door of her BMW and began to put bags inside. "What do you need to know?"

Although she'd had a bad day at the office and seemed eager to throw her boss in front of a bus, she must be paid pretty well to afford the BMW.

Raith handed her one of the bags. "We saw Kai Whittaker came to see him the day we were there. Do you know what the meeting was about?"

The assistant put the bag into the car and then straightened. "Nash shut the office door when Kai was there. I didn't hear much. They were arguing, though."

"What were they arguing about?" Raith handed her

two more bags, the last of them, and Paisley put them into the car.

She turned to them then. "I'm not sure, but I did hear Kai say the name of our Singapore office, so it must have had something to do with the components manufactured there."

"Components for night-vision equipment?" Autumn asked.

The assistant nodded. "NV Advanced has a few subsidiaries. Most of them are foreign. I think there are six altogether."

To gather technology from all over the world. That kept American night-vision equipment on the cutting edge.

"Why would Kai argue about one of NV Advanced's subsidiaries with Nash? Wouldn't that be proprietary?"

Paisley shrugged. "Yeah, I'm sure it is. But Kai is sort of an in-your-face executive. He stops by NV Advanced every so often to butt heads with Nash. Nash thinks he tries to manipulate the industry."

"What did he hope to do? Stop your company from using the components?"

"I didn't hear what they were talking about," the assistant reminded him.

"What kind of components does the Singapore company manufacture?" Autumn asked. She was coming up with some good questions.

"I don't know that much about it. It's highly technical. Optical components for night-vision equipment."

"What kind of components?" Raith asked. When she looked blankly at him, he offered, "Weapon sights? Surveillance systems?"

Paisley breathed a cynical laughed. "Yeah, sure."

Raith would do some more research into NV Advanced's business. "How well does Nash know Kai?"

"You mean, are they friends?"

"Or not. What do you know about their relationship?"

"Just what I told you."

"They're competitors."

"Yeah."

"Would Nash hire someone to kill him?" Raith asked.

Paisley's eyes widened and then she laughed. "Kill someone? Is that what your investigation is about? Someone is trying to kill Kai?"

Raith didn't answer.

The assistant thought a moment. "Nash is an asshole, but I don't think he'd actually try to kill someone, hired or not."

This was all they'd likely get out of her for now. "If you hear of anything or notice anything, would you mind calling us?" Raith took out one of his fake FBI business cards that only revealed his cell number.

"Sure." The assistant took the card.

Autumn sat cross-legged on the black leather ottoman, surfing the internet on her tablet. Raith was at the table working on his computer. Apparently, he brought his technology with him when he traveled. The only difference was he had more computers in Wyoming. Probably some secret networks, too.

She found another entertainment-news page. So far nothing about her and Raith. That was a good sign. There was an article on the party held at the Ivy mansion, and some pictures of Deangelo and other stars. Her parents had been interviewed. She saw Lincoln and Sabrina, and Arizona and Braden in one, but nothing was said about them. The photos of them had been taken outside the mansion, so they must have been willing. She and Raith had been more careful to avoid the press.

Turning off her tablet, Autumn put it on the ottoman. Raith sighed and leaned back against his chair, studying the screen. Talking to his dad had drained him. He hadn't given up much information after ending the call, only said he was meeting him tomorrow. Something else bothered him. More than reuniting with his estranged father.

Drawn to him, she got up and stood behind him. She put her hands on his shoulders, an instinctive reflex. She almost pulled back when he reached up and covered her hand with one of his, also an automatic reflex. Warmth spread through her.

"What have you got so far?" she asked to distract herself from the sparks.

He lowered his hand as though realizing what he'd just done. She moved hers to the back of the chair.

"NV Advanced Corporation is global. They have offices in Singapore, United Kingdom, France and Luxembourg. Each company does something a little different, but all are doing military-grade optics. The Singapore office manufactures subassemblies for night-vision sights. All together they manufacture eyepiece and observation devices, seeker heads, surveillance systems, warning systems, and spotter and zoom lenses for UAVs."

"Huh? Speak English, please."

"They're into some serious night-vision technology, including some new image intensifier tubes."

"What's that?"

"It protects the user from washouts caused by bright light. Nash's company must have come up with something cutting edge."

He was like a kid in a cool electronic-toy store. "And that was why Kai paid him a visit?"

"Possibly."

It still made no sense why Kai would go ranting to Nash about technology that Nash's company owned.

She moved to the chair beside him and sat.

Raith closed his computer and looked at her with new awareness. Gone was the thrill of cool equipment. Autumn felt peculiarly at ease with him.

Leaning over, he put his hand on the nape of her neck and kissed her softly. When he finished, he drew back a few inches and her whole body melted into a pool of desire.

"Are you hungry?" he murmured.

"Starving." For him. She'd like nothing more than to spend a few more hours looking at him, kissing him, touching him.

He moved back and then stood, full of energy. "Let's go out for dinner."

Autumn had suggested Italian and Raith had taken her to Tivoli's Italiano, a casual fine-dining restaurant in downtown Houston. The table was adorned with a white tablecloth and side chairs and was near a black piano, a man swaying as he gently touched the keys to create a soft, romantic tune. Through wood-trimmed glass doors, a solarium held more tables and a view of the tree-lined street. Beautiful murals of citrus trees and seaside villages covered the walls.

"How many times have you been to Italy?" he asked.

"Many." She told him how beautiful the Sea of Naples was in Italy. "And Mount Vesuvius, in a morbid sort of way. I find it hard to comprehend how so many people would live there today." While he appreciated what she said, she asked, "Have you been there?"

"Once. Most of my travels are to less civilized places."

"Rescuing people?"

"Sometimes."

What did he do most of the time? Kill people? She looked toward the pianist, trying to preserve her enjoyment of this night.

"I help those in need fight for justice," he said.

She turned back to him. "You fight for justice?" Even though he abided by no laws?

"Always."

But he was open to doing something different. He'd indicated so before. That and her belief that he fought for justice gave her a wave of soft contentment that she had to struggle to contain.

A waiter stopped by and asked if they'd like some wine. Autumn declined and asked for a sparkling water instead. Raith scrutinized her before asking for the same.

"You drank the night I met you," he said.

He'd noticed she'd skipped wine before, too. Autumn fought to keep her expression neutral. "I don't like to drink a lot. It isn't healthy."

"You're a health fanatic?"

She smiled. "No. My clothes are getting tight. Alcohol is empty calories."

She suffered more of his scrutiny. "What a tragedy if your clothes didn't fit."

"It has more to do with size. I love to shop." She often didn't wear the same thing twice. Only when she really loved whatever she'd bought did the outfit make it a second day.

Leaning back against his chair, his green eyes flitted over the top of the black dress she'd changed into. "I've been meaning to ask you something."

She sipped from the water glass that had been brought to the table when they'd first sat down.

"It's about that night."

She sipped some more water. Oh, no.

"Were you...on the pill or anything?"

His question came with a sting of shock. How would she answer that?

"Yes." She felt bad for lying. But she had been up until a few days before that.

Relief relaxed his eyes and he grinned. Damn if she didn't find that grin sexy even as he revealed how much he didn't want children...well, at least not with her, maybe not with any woman. If she was blatantly honest, she didn't want children, either. One night of careless impulse had taken that choice away from her. Careless didn't adequately describe the attraction that had begun with the first sight of him walking toward her in the elevator lobby. Natural did. That indescribable zing had intensified on their way to her room, and burned into all-out passion once they'd gone inside. No, not careless. More like destiny. Fate.

Autumn believed people made their own fate and destiny, and that night had challenged those beliefs. Had she been forging her own path, she'd have stopped to think more on the consequences. But the desire had been too gripping, too real.

"I usually check before," he said, telling her he'd spent the lapse in conversation thinking of that night, as well.

"Oh." She nodded and sipped her water again, still lost in that one-night memory.

"Is something wrong?"

Setting down her glass, she smoothed the napkin over her lap. "No. I was just...thinking."

The bustling activity around her fell away as his eyes locked her in intimate recollection. The idea of doing it again heated the energy. And just as quickly cooled the moment.

The waiter arrived to take their order, leveling the moment. She ordered first and then Raith did. The waiter left.

Autumn watched Raith for signs of suspicion. All she saw was a man content to be here with her. In fact, every time their gazes met, unruly sparks played havoc on her senses. A faint voice in her head warned that he was content because he thought she wasn't pregnant and wouldn't be, but it wasn't enough to douse the fire.

"This restaurant reminds me of a place in LA," she said. "I went on a date with my sky-diving instructor. There was music, good food and great conversation. There were no murals on the walls, only paintings."

"You dated a sky-diving instructor?"

She smiled. "He was a lot of fun."

"What happened to him—? Let me guess. The media started taking pictures of the two of you."

The dark-haired, blue-eyed instructor had charmed her that night and many others. She had liked him. And Raith was right. The media had ruined everything. She'd taken a translating job, and when she returned three months later, the instructor had found someone else.

"How long did he last?"

"Six months."

Raith whistled low and soft. "I'm impressed. That must be your record."

It was. "Stop it."

He chuckled. "You escaped the media for that long?"

"No. They caught us a few times." She looked down at the table in front of her as she remembered how much she'd thought of him while she'd been away.

"You must have really liked him."

She raised her head. "What?"

"Didn't you feel trapped when the media was taking pictures and publishing articles about you?"

"Well, yes, but—"

"And yet you put up with it."

For a while. She saw his point.

"In the end, you left." The way he looked at her made Autumn wonder if he regretted staying for the party. Had he flown back to Houston without her, she wouldn't be here right now. There would be no danger of them falling in love.

Falling in love?

Autumn sat straighter. Could she fall in love with him? Was he worried about falling in love with her?

"Have you ever been with anyone you really cared for?" she asked. He seemed to be such a loner.

The waiter returned with their meal and she thought he'd avoid answering.

"Once when I was twenty-two, and again when I was thirty-six."

Four years ago. "What happened?"

"I was gone for eight months and the first one gave up on me. The second one…" He looked away. Then he stabbed a bite of his steak and put it into his mouth.

Well, well, well. He had obviously had strong feelings for the woman. After dealing with a wave of jealousy, she pressed for more.

"How long were you with her?"

He drank some water before saying, "A year."

That was probably a long time for him. "How did you meet her?"

"She runs a café in Lander. I met her at a festival. The owner of the hardware store introduced me."

That sounded romantic. "You're friends with the hardware store man?"

"Both him and his wife. I spend my holidays with them."

"Family." That was probably the closest he'd ever gotten to one. Autumn found that sad and endearing at the same time. He must get lonely. The hardware store owners must ease the ache.

He nodded, eating more of his steak. "They're always inviting me to events. Most of the time I'm obligated to go."

She smiled, recognizing the cover-up. "You love how they care about you. Desi, too."

Putting his fork down, he sent her a fond but tolerant look.

"What attracted you to her?" she asked.

Now he cocked his head.

"Looks?"

"She is a beautiful woman."

"What else?"

"Why are you asking me all these questions?"

Because he was the father of her baby and she was beginning to think there was a chance for them. "Just tell me."

"She had a gun collection. Old guns. She liked the history of them. Studied wars and the weapons used for the time."

"She sounds rough."

He laughed briefly. "She isn't. She's actually softspoken. Kind and giving. The only reason we lasted a year is she gave me more of a chance than I deserved."

"You weren't home much?"

He shook his head.

Neither was Autumn. She understood his lifestyle,

at least the rarely home part. He seemed to realize the same thing as they stared at each other across the table for long moments, sending sparks flying.

After finishing dinner in that warmth, Autumn stepped outside with Raith. Their rental was a couple of blocks away.

Down the street at the corner, she heard the sound of a carnival going on and saw the lights. Not wanting the night to end, she took Raith's hand and tugged him in that direction.

"Come on, let's go to the carnival."

With a chuckle, he kept holding her hand as they walked down the street. Flashing and blinking lights brightened the parking lot where the carnival was set up. Laughter and screaming kids joined the sound of the generators running the rides. Autumn smelled cotton candy and fried food.

She took him straight to the Zipper. The line was long and the operator had long, dull, uncombed hair and a scraggly beard. His eyes were vacuous and a cigarette stuck out from his mouth. He didn't even squint from the smoke as he ended a ride and people began filing off.

"You would pick this one," Raith said.

It did satisfy her thirst for adventure and travel. It wasn't Milan, but…close.

"I can't believe I'm actually going to ride this."

She stepped forward with him in line. "Scared?"

"I haven't ridden one since I was twelve."

"Then you're long overdue."

"I don't see any other forty-year-olds getting on this."

She laughed, not seeing any either and hearing his teasing tone. "Man up. It's our turn."

With a chuckle, he let her in their car first.

"We just ate dinner," he said.

Autumn couldn't tame a big smile as the ride began to move. She was also very aware of Raith's big body next to her. Their car twirled as it rose to the top and they headed down toward the pavement. Screams came from the other cars in front of and behind them. A few minutes later the ride ended and neither of them lost their dinner.

She took him to two other rides before he finally protested and stopped at the Shoot Out the Star game.

"You going to win me that big stuffed bear?" she asked him.

"How many of them do you want?"

He was fun to be with. Behaving like a teenager again had its rewards. "One is enough."

He paid the operator, this one with a shaved head and dark stubble poking out with new growth and tattoos all over his arms and creeping up his neck.

Lifting the BB gun, he aimed and shot out a circle around the points of the stars and moments later the center fell down. The operator didn't look happy as he handed over the polar bear.

Autumn hugged it as they turned away.

The crying of a young boy stopped them both. The youngster stood in the middle of the walkway between a line of games and food kiosks. He must have just realized he was lost.

Autumn went to him. "Where was the last place you saw your parents?" she asked.

The boy cried louder, probably remembering being told not to talk to strangers.

"Come on." Autumn extended her hand. "Let's go find them."

The boy didn't give over his hand but pointed down the walkway.

"Okay, follow us. We'll help you find them."

The boy's crying eased and he began to follow them. Seeing a woman searching frantically through the crowd, Autumn headed there.

"Mommy!" the boy yelled.

"Jonathan!" The woman knelt down and the boy clung to her.

She raised her eyes to Autumn and Raith. When the boy quieted, she stood. "Thank you."

Autumn extended the bear to the boy. "You could probably use this more than me."

A smile lit up his tear-streaked face. "Thank you! You won this?"

Aiming her thumb toward Raith, she said, "He did it. At the Shoot Out the Star game."

"Wow! You must be a good shot!"

"I'm not bad."

Autumn eyed him, recalling how he'd shot the assassin in Reykjavik. He must have shot a lot more than that in his line of work. And it not at all resembled a carnival game.

"Jonathan tried for an hour to win something on that game," his mother said. "Thank you so much."

"Looks like I'll have to go win another one." Raith looked at Autumn with a grin and winked. Sexy shooter.

Hooking her arm with his, she walked with him back to the booth.

The operator saw them and said, "We have a one prize limit per player."

Raith took out his wallet and handed the man a hundred-dollar bill. The man smiled.

Autumn was giddy with pleasure. The operator had no doubt Raith would win her another bear. He smiled and gave a nod.

Raith took a few shots and did indeed win her another big bear.

Carrying it in one arm, she left the game with Raith and they headed for the car. He took hold of her free hand and she looked up at him, still smiling from the fun.

Breathing in the night air beneath a clear, starlit sky, she wished this pleasant glow would never end. He unlocked the doors and walked with her to the passenger side. She faced him before getting in, feeling playful and not ready to go yet.

Stepping closer, she put her hand on his chest. "Thanks for the bear."

His grin smoothed in the wake of awareness. "It's the first."

"First bear you've ever won for a girl?"

"Yes." His eyes took in every feature of her face, making her feel caressed.

"I feel special, then."

"It's a special bear."

Just as she thought of how special it would be when she gave it to their baby, he bent to kiss her. The bear squished as his arm slid around her and he pulled her to him.

Instant passion flared. All that was missing was the hissing sound a firework made as it rocketed into the air. She sank into the kiss, giving all she had, or all her heart had.

Their mouths moved in unison, the kiss deepening and desire taking over. Heat built up, starting with the soft contact of their lips and radiating from there. Autumn couldn't get close enough. Raith seemed to be in the same state, kissing her gently, reverently, and then urging for more, intense and hard.

When the kiss escalated to the next level, he pulled

back. He looked down at her, eyes ablaze, teetering on the edge of taking her right then and there. Then his breathing leveled and he lifted his head.

Autumn regained full alertness as she watched him search around them. He was looking for a cameraman. He meant to avoid being seen with her…being seen kissing her.

Fighting off the instinct to be hurt, Autumn pushed his chest with her one hand. That drew him from his paranoid surveillance. His arm left her waist, taking the last of any warmth she felt from the kiss.

"I'm interesting news, but they don't follow me everywhere," Autumn said. "It's not like I'm Hollywood's most famous actress."

"But famous enough," Raith said.

Famous enough to destroy his lonely life. Disgusted with herself and disappointed in him, Autumn moved to get into the car.

Raith stopped her with his hand on her arm, the one that held the bear. "I was just checking."

She scoffed. "I'm glad you didn't get caught with the likes of me." She tugged her arm. Yes, she was being an insecure, emotional woman right now.

"That wasn't about you."

"God forbid if you should ever be seen with me."

"I wouldn't be ashamed of that, and I wouldn't hide it."

If it weren't for who her father was…

He didn't have to say that. It's what he meant.

She tugged her arm again, and this time he let her go. It didn't matter why he endeavored to hide their unconventional romance. The fact remained that he did.

Chapter 11

Raith stepped out of the hotel elevator behind Autumn. She'd asked him three times if he was sure she should be with him and he was. Ever since that kiss last night, she'd done all she could to stay away from him. He wasn't sure if avoidance motivated her or if she felt she would be intruding. Maybe it was a little of both.

He'd almost reassured her that his vigilance for the media had nothing to do with his feelings for her. And then he'd checked himself. Regardless of how much he desired her, there was too much at stake if they were caught.

Entering the lobby, he looked for his father, not having any idea of how he'd changed. Nervous butterflies were as foreign to him as Mount Everest. His stomach knotted with them now.

He hadn't seen his dad since he'd left twenty-three years ago. This wasn't a family reunion. This was something to be dealt with. Gotten out of the way. Never to be revisited. He'd find out the reason for this meeting and be done with it. This was probably his father's sly attempt to get back into his life. Maybe he found out that Raith had money.

Seeing a man sitting on a chair in one of three seating areas, Raith slowed his steps. Was that him?

The man turned, saw him and stood. Tall and lanky, he was thinner than Raith remembered. His hair had grayed and sagging, wrinkled skin shrouded his green eyes.

Leonardo De Matteis moved slowly as he made his way around the chair. He seemed frail. At sixty-five, he was not so old that he should be moving that way, but his dad had never taken good care of himself.

"Raith." His dad smiled as though genuinely glad to see him.

Raith shook his hand, finding the grip weak.

Autumn stood cautiously next to him. He wished he could tell her to relax. She wasn't intruding. This was a casual meeting. It couldn't be anything more, not to Raith.

Raith had no idea what to say. Not "Dad," that was for sure.

"Thanks for agreeing to meet me," Leonardo said. "I wasn't the best father in the world, so I wasn't sure you would."

One of the worst. Raith still had nothing to say.

"Who's this?" his dad asked. "Are you married?"

"Autumn. No, we're not married." Raith glanced at her as she gave a faltering smile.

"Your girlfriend, then."

Autumn looked at him as though asking the same question. Or maybe she silently accused him of pretending to be her boyfriend when perhaps there was more truth to it than either of them admitted. He'd played as though she was his girlfriend before and a secret part of him wished he could admit that she was—in some fanciful way.

Raith didn't answer.

His dad nodded, clearly not expecting Raith to be inviting. He looked around the lobby. "Is there somewhere more private we can talk?"

"We can go up to our room," Autumn offered.

Now Raith second-guessed his thinking in allowing her to be here for this. That took casual to a new level.

"If it's no trouble." His dad met Raith's eyes, asking silently for approval.

Autumn hooked her arm with his dad's. "It's no trouble."

She must have caught on to Leonardo's weakened condition and wasn't going to let Raith have a say. She helped his father toward the elevators.

Craning his skinny neck to look back, Leonardo said, "You've found a real spitfire."

"Yeah, a real spitfire." He said it while thinking of their kiss.

Autumn glanced back with an impish smile.

"I hope you're treating her better than I treated your mother," his dad said, ruining the moment.

Raith clenched his teeth, biting back a caustic reply. How could his dad joke about that? Or was he? They didn't know each other. Maybe he was nervous.

"He treats me very well," Autumn said.

"I'm glad to hear it."

In the elevator, he stood opposite his dad, fighting his curiosity.

"Are you two planning to get married?"

Raith turned to Autumn the same time she turned

to him. Just playing girlfriend and boyfriend tantalized him enough. Marriage? That should set him into a cold sweat. Instead, he let the possibility linger and toy with his imagination. What would it be like if she were all his?

Neither she nor Raith answered.

"Still in the early stages." His dad laughed lightly. "Those were the days."

The days before alcohol destroyed their family.

The casual talk ended for now. Raith led them into the suite, noticing how his dad didn't miss what kind of room they had.

His dad walked into the living area, taking in the grandeur. "You must be doing well for yourself."

"We both are," Autumn said. "My dad is the movie producer Jackson Ivy. Most of my money comes from a trust fund, but I'm a translator, too."

Raith was sure she never offered that information. Now she had diarrhea of the mouth with his estranged dad. Why? Did she sense something about him? His frailty?

"It says a lot about a woman who doesn't have to work but does," Leonardo said.

"What, that she doesn't like to be bored?"

Leonardo chuckled. "What do you do for a living to attract such a fascinating woman, Raith?"

None of your business came to his mind.

"He's a private investigator," Autumn volunteered for him.

"Autumn."

She glanced at him. "You said you were okay with me being here."

Almost telling her he was beginning to regret that, he sat on the sofa.

She helped his dad sit on the chair adjacent to him.

Raith watched, curious again as to why his father was so slow and weak.

Autumn went to get something to drink while he and his dad shared an awkward moment.

She returned with some bottled iced tea that she had room service keep in the refrigerator.

"What are you doing in Houston?" his dad asked.

"Tracking down someone who contracted to kill one of Raith's clients," Autumn answered.

Raith drilled her with a warning look. She was taking over this meeting.

"Not just any P.I., huh? Impressive."

Raith ignored the compliment. Or was it that? The way his father said *impressive* sounded as though he hadn't really meant impressive.

"Do you help him with his work?" his father asked Autumn.

"No. Raith doesn't need any help."

"Then why are you here? I thought you were here on business."

"His business sort of got me involved."

With Leonardo's perplexed look, Raith stepped in. "I can't discuss the details of my investigation."

"Ah." Leonardo nodded and then turned to Autumn. "As long as you're not in any danger." He looked at Raith. "It sounds dangerous."

"Sometimes it is. Why don't we get to the reason you're here."

"Malcolm gave me your address. That's how I found you and your number."

Raith waited. Leonardo appeared to struggle with what to say next.

"He sends you Christmas cards, he said, but you two haven't spoken in a few years."

"He does. And no, we haven't." He caught Autumn's stern look. Was he being too harsh on the man? He didn't think so. His father must know Raith had money. Was that why his dad was here?

"He says you don't send Christmas cards."

"I don't."

"It's a shame that you've lost touch with your family. With your brother. Me, I understand, but Malcolm?"

"Did you only come here to talk?"

Once again, Autumn shot him a scolding look.

Leonardo lifted the bottle of tea. His hand trembled and he sipped unsteadily. What was wrong with him? Sixty-five wasn't that old. Lowering the bottle and placing it on a side table, Leonardo took several more seconds before meeting Raith's eyes.

"I have cancer, Raith."

Cancer. The word went into this ears along with Autumn's soft gasp and bounced around his brain before the meaning registered. The news gave him an unexpected, potent jolt. The father he'd lost during his boyhood and the one who had ruined his adolescence had cancer. How could he care so much for a man he'd spent very little quality time with? He supposed nothing would change the fact that he was his father, and Raith did have some good memories as a boy.

Raith said nothing while a million conflicting emotions clashed and twisted inside him.

"Colon cancer," Leonardo said, as though still in disbelief. "I've had two surgeries."

Colon cancer. Did anybody survive that?

"I'm deathly ill," he said in that same tone.

No one could comprehend their own death. Raith never tried. He wasn't afraid of dying. He didn't have to understand it. Someday he'd just be…gone. That was the simple truth.

Hearing that his father would soon reach the end of his life, something wrenched inside of him. Ever since he'd left home all those years ago, he'd cherished his freedom. He was free of his father. Had his father died without reaching out to him, he'd have felt nothing. Instead, his father had reached out, and the reaction that caused infuriated him.

"Why did you come here to tell me that?" His dad had sought him out after so many years of nothing to tell him he was dying? It wasn't fair! It was selfish. Typical of his dad. Did he mean to get close to him and then die? Torment his son one last time?

"Raith," Autumn admonished. Standing, she went to Leonardo and crouched before him, putting her hand on his where it rested on his knee. "Are you getting treatment? Do you have good doctors? Is your insurance covering everything?"

Leonardo smiled at her, not a jovial smile by any means, a smile of a man who'd accepted his fate. He'd gone through the horror of the diagnosis, learning what would happen to his body, how it would take the life out of him.

"You don't have to worry about me. I've got plenty of good care. It just won't be enough to save me." He turned to Raith. "All that matters to me now is settling my affairs before I die. I need to atone for the things I've done, the people I've hurt."

Did he think coming here would do that? Just like that?

Abracadabra.

"The doctors say up to six months," Leonardo said.

Up to six months. That wasn't much time. Just long

enough to get reacquainted, or acquainted for the first time, only to die.

Autumn bowed her head.

Leonardo slid his hand from beneath hers and touched her shoulder. She looked up, and then when Leonardo sat back on the chair with a tired sigh, she moved to sit on the ottoman behind her, clasping her hands as she leaned over her lap.

She had a lot of compassion for someone she didn't know. Raith was angry over the compassion he felt, that his father made him feel with this pity visit.

"Raith." His father brought his gaze back to him. "I'm asking for your forgiveness. I don't expect it today, or this week or month. I'm asking for a chance to earn it. I have a lot of regrets in my life. Your mother. You. Malcolm. So many things I've done to hurt you all. I can't die with those regrets."

Selfish. He was a selfish man for coming here, for waiting until he was dying to do so.

"I know you blame me for your mother's death," Leonardo said. "I blamed myself. I still do. She's the one person I'll never be able to earn forgiveness from. If I'd have been smart enough to go get help, maybe she'd still be alive." He looked down at his hands on each of his thighs. "After she died…I didn't see anything I had to live for." He looked at Raith. "It was no longer important that I fix myself. I didn't think about you and Malcolm. Malcolm was already old enough to be on his own, and you were always so independent. I never stopped to consider what your mother's death did to you, that you were hurting, too, and needed support and guidance. The moment you started getting into trouble, I should have realized what was happening."

Raith could only sit there and watch his father. So

many thoughts pummeled him that he couldn't organize them all. Anger kept everything in a tight ball.

"If I'd have stopped drinking, I might have." He stared at Raith, imploring. "I'm sorry, son. There isn't anything I can say to change the way things were. All I can say is I'm sorry. And tell you that I've changed. I've been sober for ten years now. I've thought of you and Malcolm every day since."

"Why didn't you come to see me, then?"

"I didn't have the courage."

Not until he'd been diagnosed with cancer.

"And I was a recovering alcoholic. It took a lot to quit. I struggled every day with it for years. I wasn't in a healthy enough state of mind to consider coming to see you. And I didn't think you'd welcome it."

He got that one right. "I'm not your son," Raith said.

Autumn's head turned sharply toward him and she sat straighter on the ottoman.

Raith ignored her. "If you've come here hoping to hear me call you my dad, think again."

Leonardo's mouth tightened as sadness shadowed his eyes. "I didn't expect you to, not right away. So many years have passed." He looked down at his hands again and moments later lifted his head. "You don't have to forgive me. I was never there for you and I hold nothing against you, now or in the future. I had to try, though. I had to come here and try. I can't die in peace otherwise."

Autumn's dark green eyes pooled with unshed tears as she looked from Leonardo to Raith. Obviously, she couldn't understand his indifference.

"Take some time and think about this." His dad struggled to stand.

Autumn helped him. "I'll call for someone to come and help you."

"No, no. I've said what I needed to say." He turned to Raith. "I'll be in Houston a few more days, maybe a week. Doc says no longer than a week. Is it all right if I call again?"

"Of course it is," Autumn said. Her fiery eyes pinned him.

Leonardo didn't acknowledge her. He needed Raith's approval.

Raith could feel the hardness of his own gaze. He was angry with his father.

"I'll try calling you. I'd like to meet again. Talk. But if you decide not to, I'll understand." After long seconds of staring at his son, his dad walked toward the door.

Autumn went there with him, putting her hand on his shoulder and saying something Raith couldn't hear. Whatever it was, it made his dad smile. He thanked her and left.

Now Autumn turned to him, her green eyes ablaze with outrage. "How could you?"

"How could I what?" He stood as she approached. "Welcome him with open arms because he's dying? Why did he wait until now to contact me?"

"He *needs* you."

"I needed him when I was growing up." Ain't life a bitch? He sounded childish, but he couldn't stop it.

"That's in the past, Raith. Don't turn your back on him. He's making an honest effort. He traveled to Houston to see you when he's obviously very ill."

Although he steeled himself against caring, he did care. That's what bolstered his defenses. And the building instinct to see his father again only added anger to them.

Autumn came to stand before him, a woman on a rampage of morality. "Are you just going to let him die?"

She didn't understand. She hadn't lived the way he had.

"You'd rather hold on to the past?" she pressed.

He stopped himself from saying anything. He'd rather let go of the past and forget he ever had a father, forget that father had come to see him. One last time before he died.

"Wouldn't it be better to let go and forgive?" Autumn wasn't going to give up. "Wouldn't it be better to have a good memory of your father instead of bad ones? If you have a chance to remember him in a positive light, why not take it?"

"The bad will always be there, Autumn." He was a man who never shied away from the truth, no matter how ugly or overwhelming.

"Is that all you have? Bad memories? You have no good memories of your childhood?"

She'd zeroed in on exactly what would possibly be the only reason he'd see his father again. When he was very young and his mother was healthy, yes. Then she realized what a loser she married and everything had changed. No more good memories after that.

"You do," Autumn said.

"It doesn't matter. My father was already dead to me when I left home. He was dead to me then, and he's dead to me now. So why put myself through the misery of losing him again?" *Loss* was hardly the word he preferred. *Killing* was a better one. He'd killed the memory of his dad. He would not do it again.

Folding her arms, Autumn looked at him with disdain. "Is that how you expect to be treated when it comes time for you to die? You're okay with people turning their backs after you ask for their help?"

"Leonardo isn't asking for help." He was asking for forgiveness. Not money, Raith realized. He genuinely needed forgiveness. That's all.

Seeing Autumn follow his train of thought, he moved away from the seating area and headed for the door.

He had nothing left in him to give his father.

Autumn left Raith alone last night. He didn't come back to the room until after 2:00 a.m. She'd paced the hotel suite and had to stop herself from going after him. He needed to be alone. He needed to think. She'd let him do that.

This morning she'd watched the news and then a movie. Finally, at eleven, Raith was ready for the day. Appearing in the living area in jeans and a short-sleeved shirt, he looked ragged and worn from a night of deep thinking. The hotel had slipped the daily tally of expenses under the door and she'd seen what he'd charged to the room. He'd spent the night in the hotel bar, but he hadn't overdone it. Judging from the amount, he'd only had one. What had he done all that time there? Met and talked to someone? As a loner, likely not. He'd probably left the bar and gone for a walk or something. Found some secluded place to just think.

His father's alcoholism had taught him a valuable lesson. He'd never turn to booze to ease anxiety. Autumn fell for him a little more knowing that. Raith was a good man. Grounded. Ambitious. And despite being a loner, steady.

And as much as he denied it, his father's health condition had moved him. He cared. Maybe he could admit that much, that he cared. But he fought caring. He chose to turn his back, but his heart resisted. In his heart he cared. That had stopped her from being so frustrated with him.

He parked in a visitor space at Defense Technologies Corporation. A big, bold sign over the main entrance read DT Corporation. She hadn't known they were coming here until she'd recognized the street. He still hadn't said anything to her.

When she reached for the door handle, however, he curled his hand around her left forearm.

Turning, she saw his somber eyes. "I'm sorry I left last night."

"Don't be. You needed the time alone."

Drawing his hand back, he looked straight ahead.

"I almost went after you," she said.

"Why didn't you?"

"If it was me who'd just learned the father I hadn't seen in more than two decades was dying, I'd prefer to be alone, too. It's a lot to take in."

With a grunt, he nodded. Then he sighed. "I'm going to call him."

Autumn smiled. "I'm glad. For you."

Leaning over, Raith ran his hand along her neck and tipped her head so that her lips were poised near his. She stared into his glowing green eyes, seeing the mountain of emotion coursing through him just before he kissed her.

"What was that for?" she asked.

He grinned. "Let's go talk to Kai about that company in Singapore."

Walking with him toward the building, Autumn wondered why he had kissed her. She didn't have time to think too long. Inside the building, Kai's assistant appeared to bring them to his office.

Kai stood when they entered, extending his hand to Raith and then Autumn.

"Have you found whoever hired the assassin?" he asked.

"Not yet." Raith moved one of the two chairs at his

desk to give Autumn more room to sit. She did, and he took the seat beside her. Kai sat down again.

"Why did you go to see Nash Ralston?" Raith asked.

Looking baffled, Kai glanced from Autumn to him.

"Autumn and I were there. We saw you talking to him in the lobby."

Kai's eyebrows rose and he leaned back against his chair, studying him. "I had a business meeting."

"You discussed the NV Advanced subsidiary in Singapore."

"The technology is questionable for that type of manufacturing in a foreign country."

"Why do you care about that?"

Kai just stared at him.

"NV Advanced isn't your company."

"It's in DT Corporation's best interests for Nash not to engage in that sort of activity."

Autumn didn't know much about high technology or government defense contracts, but that sure sounded like a load of crap to her. "I've been wondering something."

Both men turned to her.

"How does an assassin as good as Leaman Marshall miss a target?" When they continued to stare, she went on. "You were in your garage, right?"

Kai nodded uncertainly.

"And he drove by shooting."

Again, he nodded.

She tapped her forefinger on her lips a few times. "How does a professional killer miss? And more importantly, why would a professional killer do a drive-by shooting?"

Kai stuttered and then managed to say, "How would I know? He shot at me. I didn't know if he was professional or not." He shifted his attention to Raith. "That's why I called you."

"Why did you really go see Ralston?" Raith asked.

"I told you why. It was about the technology."

"Subassemblies for night-vision equipment?" Raith asked.

"How do you know so much about what we discussed?" Then he leaned back again. "Ah...the assistant. Nash never was good at hiring employees he could trust."

"Maybe he should treat them better," Autumn said, noticing how that comment made him turn to her and drill her with a penetrating look. And she found it interesting that he'd pinned Nash's assistant as the one who'd leaked the information. Maybe that's how he'd learned of it, through some employee, and that's what had made him go meet Nash.

"Why is the technology bad for DT's business?" Raith asked. "And why did you go see Ralston without telling me?"

Kai turned to him. "It's Ralston you should be focusing on, not me."

"Is it?"

A moment drew on while Kai assimilated Raith's meaning. Kai had obviously gone to see Ralston about something he had intentionally withheld from Raith. "Maybe I was wrong about you, De Matteis. Maybe I don't need you, after all."

"No?"

"I need someone who will help me. It doesn't sound like you're helping me. It sounds like you're investigating my business affairs."

"Do your business affairs have anything to do with Leaman's attempt to kill you?"

"I think it's time you left. And you can take your body-guard with you."

"Not very afraid for your life, are you?"

What had changed to make him feel he didn't need Raith anymore? Autumn recalled how he'd said only Raith could help him. Why had he changed his mind?

Kai didn't respond.

Whatever he wasn't saying threatened him more than the attempt on his life.

Raith stood and said to Autumn, "Let's go."

She followed him out of the office, looking back at Kai, who watched them leave beneath a grim brow.

Outside the office, Raith spoke to the bodyguard, who had no significant reaction to being told he was no longer needed, and Kai's assistant escorted them all to the lobby.

Leaving the building, Autumn waited for the body-guard to go his own way and then asked Raith, "What government contractor would manufacture U.S. military equipment in Singapore?"

"Certain parts can be manufactured that way. U.S. companies can save money by outsourcing. It's not un-usual. The Singapore company manufactures subassemblies."

Not the entire component. "We're missing something."

"That's for sure." He touched her lower back as he reached around her to open the passenger door of the rental.

"Wait," a woman's voice called, her heels clicking on the pavement as she hurried to catch up to them. She passed a limo parked along the circular driveway in front of the building.

Raith straightened and turned with Autumn. The woman was blonde and tall, wearing a short dark blue skirted business suit with a white blouse.

She slowed her pace as she reached them, slightly out of breath. "Kai's assistant told me you've been working for him on his attempted murder."

"I'm sorry, but you are...?" Raith said.

The blonde smiled at him, eyes flashing a flirtatious message. Raith was a hot guy. Most women would react to him.

Autumn pushed back an unreasonable flash of jealousy.

"Rylie Sanderson. I work at DT Corporation. I used to be Kai's assistant until..."

"Until what?" Autumn coaxed.

The woman hesitated, glancing around. "Let's go somewhere we can talk. There's a coffee shop across the street."

They walked across the street and entered the coffee shop. Tall fig trees created the illusion of private seating. The aroma and shelves of artfully displayed coffee and accessories teased the senses. Raith bought them all their choice of coffee. Autumn carried her decaf vanilla latte and sat beside Raith at a four-seat table. Rylie sat across from them, two fig trees behind her. The coffee shop was slightly busy at this hour, just after lunch.

Rylie sipped some coffee and then blurted, "I had an affair with Kai Whittaker."

Autumn glanced at Raith, seeing he wasn't sure how this was important, either.

"He broke it off six months ago," Rylie continued. Then she registered their confusion. "Kai's assistant said you were asking him about the NV Advanced Singapore company."

"Yes," Autumn said, and Raith tapped the toe of his shoe against her high heel.

"Is he blackmailing Nash Ralston?" Rylie asked.

Blackmail? Autumn kept quiet and waited for Raith to reply.

"Why would he do that?"

"He does it all the time. He warned me not to say anything, but I'm tired of living in shadows because I made the mistake of sleeping with him, a married man on top of that. Kai Whittaker is a slimeball. He blackmails other businessmen whenever it helps his own company and his position. He treats his employees terribly, and his women even worse. Except his wife. He worships her. I found that out the hard way. I don't even know why he started pursuing me. Maybe I was just a spice. He said he realized he made a mistake with me and that he loved his wife. It was an accident to him. I haven't told anyone except Kai's assistant. She hates Kai."

Both Kai's and Ralston's assistants hated their bosses. There were a lot of similarities between the two CEOs.

"How does he blackmail his adversaries?" Raith asked.

"He gets information on them, whether it's personal or professional. He backs them into a corner and forces them to do what he wants."

"What does he want from Ralston?" Autumn asked.

"Probably the new technology NV Advanced is developing. Kai told me he'd discovered something and it was big."

"What kind of technology?" Raith asked.

"Kai wouldn't say."

"How does he know? It belongs to NV Advanced. Isn't the contract between them and the United States government?"

"That doesn't matter. Kai has his ways of finding things out. He probably has someone on the inside over there, an engineer working the program or something.

He probably will try to use NV's technology and come up with something better. He's done it before."

"What is significant about the Singapore company?" Raith asked.

"I don't know, but if you find out, you might be able to catch Kai doing what he does best—cheat people out of a decent living. There are a lot of people here at DT who'd cheer you on. We'd celebrate his resignation, or his trip to jail. Nobody likes him."

Nobody liked Kai and nobody liked Ralston, and they didn't like each other.

"Does his wife know about his affair?" Autumn asked.

Rylie's eyes grew wide and round. "No. And can never find out. I feel awful about it. Kai was a sweet-talker. He made me feel as though I had a chance with him. He was lying, of course. That's the way he operates. He'll say and do anything to have his way. He took me out to lunch a few times, then occasionally to dinner. Over about a two-month period, he romanced me, and then he rented a penthouse suite and gave me a key. I should have known then that it would never work. He never took me to his house, and every time I asked about his wife, he'd give me a vague excuse."

"Why did you keep seeing him?" Autumn asked.

Rylie shrugged. "He's a powerful man. I guess I was flattered he desired me, and a stupid part of me believed I could have him. But all he was doing was living out a fantasy, getting some sneaky strange on the side." She screwed up her mouth with self-disgust.

At least she had the decency to admit her actions were immoral and wrong. Autumn despised women who betrayed other women, whether they knew them or not, by sleeping with their husbands.

"I wouldn't wish to see him killed, but I wouldn't

mind seeing him brought to his knees if he's blackmailing Nash Ralston again."

A few stunned moments passed. "Again?" both she and Raith asked.

Rylie looked from him to her. "Oh, yeah. He and Nash go way back. They've hated each other for years, long before either of them worked for NV or DT."

A woman sitting at the table on the other side of the fig trees turned to look at them. Her blue eyes were wide with what Autumn had to assume was shock. She stood and walked around the trees. Tall and blonde with dark red lipstick, she was a stunning woman. She was dressed in a black formfitting dress that revealed a good portion of her large breasts; her hips flared and dipped into a tiny waist.

"Holy hell," Rylie declared as she saw her.

"So it was you," the blonde hissed. "How could you?"

"India, I…" Rylie was appalled and flustered. "I…"

"Don't even try to explain anything."

"I swear I didn't mean to hurt you. It just sorta happened. I—I didn't plan it and I—I'm not the kind of woman who normally does that sort of thing."

India scoffed, disgusted and enraged. "I bet that's what you all say. But the truth is, tramps like you thrive on the wrongness of it. You get off knowing he's going home to another woman who has no idea that you're spreading your legs for her husband."

"No, I—I swear. It wasn't like that. He pursued me."

"Now you're blameless?"

"No. I'm sorry, I…" Rylie began to cry.

"My husband loves me. If he pursued you it was for the exact reason you yourself said. He was living out a fantasy. You aren't the real thing. I am." India ran her revolted gaze up and down Rylie's torso. "Whatever made you think you could get a man like Kai, much less hold on to him?"

Rylie stood from her chair, sniffling, tears running down her face. "I'm so sorry. I am." She turned to Raith and Autumn. "I've got to go." And then she hurried from the coffee shop.

India Whittaker watched her disappear through the door, a subtle shudder wracking her shoulders and her fingers trembling as she adjusted her purse.

"You're the one who's helping Kai?" she said to Raith.

She'd heard plenty of their conversation with Rylie. "Yes."

India's distraught state lingered. She adjusted her purse again, an anxious action. "The chief financial officer's wife and I are close friends. She told me she heard Rylie talking to Kai's assistant yesterday. I saw you walk over here with her and so I followed. I figured the least amount of damage I'd come away with would be the cost of two cups of coffee before I went to see Kai, and saw her with you. I didn't want to believe…"

Tears had begun to pool in India's eyes. Autumn stood and put a comforting hand on the woman's back.

She regained composure and asked Raith, "Was it Nash who sent that shooter to our house?"

"It might appear that way. We're still investigating."

Autumn appreciated that he'd included her. She couldn't pinpoint why. Partnering up with him? Or maybe she liked investigative work. It was almost as exciting as traveling.

India nodded, looking numb and at a loss for words. She seemed torn over caring whether her husband was killed and anger over his betrayal. Either way, she was in the early stages of devastating pain.

"Well," she managed to say. "Thank you." She stepped

out of reach of Autumn. "Thank you." The words were forced and insincere. She started for the exit.

"Mrs. Whittaker," Raith called after her.

She stopped and looked back.

"I'm sorry for what you heard today."

Her lower lip quivered as she nodded once, this time a sincere thank-you.

After India left, Autumn looked at the table where the woman had sat. There were two cups there, forgotten now.

Chapter 12

On his way home from work late that night, Kai noticed a car following him. He wasn't sure if he was being paranoid. Letting Raith go might have been rash. The man was smart and tenacious. And dangerous. Kai should have taken that into consideration when he'd hired him.

Turning onto his street, he watched through the rearview mirror. When the other car passed by, he breathed a sigh of relief. Moments later, he was in his garage and heading into the house. India's car wasn't here. She was never out this late.

Inside, he called her phone. She didn't answer.

He searched the house for a note and found none. He tried her phone again. Where the hell was she?

Leaning on the table, he looked through the back patio door, wondering if he should call the police. What if whoever sent that shooter had taken her? A movement in the yard caught his eye.

Alarmed, he went to the door and flipped on the outdoor lights. A figure ran from the yard.

Who was that? The figure stopped. Realizing it was a deer, he chided himself for once again being paranoid.

Hearing the garage door open, he went to the hall.

She entered the house, looking beautiful in a sexy black dress. Except there was something wrong. Her eye makeup was smudged.

"India?" He walked toward her.

She said nothing as she put her purse down and avoided his attempt to embrace her. She walked into the living room and straight to the wet bar and poured herself a scotch.

India never drank like that.

"India, what's the matter?" He went to her.

When he put his hand on her shoulder, she flinched and stepped away. Walking to the wall of windows that offered a view of Houston, she sipped her drink.

Kai began to fear what this was about. "India?"

Still, nothing.

"Where have you been all night?"

"Not here."

He heard the edge in her voice. She may have had a little to drink before coming home.

"I thought you had our driver take you today. You said you were coming by the office but you never did. What happened?"

"I did go to the office. But then I asked the driver to take me back home. I drove the Jaguar to a friend's house."

"What friend?"

"Lynn's"

His chief financial officer's wife. The two women had become close lately.

"Why didn't you call me?"

India finished her scotch and then went back to the wet bar. Before she could pour more into her glass, Kai stopped her. He took the glass from her and then the decanter, setting both down and searching her sad eyes.

"India…" He couldn't stand to see her like this.

"I know all about Rylie."

The shock wave that announcement brought caught him unprepared. He'd hoped she'd never find out, but now that she had, he was almost relieved. Now they could talk about it. They could work past it and get on with their lives, one he very much intended to live with her. How he handled this would determine whether that was possible.

He put up his hands. "Okay. First of all, I regret what I did. I don't even know why I did, either. I think it was some kind of weird midlife thing. She made me feel young again, the way she flirted with me."

"She said you pursued her."

"Maybe I did, after I saw that she was interested. I had no intention of acting on what was happening, the flirting. It started out innocently. People flirt sometimes at work."

"Do they?"

India hadn't worked much in her life. Kai had protected her from that.

"It was innocent at first. And then…" He'd always promised himself that he'd be honest with her if she ever found out, but now he was tempted to lie just so he could keep her.

"Don't lie to me, Kai. I know you better than anyone. Tell me everything."

He met her dejected gaze and yearned to make her happy again. Telling her this would only cause hurt.

"What happened to make it go from innocent flirting to more?"

"I took her out to lunch." He sighed and rubbed his face with his hand. "And then the next week I took her again, and that turned into more than once a week. And after a few weeks of that, we had dinner and I took her to a hotel."

"All those late-night meetings." India's eyes teared up. "I was so stupid."

"No." He moved toward her.

She stuck up her hand to stop him. "How many times did you take her to the hotel?"

"I…"

"Tell me."

"I rented a penthouse suite after that."

"Oh." She nodded slowly, her face growing paler. "You were seeing her a long time."

"A few months." He inwardly winced. The amount of months didn't matter. He'd slept with Rylie many times. "It was a phase, India. I got through it and I realized what a mistake it was. I love you. I woke up one morning and realized that, how much I love you. Being with Rylie was a mistake."

"Maybe it was one you needed to make. Would you have realized you loved me without sleeping with her?"

"I…" What did she mean?

"Why did it take cheating on me to realize that, Kai?"

"I don't know. After a while, she wasn't you, and it's you I've always loved. Being with her had nothing to do with love. It had to do with going through a life change. Rylie meant nothing to me. She was more of a…tool."

"Well. At least I know how you'll handle your next life change." India picked up the bottle of scotch and poured more into her glass. Taking the glass, she stormed off.

Kai followed. "How did you find out about her? Did Lynn tell you?"

"I overheard her talking to your mercenary."

Raith? "Why was he talking to Rylie about my affair with her?"

"That wasn't why he was talking to her. They were talking about Singapore."

Kai stopped following her, recalling everything Rylie knew. He had to do something before she ruined everything…or Raith did.

Chapter 13

A few days had passed since the encounter with India. This time when they went to meet Raith's dad, they arranged it so he wouldn't have to travel anywhere. There was a café across from the motel where he was staying. The condition of it gave Raith a sick feeling. The café was a mom-and-pop-type place, clean with home-style charm.

His dad smiled when he saw him, a big, joyous smile that lifted Raith's mood slightly.

"Don't get up," he told him when he started to stand.

He shook his dad's hand and then sat across from him, Autumn taking a seat beside him.

"Thanks for meeting me," his dad said.

"Stop thanking me. Why are you staying in a motel?"

"Don't worry yourself with my finances, Raith. That's not why I came to see you. I haven't done very well with money, but I've managed to get by. I sold car insurance after I sobered up. Earned a decent wage. Had health insurance and something of a retirement. Things were starting to look up for me. I even met a woman. But then…"

Raith stopped himself from throwing money at a father who hadn't been a father to him. He still wasn't sure he was here out of obligation or the possibility of reconnecting.

Had the woman left after she learned he was dying of cancer? She must have, and his father couldn't say it. He had to stop himself yet again. Why did he care? He was still confused and not sure he could forgive so easily.

"You never remarried?" Autumn asked.

Leonardo turned to her. "I take it Raith has told you about his mother."

"Somewhat."

"No, I never remarried." Now he looked at Raith. "When I met your mother, I fell in love with her by the end of our first date. We were starry-eyed twenty-two-year-olds back then." He smiled with the memory, his face lighting up, erasing traces of his illness, if only temporarily. "She had plans to go to college and teach kindergarten. I was a carpenter, building houses. We didn't have two nickels to rub together but we were happy. She got pregnant and we had to get married quick. It would have happened, anyway. She had to put off going to college. I felt bad for that. She was upset about it, but we both wouldn't have traded Malcolm for anything. Life happened after that. You came along, I kept working construction and she stayed home with you two. We'd come home and have a drink or two, and after a few years of that, it turned into more. We should have stopped it."

Raith remembered those days. He was a young boy and his parents would drink before dinner. It seemed normal until his dad's addiction got out of control. He turned into a raging drunk. From there, Raith watched his mother fade away. And then there was the affair.

"After she died, I lost myself in grief. I drowned it even more than I was drowning my life before that. Malcolm left, and then you. It wasn't until I was fired five years later that I began to realize what I had done. I'd drunk my life into ruin. Alcohol took the woman I loved and my children away from me. I betrayed my wife with a woman I didn't even care about. She was just another drunk in a bar that I took home one night. I was gone all night. The next morning, I could see what it did to your mother. I tried to apologize and explain, but it did no good. Her trust was gone. I destroyed her love for me. I destroyed her."

The pain in Leonardo's eyes penetrated Raith's indifference. He kept his empathy at bay and let his dad continue.

"The worst part was that I blamed her. I blamed her for not seeing that the other woman meant nothing. I was angry that she withdrew, that she denied me her love. We both were drinking a lot then. And then she got sick and died." He fell into a sorrowful pause. "That erased my anger. Then the guilt finally settled in. It took her dying for me to realize that I didn't try hard enough to earn her forgiveness. It took even longer to realize that it was the alcohol that caused all of my grief."

"How did you overcome your addiction?" Autumn asked.

Raith was glad she was here. He doubted he'd have asked any questions. He was too mixed up inside.

"I checked myself into a facility. I was there for two months, and then I joined a group and went to meetings weekly and then monthly. I still go every once in a while...or I did." He turned away with the reminder that he was dying. It no longer mattered if he went to his meetings.

"Why didn't you tell us you were getting treatment?" Raith asked. He could have sent a letter or had one of the counselors call him and Malcolm.

"I didn't feel I deserved to."

He'd been so riddled with guilt that he hadn't called for the support of his kids.

"I began to finally grieve for my wife's death during my treatment. The counselors helped me, but even afterward, I couldn't forgive myself. I still haven't forgiven myself, not completely. Enough to move on with my life, and I had begun to do that when I was diagnosed."

"Did you ever think about contacting me or Malcolm?"

"Every day. Every sober day of my life. But I was too ashamed to call you. Until now. Now it hardly matters how I feel. What's important to me is that you aren't burdened with the way I raised you, that you can let it go. You don't have to forgive me. As long as you're happy that's all I care about. Don't make the same mistakes I made." He looked at Autumn. "Which I can see that you haven't." He turned back to Raith. "The only area that has me concerned is your profession."

"My profession?" How did he know anything about it?

"Malcolm told me what little he knew of it. He said you were secretive, that once you dropped out of the military, you went underground. He called you a modern-day Rambo."

"I'm legitimate." On his own terms.

"I believe that. But why did you go underground?"

"I got tired of politics slowing down progress."

"You got tired of following rules. You lived in a dysfunctional home. You're more comfortable in dysfunc-

tion. It's time you stopped, Raith. You can have stability."
He glanced at Autumn briefly. "But only if you offer it."

"Did you have this same speech prepared for Malcolm?"

"Malcolm is happily married and has kids who are doing well in school. He doesn't drink and he has a successful job. He's not a millionaire, but he's doing well for himself and his family. He overcame his upbringing. Probably because he got out sooner than you did, and he was older when your mother died."

"Well, good for him. I don't need fixing, but thanks for your concern. I overcame, too." Realizing he sounded defensive, Raith looked away.

"You rebelled," his father said.

Catching agreement in Autumn's eyes, Raith squashed the anger that reared up. What if his dad was right?

"Your mother died. Your brother abandoned you and I wasn't there for you. You rebelled because of that."

He did harbor some resentment toward his brother for not taking care of him, just leaving him at home with a drunk.

"Are you doing what you really want to do with your life?" his father asked.

Raith had always thought he was. But hearing his dad's repentance had shifted something inside of him, something he wasn't ready to accept.

"We should get going," he said. "We'll talk again."

His dad nodded. "I'm flying home tomorrow."

"When we're finished here, we'll stop by."

"I'd like that."

Outside, Raith watched his dad slowly make his way across the street as he and Autumn headed for the rental, which he'd parked in the motel parking lot. As they neared, he noticed a man standing in a gravel alley off the small parking area behind the café. He leaned against the aging red-brick wall of the business next to the café, smoking a cigarette and looking right at him. He wore a dark blue hoodie and holey, faded jeans. Recognition came along with a rush of foreboding. He stopped Autumn to assess the situation. There was no one else in the alley. He surveyed the rental. Something hung down underneath the driver's side. They were just ten feet from the car.

Acting on instinct, he put his arm around Autumn and began to turn her away when an explosion erupted. The rental blew up. Raith saw the burst of flames and felt the powerful repercussion, the boom deafening. Shrapnel sprayed him as the force of the explosion threw him and Autumn. Raith's back came against the side of a Dumpster, his head slamming back and disorienting him for a few seconds. He regained coherency fairly soon. Sitting against the Dumpster, he searched for Autumn. She lay sprawled with her back on the ground, the corner of the Dumpster keeping her hip up. She must have hit her head on the corner.

"Autumn!" He crawled to her, his head swimming.

Her eyes were closed and a pool of blood began to spread from underneath her head. Raith leaned down and felt her warm breath. That gave him marginal relief. Removing his shirt, he gently felt her head until he found the gash. It was big. Careful not to move her much, he slipped the shirt under her and wrapped it around her head, tying it tightly.

Glancing back, he saw the rental car in a ball of flames and no sign of the man. Garvin. He'd watched the explosion.

"I called 911."

Raith looked up to see his breathless and pale father and a few other people who'd gathered.

"I heard the explosion," his dad said. He must have still been outside, in front of the motel when the explosion detonated.

All Raith could think about was Autumn. Was she going to be all right?

The sound of sirens was welcome for a change. When the ambulance arrived, he moved back to let the EMTs work on her, sick to his stomach as he watched them stabilize her neck and position an oxygen mask over her nose and mouth. Next, they put her on a gurney and rolled her in a hurry to the ambulance.

He raced after her. A paramedic blocked his path and he put an arm out to move him, not brutally, just to get him out of the way. No one stopped him. They all knew he'd been with her when the explosion occurred.

Before climbing into the ambulance, he searched for his dad. He stood behind some emergency personnel and called, "I'll take a cab to the hospital."

Raith nodded and sat beside the gurney.

"Autumn." He took her hand, a heavy dread descending upon him. She didn't regain consciousness all the way to the hospital.

When the ambulance arrived at the hospital, she was taken into the E.R. A clerk behind an enclosed desk waved him over.

"What's your relation to the patient?"

"He's her boyfriend," his dad said, appearing beside him. He handed the woman a card. Only then did Raith realize that his father had picked up Autumn's purse and brought it with him. He'd thought to look for an insurance card.

He was being a dad.

Raith struggled with how that made him feel. Gratitude. Chastisement for not thinking to do it himself. But he'd been so concerned with the danger Autumn was in that he hadn't. They finished checking Autumn in.

"Have a seat. The doctor will be out as soon as she's stabilized."

Raith stepped back from the desk. He was no good at waiting. He was a doer not a waiter.

Hospital personnel walked by. Two security officers talked, bored on a slow night. Only one woman sat in the waiting room, face glowing from the light of her laptop. A TV played a national news program. Too normal for the chaos taking place inside of him.

"Raith." A frail hand touched his arm.

His dad stood by him and draped a light jacket over his shoulders. The jacket his easily chilled dad had worn in the late-fall Houston day.

"All we can do is wait," his dad said.

For the first time in his life, he was grateful his dad was here. Slipping his arms through the jacket, Raith left it unzipped and sat next to his father on one of two chairs beneath a TV hanging on the wall. Raith wasn't interested in passing time by watching TV. If he could be in the E.R. with Autumn, he would.

"Why did your car explode?" his dad asked.

Raith lowered his head, only then realizing he'd tipped it back. "Apparently we're getting too close."

"To what?" Almost immediately after asking, Leonardo said, "Never mind. I know you can't tell me any details. Just answer me one question."

That depended on the question.

"Was it special?"

"Was what special?"

"The night you spent with her?"

Raith could only stare at his dad.

"Your personal assistant told me when I called your home phone."

Desi. Raith was going to ring his scrawny neck.

His dad didn't press the issue. Instead, he began talking about some memories he had of his mother, about how it had been in the early years when Malcolm was a toddler. The drinking had been normal back then, not every day and not in excess.

"I wish we could have stayed that way," he finished by saying.

Raith rested his head back against the wall behind him as his dad talked. The stories relaxed him and took his mind off how worried he was for Autumn.

All of that fled when he saw a doctor heading toward them. Back came the anxiety and a deep-seated fear of losing a woman he cared for, maybe more than he could handle.

Raith stood, his father slower in doing so.

"Raith De Matteis?" the doctor queried.

"Yes, that's me."

"Autumn is resting comfortably now."

Relief rushed over him before the doctor continued.

"She had quite a blow to her head. It took thirty stitches to patch her up. Fortunately, she didn't suffer any fractures to her skull. I think she'll recover just fine, however, the potential for brain trauma from a blast like this can't be dismissed." The doctor lifted his hands, palms out. "A car bomb like this one delivers two punches. First, you have the shock wave, and then you have the wind from the blast. The wind shakes your head violently and very quickly." He moved his hands to illustrate. "It's the amount of energy released in that short period of time that does the damage."

"Are you saying she's going to have brain damage?"

"Not at all. I'm saying if she does, it will be minimal. But given that she's never had any type of blow to the head or any concussion before this, I think her chances are good she'll skate right through this. She's got a pretty good concussion and a few cuts and bruises, but otherwise she's fine. Doing very well."

Raith nearly sagged with relief.

"And another bit of good news is the baby is also doing very well."

Raith froze, his mind shutting down to everything other than what the doctor had just said.

"Baby?"

His dad patted him on the back. "You should have told me, son!"

"Autumn is a lucky lady," the doctor said. "If you'd have been any closer to the bomb, she and the baby may not have survived. You, either."

"W-wait just a minute," Raith said, shaken to the core. "What are you saying? Autumn is *pregnant?*"

"Oh, boy. You didn't know," his dad said.

The doctor looked wary. "She's right around six weeks."

He didn't have to do the math. All at once he realized why she'd tried to contact him. It wasn't to ask him why he left without saying goodbye. Those times he'd noticed her mood. Not drinking. She'd been thinking about the baby. A baby, for God's sake! One she'd decided not to tell him about. Why? What had changed her mind? Nearly being gunned down? Did she blame him?

Did any of that matter?

Raith staggered backward until he felt a chair behind him. He sat down.

He wasn't happy with Autumn for keeping a secret of

that magnitude. He also wasn't happy with what it meant for his future.

He looked up at the doctor and his dad, whose illness was not apparent right now with his look of gladness. "When can I talk to her?"

"She's awake now."

Raith stood from the chair.

"Raith—" his dad stopped him "—go easy on her."

The way she'd gone easy on him? Not telling him about the baby?

"Where is she?"

The doctor told him which recovery room she was in and he headed there.

Autumn's head hurt so much she was nauseated. Or maybe it was the pain medication. She couldn't tell. She just wished it would stop. The gash was on the left side of her head toward the back, so she could at least rest her head without putting pressure on the wound.

Hearing a sound at the door, she looked there and saw Raith. He bore an intensity that went beyond concern for her. He had to know she was all right by now. Had the doctor told him about the baby? They'd run some tests to make sure the baby was okay. They must have communicated that to Raith and his father, who entered the room behind him.

Raith stopped beside the bed. "How are you?"

"I'll be fine." She met his green eyes warily.

He didn't say anything else, and Autumn could feel the unasked questions.

"Raith…"

He put his hand on hers. "Not now. We can talk later. You look like you're in a lot of pain."

Her heart melted all over itself in response to his

thoughtfulness. Maybe he wasn't so mad, after all, or disappointed.

"I'm going to go find Garvin," he said.

"Why Garvin?"

"He was there when the car exploded."

He was? "Garvin planted the bomb?"

"Why else would he be there?" He gave her hand a halfhearted squeeze. "Get some rest."

"I'll stay here with her," Leonardo said.

Raith gave him a nod. "Thanks." With that, he turned and left.

Her melting heart cooled. He was obviously upset over the news, probably angry with her, too.

Leonardo moved to the chair beside the bed and sat with an exhausted sigh.

"I wouldn't worry," Leonardo said. "If he's talking to me, he'll easily forgive you."

"You're his father."

"You're his girlfriend. Soon to be more, I'd venture to guess."

"I'm not his girlfriend."

"You're something if you're pregnant by him."

"That was a one-night thing." She found it peculiar how easy it was to talk to him. "The only reason I'm with him now is because I got in the way when he was after someone in Iceland."

"What were you doing in Iceland?"

It wasn't a typical destination. She explained what happened and everything up until the explosion.

"Well." Leonardo marveled over the tale. "I knew Raith had a dangerous job, but I'd never have guessed he was some kind of secret agent."

"Rebel."

"But an honorable one, judging from what you've told me."

Yes, honorable.

"He was always that way when he was a kid. Loved superheroes. His mother bought him action figures and movies, coloring books, you name it. If it had anything to do with superheroes, Raith asked for it."

"Is that why he went into the military?"

"No. He joined that to get away from me. But he went into politics for that reason. He dreamed of changing the world."

"But then he realized what everyone else does. Politicians don't change anything. They just get rich and make all their friends rich."

"When they follow the rules."

Autumn breathed a laugh that hurt her head. As she winced, she said, "That's the part that drove Raith out of politics."

"Rebel. You should get some rest."

"You should, too."

"I'll sleep in the chair. I won't leave you here alone."

Autumn sighed and felt more relaxed than she had since long before the explosion. "You're a good person, Leonardo. My baby is lucky to have a grandfather like you."

Leonardo didn't respond right away. She sensed he was a little choked up by her compliment, and sad that he most likely wouldn't be around for the birth of his grandchild.

"Did you meet Malcolm's kids?" she asked.

"Yes."

That was a blessing. "Good."

A few moment passed before he said, "My son will be a fool if he lets you go."

* * *

Garvin wasn't at the gun shop and shooting range, but Raith had convinced the man behind the counter to tell him where he was. Raith pulled up as Garvin was leaving. The muscular, five-eleven man turned to another one who'd followed him out of the restaurant. Ralston. Garvin and Nash Ralston had met for a lunch meeting?

Raith ducked into the covered entry of the neighboring business as the two shook hands. Ralston climbed into a sedan waiting at the curb and Garvin walked down the sidewalk in Raith's direction.

He waited for the man to pass, turning toward the door and pretending to be about to go inside as he passed. Then Raith followed Garvin. Two blocks later, Garvin walked into a parking lot.

Raith stopped him at a white Dodge pickup truck. "Garvin Reeves?"

Garvin froze as he reached for the door handle of the truck. "You again."

Raith walked around to the driver's side and shoved the man so that his back was against the side of the truck. "The last time I saw you, you watched your handiwork. You almost killed Autumn." And her baby. His baby. Their baby...

"What? You think..." Garvin pushed Raith's arm, breaking his hold on his shirt. Raith was too distracted by his thoughts to prevent it.

"I didn't set that bomb if that's what you're suggesting," Garvin said.

"You were standing right there. I saw you."

"Yeah, so?"

"If you didn't plant the bomb, who did?" He didn't believe for a minute that Garvin hadn't done it.

"How the hell should I know?"

"What were you doing in that alley?"

"Having a cigarette."

Raith grabbed him and shoved him against the truck again. "Why were you there?"

"I didn't see who put the bomb on your car," he said. "I got there too late."

"I'll ask you again—why were you there?"

Only a stony silence answered.

Raith debated forcing the truth from him, but the doctor's announcement snuffed that otherwise natural instinct out. Violence could make Garvin talk. Well-strategized violence. Violence that didn't kill, but violence nonetheless. But he wouldn't use it now. Somehow learning he was going to be a father changed him. What kind of role model would he be if his profession led him to beat people up to get information?

Without a word, Raith turned away, certain of only one thing—he was finished with violence.

Chapter 14

Autumn was released from the hospital and her head hurt unbearably by the time they reached the hotel room. In the elevator she began to feel nauseated. She saw Raith watching her and Leonardo watching the both of them. Raith had had a hands-off attitude ever since he'd heard she was pregnant, but she was too sick to care. All she wanted was a hot bath and a cozy bed with a chick flick and painkiller that was safe for the baby.

The elevator doors opened and Autumn pushed off the wall. Her stomach churned.

Raith appeared next to her and put his arm around her. She leaned gratefully against him.

Leonardo took the room key from Raith and opened the door for them.

"Oh, for God's sake, Raith," Leonardo said. "Carry her."

Autumn saw Raith glower at his father before lifting

her. She felt so terrible that she couldn't protest much. "You don't have to carry me."

"Too late."

"You're only doing it because your dad told you to."

"I'm not twelve, Autumn."

"If you were twelve you wouldn't be able to carry me."

That triggered the hint of a smile, which amazed her. They needed to talk, but she wasn't well enough yet, not for a conversation like that.

"Where to?"

"I would love a bath and then bed with a movie."

He looked down at her, any trace of a smile vanishing. She had her arms around his neck. Warmth enveloped her as she felt snug in Raith's arms. Even if it was short-lived. Even if temporary. She felt so lousy that she sponged up this brief sparkle of good feeling.

"I think I'll retire to my own room," Leonardo said. He'd told her that Raith had arranged for him to have the adjoining suite.

Raith stopped with Autumn in the middle of the living room and turned to look at his dad. "Are you all right?"

A cheerful but cynical rise of Leonardo's brow accompanied his grin. "Fine. Going off to bed. You take care of her." He walked to the door of the adjoining room.

The click of it closing left her alone with Raith. She looked up as he looked down. Their eyes met.

She almost told him he could leave her alone when he walked with her to the bedroom. He set her down near the bed.

"I'll get your bath ready."

"You don't have to." Standing with a throbbing head, churning stomach and legs that barely supported her, she sat on the bed and put a hand on her forehead.

Raith went into the bathroom without comment. She

listened to the water pour into the tub and yearned to be in it more than she'd yearned for anything in a long, long time.

Emerging from the bathroom, Raith asked, "Is there anything I can get you?"

She bit her lower lip, hesitating. She immediately thought of candles, sparkling mineral water, bubbles... the works.

"I'll call room service."

His announcement had the same effect of medication to alleviate her current symptoms. Heat against sore muscles. Relief from an aching head. Calm.

"Get ready for your bath," he said.

She smiled through her haze of pain. He spent a few long, intimate seconds looking at her before he first turned the water off in the bathroom and drained it so it wouldn't get cold and then left the room. While Autumn undressed, she listened to his deep voice asking for candles and sparkling water and bubble bath. She hadn't told him what she desired. He even added flowers.

Slipping into her thin, soft pink robe, she reclined on the bed to wait, resting her head back against pillows. About ten minutes later, room service arrived and Raith directed the man into the bedroom. The hotel attendant pushed a cart that had several candles, three bouquets of colorful flowers and a bottle of bubble bath.

Raith stood in the doorway, fingers stuffed into his front pockets, looking like an awkward teenager. The man set up the bathroom and turned on the faucet before coming back into the room. Raith tipped him and then the man left.

The smell of a fragrant bubble bath lured Autumn off the bed. Raith saw how slowly she moved and came to help her. She welcomed it, so exhausted and achy that even being naked in front of him didn't bother her...or have the effect it ordinarily would.

The hotel attendant had placed two bouquets on each corner of a marble ledge that ran along the wall and some candles between. The third bouquet and more candles were between two sinks on a marble counter adjacent to the tub. A wonderful aroma filled the bathroom. Beyond the end of the tub, a floor-to-ceiling window displayed a view of city lights. The toilet was in a separate enclosure and the shower was behind the tub and sinks.

"I feel better already," she said, placing her book on a marble ledge beside one of the bouquets. She always brought a book with her when she traveled.

He said nothing while he waited for her to undress. The warm, bubbly water, the candles and flowers, and the magnificent view she'd have during her bath kept her enthralled until she glanced at him before stepping into the tub.

His eyes smoldered with restrained desire.

She reached out her hand, asking for help. He stepped forward as though jerked out of a stupor and held her around the waist. The feel of his muscles through clothing redirected her pleasure from bubbly water to him.

He lifted her and deposited her in the water, then guided her to sit. She sank back, her body going beneath a thick layer of bubbles. She stared up at him as he lingered. His gaze traveled down as though seeing through the bubbles to what lay beneath.

Then he straightened.

He stood there as though undecided as to what to do. Something told her he'd like to stay with her. Something else told her he was still upset about the news that had surely rocked him. A man like him didn't think about babies. Preventing them, maybe. Not having them. He thought about doling out his own brand of justice. They hadn't had a chance to talk about it.

"Raith, I'm sorry about the way you found out," she said.

She noticed how he tensed and wasn't sure he'd reply, but finally he did. "When were you going to tell me?"

She remained silent. She had gone back and forth between deciding to tell him and not.

"You wouldn't have told me?"

Seeing the degree of his dismay, she quickly said, "That's why I came to Houston, why I met with Kai." To find Raith and tell him. "But then…"

"But then you saw what a lawless rebel I was and changed your mind."

"I wasn't sure."

He held up his hand. "I don't want to talk about this."

"We need to."

He shook his head. "I'll be back to check on you." He started to turn.

"Wait." She pointed to her book, a really good adventure story that was a bestseller. "I need a towel."

Seeing her wet hand, he slid a hand towel from the rack and handed it to her. She dried her hands and dropped the towel to the floor before reaching for the book. Wincing with the strain on her muscles, she leaned back and closed her eyes for a second. Holding the book above water kind of hurt, too. Not terribly, but it would ruin her bath.

She leaned to put the book back on the table. "I don't need to read." She shut her eyes.

Raith leaned over and snatched the book, annoyed but unable to leave her.

"You don't have to read to me. I'll just enjoy the view."

He leaned against the sink counter and crossed one ankle over the other. Opening the book to the page she had marked, he set the metal bookmarker onto the counter and began to read. His deep voice tantalized her senses. She closed her eyes, listening to how his tone began stiff and slightly irritated, to smooth and engaged with the story. He enjoyed a chapter with her.

Autumn opened her eyes as he continued to read, looking over at his handsome face until the sight became too much of a stimulus. She closed her eyes again. His reading stopped.

Opening her eyes, she saw him watching her in that smoldering way. Then he resumed reading. She looked out the window. Candles, flowers, the view and his voice all worked to lull her. Even her head didn't ache as much.

He finished a second chapter. "Don't fall asleep in there."

"The water is cooling." She sounded as letdown as she was.

"Poor baby." Raith set the book down and retrieved some towels from the rack under the sink. Setting those on the counter, he stepped toward her with reaching hands.

She sat up and put hers in them and he lifted her, bubble bath dripped down her body. He didn't miss a single curve they slid over.

"I need to rinse off," she said.

With his hands on her ribs, he lifted her from the tub. Her feet came down on a soft rug and she stood still, stirred by his face, her hands putting wet prints on his shirt.

He stepped back.

Growing acutely aware of her nakedness, she walked to the shower, feeling his gaze on her backside and then her profile as she started the water.

While she waited for the water to warm, she looked

over at him still standing where she'd left him, that smoldering look harder with restraint.

Then his eyes traveled down, catching on her stomach and dousing the heat in his eyes.

Autumn got into the shower and took her time rinsing off as best she could without getting her stitches wet. By the time she dried off and emerged in her nightgown, she felt exhausted again.

In the bedroom, Raith sat at the end of the bed, surfing channels. He stopped when he saw her.

She went to the bed, pulling the covers back and climbing in.

Raith found a funny movie and put the remote on the bedside table. "Do you need anything else?"

Lying in here and watching a movie alone didn't appeal to her. "Will you sit in here for a little while?" Maybe it was her concussion that was making her needier than usual.

He hesitated but walked over to the other side of the bed and reclined there. Autumn resisted the urge to move closer and cuddle against him. But he extended his arm in invitation and drew her there.

She made it only a few minutes into the movie before drifting into deep, contented sleep.

Raith looked down at Autumn's sleeping face and felt a myriad of emotions. Protectiveness. Dread. Love…

In fact, he was pretty sure it was love that had made him carry her into the room and then order all those romantic items for her bath. She hadn't had to tell him what she was thinking. She looked so exhausted and he could tell she ached from being thrown in the explosion.

Running away would have spared him having to face that. But Raith never ran from anything. He was a fighter.

What was there to fight with Autumn? How could he fight having a child with her? And how could he not?

Disconcerted, he got up from the bed. She'd be all right until morning. He had to get out of here. He had to stay busy...and away from her.

The following night, Raith waited for Ralston to leave work. It was after eight and he appeared a few moments later. He didn't care if he was noticed. In fact, it was better if Ralston did notice that he was being watched. If he was the shooter, he'd think twice about going after Kai.

He didn't notice at first. He drove all the way to a hotel and parked. Raith parked nearby and watched Ralston walk over to him.

Raith got out of the car as he approached.

Ralston seemed annoyed that he'd been followed. "Why are you following me?"

"Who are you meeting here?"

"I often have meetings in the conference center here."

Raith wondered if he was telling the truth. "Isn't it late for a meeting?"

"I didn't try to have Kai killed."

"Then tell me why he came to see you that day." It was that simple.

"It's not me you should be following."

"Who should I be following, then?"

"That's your job to find out. Just stop following me. I didn't do anything to Kai. I've never done anything to him." Ralston walked toward the hotel.

Then something Raith hadn't expected happened.

Kai appeared. He walked toward Ralston, who saw him and turned.

Raith jogged toward them, seeing Kai pointing his finger in Ralston's face.

"I'm going to kill you!" Kai shouted, swinging his fist.

Ralston took one on the face and then swung back. The two collided in a brawl, grunting and growling swearwords.

Raith hooked his arms around Kai as he tackled Ralston to the ground and was about to attack him with more punches.

"Let me go!" Kai twisted and wrenched his body, fury propelling him to go after Ralston some more.

Wiping his bleeding face, Ralston got to his feet, eyeing Kai in disgusted befuddlement. Raith gave Kai a shove to separate him from Ralston. Kai immediately lunged.

Moving into Kai's path, Raith gave him another shove. "I'd think twice about that if I were you."

Kai's face, crazed with fury, eased some. He became aware of Raith's threat and didn't try to go after Ralston again.

"What is the matter with you?" Ralston demanded.

Kai shook his finger at Ralston. "I'm going to destroy you!"

"Haven't you already done that?" Ralston charged this time.

Raith planted his hand on Ralston's chest, sending him bouncing backward.

"What are you doing here?" Raith asked Kai.

"He deserves everything that's coming his way," Kai answered.

"I wish that shooter hadn't missed!" Ralston hissed, going after him again.

Raith had to give him another shove to put him in check.

"Is there a problem out here?"

Raith saw the security guard walking over. Now

Ralston and Kai would never reveal what was going on between them.

"No, no trouble," Ralston answered.

"We were just leaving, weren't we?" Kai drilled a threatening look at Ralston. He would not let him go into the hotel.

Who was in there?

With a brief hesitation, Ralston started toward his car. Kai trailed behind and Raith walked with him.

"What was that all about, Kai?"

"Leave me alone." Kai walked faster and Raith let him go. He wouldn't give away a thing without being forced. Raith would resort to that if he had to. He'd give this another week first. Then it would be time to play hardball.

A week later, Autumn felt like herself again. Her head didn't hurt and her wound was healing. She'd spent a lot of time with Leonardo and had grown rather attached to him despite his love of movies and the stars in them. He'd asked her lots of questions about her dad and the movie business but in a nonintrusive or overly awed way. He'd been interested, that's all. The conversation had transported him to a place outside of his dying body, which had pleased Autumn.

Ever since pampering her the night she was released from the hospital, Raith came back late at night and generally avoided them. Going on eight tonight, he, of course, wasn't here. She and Leonardo had just finished dinner. He had to leave the day after tomorrow to make a doctor's appointment later in the week.

"What is your appointment for?" she asked.

He seemed to hesitate. "To discuss some experimental treatment."

Carrying a magazine, Autumn moved from the kitchenette to the seating area where Leonardo had turned on the television and was watching a movie. "Is it promising?"

He looked up at her grimly. "I don't see how. They don't usually offer experimental treatment until they're sure you're going to die. They figure you have nothing to lose, so why not try anything? Human experimentation."

She stopped near him. "What kind of treatment is it?"

"Apparently, something kind of new. It's a pill that contains a chemical that theoretically gives your immune system a boost, tells it to attack a type of protein cell in the cancer. Works on some, doesn't on others."

"You don't seem very hopeful."

Leonardo smiled at her. "I'm as hopeful as a dying man can be."

And he had nothing to lose, as he'd said. She didn't say anything, but she felt as though he did have at least something of a chance. She'd heard about that type of experimental treatment. It did work on some. But Leonardo was right. It didn't work on everyone.

The hotel-suite door opened. Raith was back early tonight. The sight of him gave her heart a lurch, painful and warm at the same time. She hadn't seen much of him. He slept late and walked out the door as soon as he was ready. She wondered why he was home so early.

He walked into the suite slowly, taking the sight of her in and then his dad.

"Welcome back," Leonardo said with a hint of sarcasm.

He didn't approve of the way Raith was managing the news that she was pregnant. Autumn wavered between agreeing with him and not faulting Raith. It had shocked her, too. Maybe he just needed time to adjust.

"Anything new on Garvin?" she asked. Raith had said

he was watching the man, hoping he'd lead him to the one who'd hired Leaman.

"No. He's kept a regular schedule. Ralston, too."

So, he'd been keeping an eye on Ralston, as well. Did the two men know they were being watched? Were they being careful?

Raith came to stand a few feet from her. She grew uncomfortable, unable to tell if the energy radiating from him was animosity or attraction.

Leonardo made a show of yawning and stretching. "Gosh, I'm tired." He groaned as he stood. "I'm going to go to bed now. Good night, you two."

"Good night, Leonardo," Autumn said.

"Good night," Raith echoed in his deep voice. He was still rather aloof with his father, but there was some warming going on there.

Leonardo disappeared into his suite and Autumn was left alone beneath Raith's observant gaze.

"You look like you're feeling better," he said.

"Yes. Much." She dropped the magazine she still held onto the side table by the couch.

"Good."

When she straightened, they fell into a long stare. The issue of the baby made it infinitely more tense. Several more seconds ticked on.

"Raith…" She'd tried to talk to him before but he didn't give her a chance. "We still haven't talk about—"

"Not now." He started to turn away.

She grasped his forearm. "Don't you think we *need* to talk about it?" What were they going to do? They should make plans. Get an idea of what each expected and come to terms with whatever that was.

"I'm not ready to talk about it."

She wasn't ready to be a mother. "What if I am?" She let go of his arm. "What about me?"

He blinked his acknowledgment. At least he had empathy for her. "Why did you lie to me when you said you were on the pill?"

Although he asked nicely, she could see it upset him a great deal. Maybe that was why it was so hard for him to talk about it. "I didn't…I didn't really lie. I was on the pill up until two days before."

His brow came down and Autumn was forewarned that he didn't like that. "Why didn't you tell me?"

She put her hands on her hips. "Why didn't you think to use protection if you were so worried about getting me pregnant? That wasn't all my responsibility. You played a part in that as much as I did."

He sighed and pinched the bridge of his nose with his fingers.

She probably would have told him everything if that man hadn't started shooting at her. "You don't have to worry. You're off the hook." She began to regret coming to Houston.

He lowered his hand and pinned her with a hard stare. "What do you mean, I'm off the hook?"

"The reason I didn't tell you about the baby is that I was afraid you'd feel obligated to…do something."

"Like be a father?" he asked, his voice raised.

He seemed angry that he was being forced into being one. And how could she tell him that with him, trouble soon followed, and she wasn't sure he'd *make* a good father. "I meant…the rest that goes along with that."

"Family."

"Yes."

"Marriage."

"Yes."

His gaze remained hard.

"You shouldn't commit to anything out of obligation. And I wouldn't stop you from being part of the baby's life."

"Which part, Autumn?" Although he kept his tone calm, she sensed his tumultuous emotion. "The part where the media follows me everywhere? The part where my job is destroyed? My privacy?"

Understanding where his anger came from, she didn't condemn him for it. But he wasn't looking at the whole picture. "Think of all the traveling I'll do."

The quip didn't go over well with him. His eyes grew stormy and his jaw clenched.

"Sorry. It's just that I can't feel sorrier for you than I do for myself. You talk about how the media will affect you. Well, what about me? Have you stopped to think how this is going to change *my* life?"

When he didn't respond, she went on. "I didn't plan to get pregnant, Raith. I didn't ask for this. I loved my life exactly the way it was. When this baby is born, my freedom is gone. I'll have to plan everything around that. I won't be able to do whatever I want. I'll have a baby I'll be forced to consider. And then a toddler who will have to be enrolled in school. I can't drag a child along with me whenever I feel like taking a job in another country. So don't look at me and expect sympathy. You won't get it."

At last his anger abated. At last he began to see this from her point of view along with his. He wasn't the only one whose life would be turned upside down.

"I don't blame you," he said. "It was just… I'm angry because it was such a stupid thing to do." He shook his head. "That whole night. Stupid."

Oh, is that how he thought of it? She tried to steel herself against the sting of hurt, but it got to her, anyway.

"I didn't mean... I..." he stammered.

"No, you're right. It was stupid. I've never done anything so *stupid* in my life."

"I didn't mean you and me."

He was talking about the sex and nothing more. That placated her some. More than placated. He warmed her with that revelation, that admission of truth. "Did you think about calling me after that night?"

She saw by the way he blinked that he had. As that knowledge heated her blood, it also became too much to bear. If it had meant that much...

Him and her. Them. Together. Connecting powerfully.

"You didn't call because you found out who my father was." She clung to that. Surrendering to love with this man frightened her more than ever.

"Autumn. I—"

"You regret that night. And you wish I'd have never shown up in Houston. Believe me, I wish the same."

The lack of truth in that statement hung between them. How could she regret a night that had lit her up inside like never before? And if she looked deep down inside, she couldn't deny that she was glad she'd come to Houston. Even with all of the danger, at least she was with him.

"I don't regret it and neither do you," he said.

Autumn turned and walked to the window overlooking downtown Houston, folding her arms. She felt and heard Raith approach. He stood behind her and put his hand on her upper arm.

"What are we going to do?" she asked, speaking her thought aloud.

He lowered his hand. "I don't know yet."

Fair enough. At least he was honest.

His cell phone began to ring.

Autumn turned from the window and watched him

answer. As he listened to the caller, his eyes met hers and intensified with something new.

When he hung up, he said, "Paisley has something for us."

Autumn accompanied Raith to meet Paisley, who didn't want to be seen, so she asked them to come to her mother's house. They passed through a wrought-iron gate between two four-foot sandstone-colored brick pillars and walked up a narrow sidewalk to the taupe-sided, white-trimmed Queen Anne–style house. The roof gabled on the right and ran into a second story balcony. Stepping up to the covered porch that stretched the entire length of the house, Autumn noticed how Raith searched their surroundings to make sure no one was watching. No one was. Paisley hadn't been followed and neither had they.

Autumn was at odds over Raith and the talk they'd had. She had received mixed messages. Was he angry that she didn't expect him to feel obligated? That sort of suggested he was daddy material...

Or was he angry because of what he'd said—the media would destroy his life?

The door opened before they reached it and Paisley ushered them into the dark wood–floored foyer. A hall-way straight ahead led past a stairway, and arched door-ways opened to a living room to the right and a dining room to the left. Paisley took them into the living room.

Yellow walls and crown molding gave the room a crisp and modern appeal. A white sofa with brown-and-white pillows and two wooden accent chairs faced an oval cof-fee table atop a colorful mosaic area rug. At the end of the seating area the white wood trim of the fireplace rose to the ceiling.

Her mother sat on the sofa, hands clasped on her lap.

Her dyed-blond hair was cut into a chin-length bob and she wore moderate makeup, blue eye shadow and blush, trying to conceal mild wrinkles.

After introductions were made, Paisley's mother said, "I keep telling her to stay out of this. That boss of hers is no good. And he treats her so badly."

"Mother," Paisley cautioned. "I'm going to do this."

"You're trying to take down your boss, and I just don't think this is the way to do it."

"Mrs. Orman," Raith said. "I won't let anyone harm your daughter."

The woman eyed him as though skeptical.

"He does this for a living," Autumn said.

Mrs. Orman frowned. "Are you a policeman?"

"No. Something better than that."

After a bit more wavering, Mrs. Orman said, "Paisley did tell me you were capable." She gave him an up-and-down look. "And you do look it."

"Mother." Paisley went to an antique buffet table and retrieved a folder. She handed it to Raith.

Raith opened it up.

"I got this from one of the engineers at NV Advanced," Paisley said.

Raith looked over what appeared to be engineering documents and something called a technical assistance agreement.

"I shouldn't be showing any of this to you, but the engineer said this is the technology that he's been asked to send to Singapore. He also said he doesn't think the agreement that's in this folder covers the export."

Autumn and Raith had already suspected the technology was questionable to be sending to a foreign country for manufacturing.

"How did you know this engineer was working with this?" Raith asked.

"I knew who was working with the Singapore office. He was the only engineer, so I just asked him. He didn't talk to me at first, but when I convinced him I had outside help—you—and you were investigating Nash Ralston, he changed his mind. He said Nash fooled him into sending unauthorized technology to Singapore. He said NV Advanced tried to get an export license for some data that included information on some new image intensifier tubes, but that was denied."

"But they sent the data, anyway?" Autumn asked.

"Nash didn't tell the engineer about the ruling and the engineer didn't find out until after the exports occurred."

"So now we have a national security issue," Raith said. "Image intensifier tubes have to be highly sensitive U.S. technology."

"NV Advanced would be fined millions and Nash himself could do prison time."

"Why would he risk that?" Raith asked.

Paisley shrugged. "I wouldn't know anything about that. I'm just telling you what the engineer said."

Autumn was sure Raith hadn't asked her that question because he thought she could answer it. Even if manufacturing components in a foreign country saved money, why would any company take that kind of gamble? Moreover, why would a CEO take that kind of gamble? Prison? Was any job worth that?

Raith was silent awhile as he thought things through. At last, he looked at Paisley. "I don't want you involved anymore. It's too dangerous."

That seemed to please Paisley's mother. She leaned back with a smile as she looked up at Raith.

"I have to go to work in the morning," Paisley said.

"Do you have any vacation time?" he asked.

"Y-yeah…" she said warily. "Three weeks or so."

"Take them. Stay here with your mother and don't contact anyone at NV Advanced until I call you."

Paisley looked concerned. "What do you think Nash will do?"

"Let us find that out. I need you where I'm sure you'll be safe. Will you do what I tell you?"

After a moment, Paisley nodded. "Nash won't like it when I tell him I'm not coming in."

"Tell him it's a family emergency. When this is over, I'll make sure you don't lose your job."

"Maybe I'll spend the time looking for a *new* job."

"If Nash is doing what you say he is, then it will probably be him who gets fired."

Paisley put her hand on her chest and raised her eyes heavenward. "A dream come true."

Raith and Autumn bade farewell and left. Outside, Autumn walked with Raith toward their new rental.

"What now?" she asked.

"We go see Ralston tomorrow. Something tells me he'll be in a better mood to talk to us." He held up the folder.

Chapter 15

Late the next afternoon, Raith left the evidence in the rental and walked with Autumn into NV Advanced Corporation. They were told that Ralston was in a meeting. Raith wasn't sure if that was a delaying tactic because Ralston was avoiding them, but it didn't matter. They weren't leaving until they had a chance to talk to him.

Twenty minutes after checking in at the front desk, a different woman than Paisley came to greet them in the lobby. She took them to Ralston's door, and then went into her cubicle outside another executive's office.

Ralston sat behind his desk in his posh corner office and locked his computer when he saw them enter. "Please, have a seat." He stood and walked over to the black leather sofa, extending his arm to invite them to join him. Raith sat on one of the chairs opposite the sofa, Autumn taking the one beside him, a coffee table cluttered with space newspapers between them.

"You got my attention with your call," he said. "What's this about technology being transferred to Singapore?"

"We know you're sending it there illegally," Raith said.

Ralston didn't move. His eyes remained steady as he stretched one arm along the back of the sofa. "I'm afraid I'm not following you."

Raith leaned forward, resting his forearms on his knees and clasping his hands in a professional manner. Autumn found the impression opposed to his true self and wondered if he was about to become cynical.

"Let's stop avoiding what we both know is going on here," he said. "You stand to lose a lot if those exports are discovered."

Straight to the punch.

Ralston's eyebrows lowered. "How do you know anything about NV Advanced's exports? All of that is proprietary."

"I have my own way of getting information that isn't voluntarily disclosed to me." Raith let a strategic moment pass before continuing.

"I can't imagine the government will react positively to learning you're exporting information on image intensifier tubes to Singapore," Autumn chimed in.

Ralston looked from her to Raith. "Who have you been talking to? Someone who works here must have told you. Who was it?"

"Then it must be true," Autumn said, enjoying how Ralston was no longer treating her like a dumb redhead whose only worth was looking good.

Ralston ignored her. "How do you know so much?"

"I hacked into your system."

He could lie really well when he had to. Autumn may have to watch that about him. As soon as that thought came, another wiped it clean. Raith was a trustworthy man.

"You hacked into my system," Ralston repeated what Raith had said. He crossed one ankle over his knee.

"Why did Kai come to see you the last time we were here?" Raith asked. "Does he know about the exports?"

Ralston's expression grew angry. "I had nothing to do with the attempt on Kai's life. Why don't you believe me?"

"Because you look guilty, Ralston. Real guilty. You have something to hide and that something just might be enough to kill to keep hidden. Don't they send people like you to prison for willfully harming national security? The company might suffer some reputational damage and maybe a hefty fine, but you..."

"What's it to you, anyway? You're not a cop."

"No, but I'll bet the cops would like to have an earful of what I could tell them."

Ralston's faced iced over, clearly incensed that Raith had him.

"Why did you do it? Why do the exports?" Raith asked.

After another long and tense silence, Ralston said, "What our government considers a threat to national security isn't always that."

"In other words, you didn't think you'd ever get caught."

Ralston pulled his arm from the back of the sofa, lowered his foot to the floor and leaned forward like Raith. "Kai came here to blackmail me. If I didn't hand over the new technology NV Advanced is developing, he'd tip off the Department of State about the exports to Singapore."

Autumn sat back against her chair. So, Kai was blackmailing Ralston to gain a competitive edge. Not a news flash. It was nice to have the truth finally come out.

"Was that the first time he threatened you?" she asked, sure that Raith had been thinking the same as her.

"About the exports? No. He's threatened me before." He turned to Raith. "He was afraid you'd find out about them. That's why he came to my office that day you were here."

"And if I found out so would the government and he could no longer threaten you."

"Exactly. He wants the technology."

"Which you won't give him."

Ralston smiled slyly. "No."

Raith just looked at him, waiting for him to connect the dots.

"I didn't kill Kai, and I didn't hire anyone to kill him."

Still, Raith continued to look at him.

"Why did you risk the exports?" Autumn asked.

This time Ralston relented, sighing heavily. "Believe me, I wish I hadn't now. Our government makes it exceedingly difficult for companies like NV Advanced to do business in this country. The purpose of International Traffic in Arms Regulations is to protect critical U.S. technology. Night-vision equipment certainly qualifies as critical technology, but what our government does a poor job of is dealing with the reality that other countries are developing the same technology."

So he'd justified the exports that way. And thought he was invincible—until Kai started blackmailing him.

"They develop it based on ours, though," Raith disagreed.

Ralston opened his palms nonchalantly. "In some cases. But not at our Singapore company. They have the same technology."

"Then why the need to export it?" Raith asked.

"It's a subsidiary of NV Advanced Corporation. I've done no harm in sending the technology."

"Not unless there are some dual nationals working there, say, maybe from Iran?" There was an edge to Raith's voice. That kind of technology getting into the wrong hands would definitely harm national security. Raith was against that, powerfully so.

"I'm under tremendous pressure from the board to get our next-generation night-vision goggles delivered to the military," Ralston argued. "They're expecting significant revenue from the program. I can't deliver what they're demanding with U.S. development costs."

It was no less than she and Raith had already surmised.

"If Kai tips off State, then I'll deal with the investigation. I have proof that the board pressured me into performing the exports. I won't be the one to go down if ICE comes knocking on our doors."

"ICE?" Autumn queried.

"Immigration and Customs Enforcement," Raith answered, and then to Ralston he asked, "Why didn't you tell us this before?"

"It was a little obvious that you might suspect me of trying to kill my competition."

"Garvin is a good friend of yours," Raith reminded him.

"Not that good. I told you before that I use his shooting range."

"Yes, and Garvin sold guns to Leaman Marshall."

Autumn watched for a reaction from Ralston and found only confusion.

"Who?"

"I wouldn't expect you to reveal your association with an assassin."

"An assassin? What's this all about?" Ralston acted outraged.

"You sent an email to Garvin expressing your condolences over Leaman Marshall's death."

Ralston looked from Raith to Autumn and back again. "I did no such thing."

"I have a copy of it," Raith said.

"I don't know anyone named Leaman Marshall. I've never sent Garvin any emails. I only use his shooting range."

"You've got motive to kill Kai Whittaker, and I can link you to a known assassin."

Ralston only stared at him, unable or unwilling to respond.

"Is Garvin in on it? Maybe he agreed to help you after Leaman failed."

"Maybe Kai paid him to fail," Ralston said.

Autumn agreed that an assassin missing his mark was a little strange. What kind of sniper did a drive-by shooting?

"This has the stink of something Kai would do," Ralston said. "He's trying to make it look like I tried to have him killed."

Raith neither agreed nor disagreed. He stood and Autumn did the same. "We'll be in touch."

At Raith's guidance, she walked ahead of him to the door.

"I didn't try to have Kai killed," Ralston once again said as they left.

Outside, Raith called Kai's cell phone. It rang and went to voice mail. Next, he called his office. There was no answer there, either. Why wasn't his assistant answering?

He called DT Corporation's main line. "Kai Whittaker."

"One moment."

"Don't transfer me," Raith said. "He's not answering his phone."

"Mr. Whittaker isn't in today."

Not in? Where was he? Raith hung up and then called his home number. India answered after the first ring.

"Kai?" she asked.

"No, it's Raith. I need to speak with him."

India began to cry. "I don't know where he is."

"Why not? Did something happen?"

"I—I don't know. He didn't come home from work last night. He isn't answering his phone and no one from work knows where he is." She sobbed some more. "Has… has…he called you?"

"No." Kai was missing?

"Will you find him? Please find him."

"Have you called the police?"

Autumn looked over at him.

"Y-yes," she wailed. "There's nothing they can do. Please. I'm so worried."

"Did he say anything to you the last time you saw him?"

"We had a fight…about that woman he had an affair with. He apologized. He said he loved me. But I was…I was so upset."

"Did he leave after you fought?"

"Yes."

"And that's the last you saw of him?"

"Yes." She cried harder.

"Would he have left you? Did you ask for a divorce?"

"No. He wouldn't have left me. Something's happened to him. Please, Raith. You have to find him. I would have called you but I didn't have your number. Only Kai had it."

"I'll do what I can. Is there someone who can stay with you?"

India regained control of her crying. "My daughter is here."

"Okay. Stay in the house and don't go anywhere. Make sure all your doors and windows are locked and your security system is set, okay?"

She sniffled. "Okay."

Raith ended the call and turned to Autumn. "Kai is missing."

After questioning Kai's assistant, Raith checked Kai's email and found nothing unusual. His assistant confirmed he'd left work at his normal time and said he was going home. He'd called his wife from the office. Security checked camera recordings and confirmed Kai had left the building shortly thereafter. Something had happened to him between there and arriving at home.

Had Ralston hired someone else to kill him? Had Garvin done it? Raith called NV Advanced and found out that Ralston had left at five.

Kai had left at six. That gave Ralston plenty of time to intercept him.

"I think it's time we called the cops," Autumn said when they left the building.

"And tell them what? That I killed an assassin and now the CEO of a competing night-vision equipment company may have taken matters into his own hands?"

Autumn's long, silky hair flowed in a slight breeze as she walked beside him toward their rental. "Well, we can leave out the part about killing the assassin." Her big round sunglasses hid beautiful, dark green eyes, but the tilt of her head and impish curve of her mouth lent her an animated spark.

She could turn the most awful statement into something adorable. She said it so matter-of-factly, so innocently.

"We could, but I'd rather not. India already called the cops."

"Yes, but she doesn't know what we know about Ralston."

"What do we know? That he emailed Garvin expressing sympathy over the loss of his friend, the assassin we aren't going to mention?"

"All right. I see your point, but the police don't know that Kai was blackmailing him."

"And if they did, they'd have to inform the Department of State."

"That's going to happen, anyway."

"Only if Ralston hired Leaman."

She stopped at the trunk of their rental. "So, you're saying you'd keep Ralston's secret if he ends up being as innocent as he claims?"

"I wouldn't keep anything secret. I just wouldn't take it upon myself to call the Department of State."

"Paisley might do it."

"Better her than me."

Autumn folded her arms. "You're making sure they don't find out you're involved."

"I'd have to explain why I was involved." And that would force him to talk about Leaman, which is what he wasn't going to do.

"Don't you get tired of always keeping secrets?" she asked.

And he realized this wasn't about calling the cops. This was about how she felt about him.

"I've never really thought about it. I just do what I have to not to get caught."

"Right. Doing something illegal, like killing someone." Her mouth curved downward now, no longer adorable.

"Leaman Marshall was a bad person. He would have killed you just because you saw his face."

"You break the law for a living."

"Not always."

Swinging her arms down roughly, she pivoted and marched to the passenger side of the car.

Raith got in and looked over at her pouting in the passenger seat.

"Why are you so mad?"

"I'm not mad."

"You're mad."

She folded her arms again. "Just drive. Where are we going now?"

"Nowhere. Tell me why you're mad." Maybe he didn't want to know. Maybe he already knew. And maybe he longed to do something about it. She could add that to the secrets she thought he kept.

Turning her head, she angled it and he could feel her sarcasm.

She was thinking he should know damn well why she was mad. She was pregnant and he wasn't the best father material because he broke laws and kept secrets. He wasn't sure if he'd make a good father, but he didn't like her thinking he wasn't.

He drove to Ralston's residence. It was going on six at night and he may not be home yet. Raith would wait and see. If he'd done anything with Kai, he doubted he'd do it here. At least Raith wouldn't. Some people didn't think in that much detail. They didn't think about leaving forensic evidence. Or hiding it. But Ralston, if he was guilty, had spent a lot of time premeditating.

He parked out of sight and waited, Autumn quiet beside him.

They didn't have to wait long. A car drove up and it wasn't Ralston. A sleek Jaguar pulled into the driveway. A woman got out, one he recognized.

"Hey," Autumn exclaimed in a whisper. "That's Kai's wife."

"It sure is. You don't have to whisper. She can't hear us."

She sent him a glare before turning back to India.

They watched her go to the door and ring the bell, glancing around. She saw their vehicle but must not have thought anything of it. The door opened and Ralston appeared, kissing her before letting her inside.

"I thought Ralston was married," Autumn said, talking in a normal tone now.

"He is."

"She must be out of town." She stared at the closed door. "Ralston is having an affair with Kai's wife. Oh, my God."

"Yeah, how's that for a surprise?" Raith started the engine and did a U-turn in the street. There was nothing they could do tonight. He wouldn't give Ralston any clue that he knew about the affair.

"What do you think it means?" Autumn asked.

"If Kai knows his wife is sleeping with his nemesis, he might have set Ralston up out of revenge." Kai loved his wife. Raith didn't doubt that. He'd try to keep her.

"I bet she doesn't know Ralston tried to kill her husband."

Raith recalled how distraught India had been on the

phone. She must be riddled with guilt. Is that what had brought her here?

Raith picked up his phone from the cup holder where he'd put it and called Paisley. He asked her if she knew Ralston was having an affair with Kai's wife, and after she'd recovered from shock, told him no. He'd kept India a deep dark secret.

"Why would Kai go to all that trouble, though?" Autumn asked.

"I thought you didn't believe an assassin would do a drive-by."

"That is a little odd, but so is someone like Ralston hiring a highly sought-after assassin. Why not find a regular hit man? Someone who isn't wanted by the FBI?"

"Maybe it was more of a favor and Leaman underestimated how hard it would be to kill him in a drive-by."

"Now, *that* I believe. Ralston is acquainted with Garvin, whose best friend happens to be an assassin. Maybe Ralston paid Garvin, and Garvin lined Leaman up in return for a really nice rifle."

Raith grinned over at her. "You're pretty good at this."

She smoothed the hem of her dress, drawing his attention to her knees. "Are you going to start introducing me as a P.I. now?"

"Agent isn't working for you?" He looked at her breasts, a portion of cleavage showing.

"P.I. is more attainable."

He chuckled as he pulled to a stop in front of the hotel. Tipping the valet driver, Raith walked to the passenger side of the car and put his arm around Autumn as they headed for the doors. It was an automatic movement, one that made Autumn stop walking.

They stood on the brick walkway in front of the entrance, cauterized by the warm contact of their bodies.

Everything but where he felt her against him fell away. Slipping his other arm around her, he brought her to him fully and without much thought other than the way he felt right now, kissed her.

Her hands slid up his chest and she looped them over his shoulders, angling her head and welcoming a deeper caress. Raith could have kissed her for hours. The sound of a car driving up and people walking past brought him back to earth. He stopped kissing her but looked into her eyes, so drugged with sexual arousal that he considered taking her hand and rushing her up to the room and straight into the bedroom.

"Why does that feel so good?" she murmured.

"It could feel even better." Why he'd said that he hadn't a clue.

She answered with a sultry nod.

Swearing, growing as hard as a rock, he stepped back. She entwined her hand with his as they walked into the hotel. All the way up in the elevator, he stared at her, fighting the instinct and urgent drive to be inside of her.

At the suite door, she turned to him. Her arms went around him and she rose onto her toes to press a kiss to his mouth.

More swearing went through his head, but he put his hands on her rear and took over the kiss. She groaned, panting for breath.

Raith fumbled with the room key and managed to blindly unlock the door. He pushed it open and it swung, hitting the wall with a bang. Autumn laughed as they tripped over their feet and stumbled into the room.

After regaining his balance, he pulled her to him again. Over her head he saw his dad getting up from the sofa. He stopped kissing Autumn.

She groaned a protest and kept kissing him.

"Autumn." He put his hands on her shoulders and set her back a step. While she pouted, he said, "We have company."

She turned. "Oh."

"I'll go back into my room," Leonardo said.

"No, no." Autumn walked over to the seating area. "It's all right. Stay."

"No. I should go." He looked at Raith with a grin. "Take good care of her."

Raith couldn't imagine a more awkward thing for his dad to say. The adjoining-room door shut and he and Autumn were alone.

Smoothing her hair, Autumn cautiously shifted her eyes to him.

"Um…" she murmured.

"I'll call room service." They hadn't eaten yet.

"Good idea. I'm…um…I'm going to go change into something more comfortable."

He didn't respond, thinking of sexy lingerie and long, slender, naked thighs open for him.

Chapter 16

The next morning, Raith and Autumn waited for Leonardo to finish gathering his things. Raith had a car waiting in front of the hotel. Autumn hadn't slept well last night. Room service had distracted them enough to prevent another reckless night in bed together, but she had ached for Raith for hours before falling into a restless sleep full of steamy dreams.

He didn't seem bothered at all, not over her, anyway. He would say goodbye to his father and it might be the last time he saw him.

"Did Leonardo tell you about the experimental treatment he's going to try?" she asked.

Judging by his look, she guessed not and explained what Leonardo had told her.

"Those treatments don't work."

"This particular one might. I read about it online. It

has a pretty impressive survival rate, higher than any other that's come along."

"He has advanced colon cancer. Cancer, Autumn. When the doctors say you only have months to live, that's not good news."

He sounded so angry and she understood why. He fought against hope because if he hoped to have a father—a real father for the first time in too many years—he might end up losing him.

Leonardo appeared through the adjoining door. His grayish pallor and stiff movement revealed his exhaustion. He must not have been feeling well today.

"Are you sure you don't need us to go with you to the airport?" Autumn asked.

"Yes. I'll be fine. There will be plenty of help once I get there." He left his carry-on luggage and looked at Raith, studying him as though committing him to memory.

"I hate goodbyes, so all I'm going to say is thank you for letting me back into your life," his dad said.

Raith stepped forward and gave his dad a hug. "Good luck with your new treatment."

Moving back from the embrace, Leonardo glanced at Autumn, realizing she'd told Raith. She wondered if he'd intended to tell him himself.

"I'll call you," Leonardo said.

"I'll be in touch, too."

Leonardo patted Raith's arm. "Be happy, son."

Raith took the handle of the luggage and rolled it to the door. Out in the hall, they went to the elevator.

"Oh," Leonardo said. "I almost forgot to tell you. I watched an entertainment program this morning." He leaned to look at Autumn around Raith's big form. "I've taken to watching this channel ever since I discovered my son's girlfriend is Jackson Ivy's daughter."

Oh, no. What had he seen on the program? He couldn't guess what a sore subject this was.

"There was a brief blurb about the two of you. They had a picture. You were kissing outside this hotel." Leonardo smiled, his sickly color slightly improving. "A real handsome couple you make. And that kiss looked like the real thing."

"Someone took our picture?" Autumn asked.

Raith's mouth pinched into a tight line and his eyes narrowed in reaction.

"Someone at the party you attended at the Ivy mansion spilled the beans about the baby. You're a hot topic right now." He leaned over again. "I won't ask you how you got your reputation as a heartbreaker. That kiss and the baby stirred up a buzz. The two big questions were *will this new mystery man last? Will the baby make you commit?*" Leonardo chuckled and then had to catch his breath. "They don't know who you are," he said to his son.

"Thank God for small miracles," Raith said.

"You going to marry her and give that baby a name or not?" Leonardo braced his hand on the elevator wall and put his other hand to his stomach, taking a few deep breaths.

"I'm glad you made contact with me, Dad, but don't push it."

Had Raith noticed his father's condition?

"Scared of the press?" Leonardo shook his head. "Didn't think anything scared you."

"This isn't something I feel like discussing with you."

"Fair enough." The elevator doors opened and Leonardo was slow to push off the wall to follow them out.

Autumn waited for him and hooked her arm with his. "Are you all right?"

"I need to get home and rest."

Raith stood in the opening to the lobby and watched them, becoming aware of how slow his father was moving.

They walked at Leonardo's pace through the lobby. Outside, a dark sedan and driver waited. The driver opened the back door and Raith handed him the luggage.

"Are you sure you're up for traveling today?" Raith asked.

"I have to be."

"Your appointment can be rescheduled," Autumn said, concerned for him.

He went to her and gave her a weak hug. "I'm so glad I had a chance to meet you."

"The feeling is mutual."

Leonardo faced his son. "You take care now. With any luck, I'll live long enough to make your wedding and the baby's birth."

Autumn didn't think he should travel. Maybe he needed a doctor.

"Call us and let us know how the treatment is going," Raith said.

"Will do." He turned to the car and took two steps before bending over, one hand going to his stomach and the other on the side of the car.

Raith moved toward him and put his arm around him just as Leonardo began to collapse.

Autumn dug into her purse for her phone and called 911.

"Nine-one-one, what's your emergency?" she heard the operator automatically answer.

"A man has collapsed in front of the Four Seasons

Hotel. He has colon cancer." Autumn watched as Raith laid Leonardo down onto the pavement.

Leonardo grasped his shirt and looked up at his son as though he believed he was dying.

"Is he conscious?" the operator asked.

"Yes."

Just then Leonardo's eyes slid shut. His body slumped in Raith's arms and he went still.

"Oh, my God. Raith!"

Raith leaned down. "He's breathing."

"He's breathing. But he just lost consciousness," she told the operator, kneeling on the other side of Leonardo and looking at Raith's grim face.

She searched for the lights of emergency vehicles. An endless few minutes passed before the sirens gave her some hope. Firefighters, along with two paramedics, gathered, and Raith answered all of their questions. Then Raith stood beside her and watched helplessly with her while they worked on Leonardo. When the paramedics loaded him into the ambulance, Raith and Autumn climbed in with him. One of the paramedics monitored Leonardo's vitals while the other drove.

Autumn sat on a bench along one side and Raith sat beside her and next to the paramedic, who finished inserting an intravenous line. Then Leonardo's body convulsed as though going into a seizure.

"We're losing him," the paramedic called to his partner, who was driving.

"What's happening?" Autumn asked, taking Raith's hand. His father couldn't die like this after just reuniting with Raith.

"Ventricular fibrillation," the paramedic answered, working with quick and experienced hands as he set up the defibrillator and attached the patches to the old man's chest. Leonardo began gasping for breath every few seconds.

The paramedic shocked him. Autumn watched the heart monitor as it began to show signs of life again. The paramedic began to administer CPR and after a few minutes Leonardo's heart began to beat on its own. Autumn leaned back with a breath of relief.

"Not breathing," the paramedic said.

The ambulance stopped in front of the E.R. and his partner radioed the hospital, reporting the cardiac arrest and no breathing. Then he rushed to the back to help the other paramedic.

Autumn and Raith jumped out of the vehicle to allow them more room. She covered her mouth as they inserted a breathing tube into Leonardo's throat and set the defibrillator up again.

Autumn's heart climbed into her throat, her pulse quickening. She took Raith's hand as emergency hospital staff joined the paramedics and removed Leonardo from the ambulance. He was wheeled inside, medical staff running alongside him.

Raith stood there a few moments and then tipped his head back with closed eyes. Autumn put her hand on his shoulder.

"Let's wait for the doctor," she said.

He turned his somber face to her, eyes heavy with worry and dread. "What if he dies?"

"He won't. We have to believe he won't." Thinking positively couldn't hurt.

"Come on." She took his hand and urged him into the emergency room, going to a near-vacant waiting room.

She sat next to Raith, who stared at the closed double doors where Leonardo had been taken.

"Why did he have to come here?" Raith asked.

Autumn was appalled by that statement. "You'd rather he died without doing so?"

He straightened his head and she saw the ravaging emotion in his eyes.

"You'd rather not care," she said. "Maybe that's why you do what you do. You can be a loner and never care about anyone other than yourself. It's easier that way, right? Not caring is so much easier."

"Isn't that what you do? Travel to faraway places so you don't have to care about what the media is saying about you?"

"We're talking about you right now. Your father might be dying in there and you wish you didn't care." If he cared enough about her and their baby, the media wouldn't matter at all.

"That's right. I wish I didn't care. He was a horrible father. Why should I care now that he's dying?"

"Is he a horrible father now?"

Raith turned away.

No, his father was not horrible anymore. "Alcohol is what was horrible. It was never him. It was his addiction. He overcame that addiction and reached out to you. So what if he waited too long. You should be grateful that you had one last chance to see that he isn't the horrible man you grew up with."

Standing, Raith walked over to the window and leaned on the sill, looking outside. Autumn left him alone.

His comment about the media didn't ring as true as it normally did. That had her a little perplexed. She had no desire to take on a new translation assignment, and she had no desire to travel to a faraway place. Moreover, she didn't feel trapped with Raith. She didn't feel like everyone saw her as a celebrity, either. She wasn't Jackson Ivy's daughter with him. She was just Autumn Ivy, the translator who loved to travel. She had a feeling that the next time she traveled it wouldn't be to escape the media. It would be for the adventure.

Why didn't she feel trapped with Raith? With the boyfriend who'd lasted six months, she'd felt trapped. She'd liked him a lot, but she'd still felt trapped. In the end, that's what had driven her to take a translation job. She'd escaped.

Looking back, she realized that she hadn't felt as though she could be herself with him. She had liked many things about him, but he hadn't liked her for herself. He'd been impressed over who her father was, but he hadn't madc her feel as if that was the only reason he was with her. It had mattered to him, though, and it had changed how she behaved with him. She was the bimbo again.

She was no bimbo with Raith. She was Autumn Ivy.

That insight didn't go over so well with her. Her mood plummeted and added to her worry for Leonardo. As she turned to look at him staring out the window, tall, dark and brooding, she ached for him again, for his touch and the man who tugged at her in a deep, intimate way.

Maybe this time the heartbreaker would become the heartbroken.

"Let's go get coffee." Raith pushed off the window sill, jarring her.

She walked with him down a long, bright hall, following the signs to the cafeteria: a large, open room filled with beige-topped tables and wooden chairs with a food counter along the opposite wall. Beverages were situated along the adjacent wall on a smaller counter.

She and Raith went there.

Autumn poured some creamer into her cup while he poured his.

"This reminds me of when my mother died," he said.

Looking up at the ceiling and all round the room, he carried his cup to the register at the end of the food counter. There weren't many people in here. A solitary man sat at one table and a couple at another.

Autumn waited for Raith to continue. This was the most open he'd been about his mother.

"My dad took me to the cafeteria so he could get coffee." He paid for both of their cups.

Autumn led him to a table by the windows, which ran the length of one side. She sat across from him and watched him stare out the window.

"My mother was sick in bed when I left for school that morning. I didn't think anything of it. She had pneumonia. Death was the last thing on my mind."

"You were fourteen," she said.

He turned to her, his eyes a window into the past. "I didn't think of her at all that day. I flirted with a girl in science class."

She held back on commenting, sensing he needed to talk about this, also sensing he had never done so before now.

"I thought I had a chance with her. I thought about her all the way home. I was in a good mood. Happy. It was one of the rare days when nobody yelled or fought." His eyes focused on her then. "She was too sick to fight him."

"Raith…" Reaching for him, finding only the cold surface of the table beneath her palm, tears burned her eyes. Pregnancy hormones intensified the reaction. Autumn was not known for her weepiness. She rarely cried.

His eyes became unfocused again, lost in memory. "When I got home, she was still in bed. I went in there and noticed right away that something was wrong. My dad was on the couch watching a football game. He was drunk." He paused, the traumatic emotion of that moment so strong Autumn could feel it herself. "My mother…" He lowered his head, a powerful man choked up over the death of his mother. A few seconds passed before he was able to lift his head, his eyes still clear. "My mother's face was a grayish-white color…pasty…and more wrinkled than usual. She was dehydrated. I went to her and tried to talk to her. She opened her eyes and mumbled something." Raith shook his head slowly and fractionally. "I've been haunted all my life wondering what she said."

Autumn couldn't stop the trail of first one then another tear down her face.

"I ran out to my dad and shouted for him to go help her. He yelled at me. He told me to go to my room. I flew at him then. I punched him and told him he'd better go help my mother. He hit me and I fell backward onto the ground. He was going to beat the hell out of me, so I ran away. I had to sneak into the kitchen to call 911."

Autumn wiped her face.

"When the paramedics arrived, my dad wasn't going to let them in. You see, deep down he was ashamed of what a drunk he was. He couldn't let anyone see him like that. My mother was deathly ill and he wasn't going to let the paramedics in." Raith's jaw clenched. "I grabbed the nearest hard object I could find. A picture on the wall. And I hit him in the head as hard as I could. I wanted to kill him. I was hoping he'd die."

Autumn found herself barely able to make the connection between Leonardo and the man Raith described.

"While he lay there unconscious, I unlocked the door and let the paramedics in. They worked on my mother. I stayed with her. I rode with her in the ambulance."

His jaw clenched again and he had to stop and look out the window. Wrenching emotion gripped him. Autumn was certain he'd never felt it so strongly before. He'd been with his mother. He'd tried to save her.

She couldn't fathom how he could be so stoic.

"She kept looking at me."

Autumn stifled a sob.

"She had brown eyes. Beautiful, golden-brown eyes. I could see her love. She thanked me for helping her."

Sniffling, Autumn said, "That's awful but at least you have something good from the memory, Raith."

He didn't hear her. "She had thick dark hair. It wasn't even graying back then. She looked ten years younger than she was. Not then, though. She was thin. Sickly. I didn't see it until then. Until I was on the way to the hospital with her."

He sipped his coffee and put the cup down.

"It's not your fault."

"Oh, I know. I was just a kid."

"And that's why you blamed your father all these years."

He nodded once, firmly and with conviction. "When we arrived at the hospital, I kissed my mother on the forehead and told her I loved her and she was going to be all right. She smiled. It was a weak smile. She believed me, I think. That she was going to be all right."

His mother had believed her son had saved her life. She may have died believing that.

"She held my hand and kissed me back and then the paramedics took her away. I followed, but they put her into intensive care. A doctor came out later and said she had pneumonia and the infection had spread to her organs." Raith looked out the window again, not seeing, staring. "He said there was nothing they could do. That it was too late. If he'd gotten her sooner..."

He looked at her. "I was allowed into the room. The

doctors had her heavily sedated. That's what they do for people they know are going to die. Numb them so they aren't aware. I held my mother's hand while the heart monitor slowed until it stopped. It took several minutes."

That was terrible for a young teenage boy to go through. "Did...did your father ever show up?"

"No. And neither did my older brother. I didn't call him. It took years for him to forgive me for that. My dad? He declined medical care that night and passed out on the sofa. He was there when I eventually made it home. I walked. He heard about it in the morning. From me. I told him if he ever touched me again I'd kill him. And I would have."

That must have been his turning point. He'd gone to college with the intention of going into politics, but his heart had already made up his mind for him. He'd veered off his path and done what he couldn't do for his mother.

"Do you see now why I never wanted to see my father again?" he asked.

All she could do was nod.

"And why I dreamed of killing him? Why I hoped he'd give me a reason?"

Again, she gave a nod. "And he's been dead to you all these years...until now." That had to be why he was telling her all of this, and in such detail.

Long seconds passed before he finally said, "Yes. It's different now."

"You want him to live." He'd forgiven his father, or had begun to. "That's good."

He shook his head. "I'm not so sure about that."

"*Be* sure."

"Why? He's going to die. My wish is coming true."

Was he beating himself up over that? "Your father would never blame you for that. You could tell him every one of your dark thoughts and he'd forgive you. It's your forgiveness he needs, nothing more."

Leaning back, he stared out the window awhile, drinking coffee. After a few moments, she saw and heard him sigh. His eyes took on a more animated shape, not so drained by the past. Talking about this had lifted a great burden from him.

When he turned to her again, he was still somber, but a much different man than the one she'd seen before, confessing something he'd confessed to no one else. She felt honored.

Autumn sipped her coffee and stood. "Let's go back to the waiting room."

Raith stood and walked with her out of the cafeteria. As they approached the waiting room, a doctor appeared.

"Raith De Matteis?" the doctor asked.

"Yes." He sounded shaken.

Autumn took his hand, leaning against him in support.

"Your father is stabilized and resting," the doctor said. "His cancer has advanced rapidly. He had an infection that caused sepsis in his body. That affected some of his organs, the most significant being his heart. In his weakened state, he also experienced cardiac arrest. We got him in time, however. If he had gotten here minutes later, he would have died. We came very close to losing him."

Raith's head went down briefly with that news, like a flinch from the emotional pain it caused.

"I spoke with his oncologist," the doctor went on. "He told me about the experimental medication they were going to try. We've decided to go ahead with it here. He's too weak to move or travel and time is going to be precious over the next week. We can't afford to wait."

Raith met her look. The weight was back in his eyes. Where he'd felt it for one parent, now he felt it for another. Losing his dad this way, at the last hour, too late to do anything, would devastate him.

"Experimental treatment might work, Raith," she said. He needed encouragement, her dark, sweet, sexy hero who obeyed no laws but didn't need to.

"Is he conscious?" he asked.

"Yes. We're going to keep him in ICU for a few more days. Then he'll be moved to a recovery room for a few more. We'll see how he does. His release will depend on how quickly he regains his strength."

If he ever did. That part was left unspoken.

"Have you started the experimental treatment?"

"Yes, but as I've said, his cancer is advanced and he's so weak…"

"What do you think his chances are?" Raith asked.

The doctor sighed and took a moment to reply. "Depending on how he recovers from the septic shock, it will still be difficult to predict. Each patient responds differently to the treatment. We'll monitor him closely over the next week."

The doctor said depending on how he recovered, but what he was really saying was *whether* Leonardo recovered.

"Can I go see him?" Raith asked.

"Of course, just keep in mind that what he needs most right now is medication and rest."

Raith turned to her, eyes clouded with apprehension. He had an opportunity to bond—one last time—with his father.

"You go alone," she said. "I'll wait out here."

As she watched him go, Autumn felt her feelings shift to another level. Raith had given her a glimpse of the boy who'd tried to rescue his mother and who'd grown into a man with unwavering drive to rescue anyone else he could. No lawless rebel. Just the opposite.

Raith entered the room. His father lay semi-reclined, pale and wrinkled, tubes in his nose and arm, and another surgically implanted into his chest, feeding his body with powerful antibiotics to fight the septic shock. Raith stopped at the sight of his father's body so vandalized by sickness.

"You weren't supposed to see me like this," his dad said, his voice gravelly from the breathing tube.

Raith moved toward the bed. "I'd much rather see you climbing Mount Everest, but walking out of this place will do."

His dad laughed feebly. "I did do a lot of hiking in the Selkirk Mountains a few years ago."

"You shouldn't talk too much."

His dad patted the bed in dismissal. "That was a good trip. Have you ever been there?"

"The Selkirks? No, but I've heard of them."

His dad took a few breaths through the tubes in his nose. "Have you ever taken a trip for yourself?"

He hadn't. "I've been all over the world."

"Anywhere for fun?"

Nowhere for fun. Raith stepped forward and sat in the chair beside the bed.

"You should stop burying your past in rebellion, Raith." He took some time breathing again. "Do it now while you've still got several good years left."

Maybe he had rebelled by getting into the kind of work he did. But he'd also had a passion for it. Upon reflection, that passion had waned in the last few years. He'd grown tired of traveling so much, especially to third world countries.

"Do you have any great memories from any of the trips you've taken?" his dad asked.

Great memories? He had to think long on that. He wouldn't call any of them great. Successful. "I do things for fun, Dad."

Leonardo smiled a little and Raith realized he'd called him Dad. But his father was careful not to point it out. "Like what?"

"Festivals. Home projects."

"Alone?"

"I have friends in Lander."

"But not family."

"They're like family."

"You need the real thing, Raith. Festivals and home projects and close friends are a nice start, but you need a wife and some kids. Maybe a dog and a job where you don't have to travel."

The truth was he could retire now. "I'm happy with the way my life is."

"I don't believe you."

Raith didn't, either. As soon as he spoke it aloud, he felt the lie.

"You can be happier," his dad said. "Don't make the same mistakes I made."

"You shouldn't be talking so much. Rest."

His dad rolled his head from side to side. "I need to say this. I had a family and I threw them away. I've lived alone a lot of years. It's not a natural existence, Raith." He took some time to breathe through his nose. "Autumn is a fine woman."

"Let's not talk about that."

"Why? So you can keep burying your past? No, Raith. If there's one thing that would make me die a happy man, it's knowing you've changed your ways. Your forgiveness would be the icing on the cake, but I'd settle for you letting go of what a bad father I was and..." He breathed deeply awhile. "Moving forward with Autumn and the baby."

"Stop talking like you aren't going to make it." And stop talking about Autumn and especially the baby. It had just made him break out in a cold sweat.

His dad grunted weakly. "I might not. Chances are in favor of death. Doc didn't say it, but I saw it in his eyes and heard it in his voice."

Raith reached over and put his hand on his dad's frail arm. "You want me to tell you I'm going to marry her and we're going to live happily ever after?"

"Only if you mean it." His dad shifted his head on the pillow so his eyes could search Raith's. "Do you love her?"

Raith leaned back against the chair. "I don't know."

"You know."

He was burying it. That's what his dad was saying. He buried anything that resembled a chance at a normal, happy life. Being a loner, he wasn't in any danger of feeling too much, of hoping for too much. Like the love of his father—something he was getting a good dose of right now.

"It's too soon to talk about love with Autumn."

"You could love her if you let yourself."

That felt true enough to him to scare him.

"She loves you."

Raith looked at his father, only then becoming aware that he'd turned away to stare out the window.

"I can see it every time she looks at you," his dad said. "She holds back, though. Because you aren't there for her. You close yourself off to her and the baby."

"Dad…" Autumn didn't love him…did she? And why did he keep calling him Dad?

"Don't do it, Raith. If it takes my last breath, I'll keep saying it until you listen to me. Don't bury love. Don't shut Autumn and the baby out. Let them in. Don't do what I did. You learned how to shut those you love out from me. With you, it's your job that enables you to do that. With me, it was the booze. Don't make the same mistake."

"Autumn is famous because of who her dad is. I can't have my picture all over the place."

"You can if you change your ways."

"You think you have me all figured out. How is that possible when you've been out of my life for so long?"

"I wasn't drunk all the time."

When he was a kid, his dad saw him as the superhero of Raith's imagination, not a mercenary. Raith didn't consider himself a mercenary, but that's how his dad saw him now.

"If you love her and you let her in, you'll find a way."

How did he feel about Autumn? Terrified of her pregnancy. Sexually, he desired her like no other before her. And he loved her independence. Her adventurous spirit. And her warmth. Underneath her fearless verve was a kind, gentle and loving woman. She'd make a good mom.

"I wish I could be around to see you do that," his dad said.

And that made Raith lean forward and touch his father's arm again. "Don't talk like that." He hadn't had the chance to say goodbye to his mother, and now he realized it didn't matter. His mother had said goodbye with only a look in her eyes. Goodbyes could come in any form. As long as there was love.

His dad scoffed softly, with what little energy he had left in his body. "Don't face the truth?"

"It isn't true until it happens."

His dad reached over with his other hand and patted Raith's where it rested on his arm. "I'm proud of you no matter what you decide. I just think you'd be happier with Autumn."

"Maybe you're right." He'd let his dad think it, anyway.

A twinkle beamed through his dad's illness in his eyes. "I'm so glad I didn't give up on contacting you."

"I'm glad, too." And Raith meant it. Autumn had been right. He would have regretted turning his dad away.

"Are you?"

It seemed his dad needed some reassurance. "Yes. And I forgive you."

Although he said it to put his father's mind at ease, he felt the reality of it deep in his heart. He did forgive him.

"The way you've been now is the way I remember you when I was a young boy, before you started drinking so much," Raith went on.

Tears pooled in his dad's eyes. "I wish we had more time."

"Maybe we will."

Chapter 17

Raith was quiet after talking to his dad. Autumn didn't push him for answers, although she was hugely curious about what was discussed. Whatever it had been, Raith had taken it to heart.

They'd left the hospital after Leonardo fell asleep and now drove into the parking lot of NV Advanced. Autumn walked with him inside. The lobby was quiet today and the security guard behind the desk looked up from his computer screen, covering a yawn.

"How can I help you?"

A door off the lobby opened and a woman entered.

"We're here to see Nash Ralston," Raith said while Autumn noticed the woman stop short when she saw them.

"He isn't in today," the guard said.

The woman was dressed expensively in a beige dress, decorated with diamond jewelry hanging from her neck and ears and bulging from her fingers. She had blond hair, a striking face and bright blue eyes.

She approached the desk. "Are you that couple who came here about Kai Whittaker? The FBI agents?"

"Yes," Raith said. "And you are…?"

Autumn was glad he was the one who took on the lie and she didn't have to say it. FBI agents…

She should probably worry about how well he did that. But she wasn't. Underneath the rebel was a good man.

"Adele Ralston. Nash's wife."

She certainly fit the profile. Beautiful. Big breasts. A real trophy. She moved away from the front desk and Autumn and Raith followed.

Adele stopped and faced them. "Nash has gone missing as of last night. He never made it home from work."

Autumn glanced at Raith. Kai was missing, too. What was going on?

"I thought he might be with India but she hasn't seen him, either."

"You know about his affair with her?" Autumn asked.

She didn't seem upset about it.

"I've known for a while." Her head lifted haughtily. "I let him get away with it long enough for me to hire a good lawyer. I was going to have him served at work this morning, but he's gone and disappeared." She sounded put off and annoyed.

"What an inconvenience," Autumn said.

Adele turned to her unapologetically. "Why do you need to see him?"

"Has he spoken with Garvin Reeves lately?" Raith asked.

"Garvin came to the house the night before last. Why do you need to talk to Nash about him?"

"Why did Garvin come to see him?" Autumn asked.

"They went into Nash's office and closed the door. Nash had that damn office soundproofed when we built our house. I didn't hear anything that was discussed, but after Garvin left Nash was anxious. I asked him what was wrong but he wouldn't tell me, and to be honest, I really didn't care."

"Are he and Garvin close friends?" Raith asked.

"I wouldn't say close. Nash has always had a special interest in guns. He has a pretty impressive collection of antique rifles. He went to Garvin's shooting range every week. They're friends, but Garvin isn't in the same league as Nash. To be close friends with Nash, you have to have money and a reputation to go with it. Nash isn't the most genuine person on the planet." She tapped her bejeweled fingers on her folded arm.

"Kai Whittaker has gone missing, too," Raith said.

That came as a surprise to Adele. "Do you think they're both in the same danger? Do you suspect Garvin?" She searched Autumn's and Raith's eyes. "Why?"

"We appreciate all you've told us, Mrs. Ralston." Raith put his hand on Autumn's lower back. "We can't discuss the case."

Adele waved her arm. "Just as well. I had to force myself to care he went missing. Good luck with your case."

"Do you think your husband could have killed Kai?" Autumn asked.

"Killed him?" She scoffed. And then she saw that Autumn was serious. "I would imagine Nash is capable of anything he puts his mind to. Do you think Kai is dead?"

Both of them could be. The only question then would be who had done it? Garvin? And if so, why?

Raith took Autumn to a restaurant in a converted old house for lunch. Someone had followed them from NV

Advanced. Now he walked outside with Autumn, searching for signs of the vehicle. It wasn't the same as the one that had chased Autumn before, and had stayed far enough away that he couldn't see who had driven. He purposely hadn't told Autumn, intending for the driver to assume he wasn't aware.

Spotting the car and a person inside, he had time to see the man wore a hat and a sweatshirt. The driver could be Garvin, but he couldn't be sure. An instant later, he saw a gun go up.

Ready for action, Raith pulled Autumn down just before a shot fired. She screamed. He'd kept parked cars between them and the car in case this happened. Drawing his own gun, he inched up and aimed, firing at the other vehicle.

To his amazement, the person got out of the car and started to come after them. If Autumn wasn't with him he'd have stayed for a gunfight. He took her hand and propelled her toward a gift shop behind them. Going inside, making her go first, he looked back and saw the man following. He had on dark sunglasses and was about the same height as Garvin.

Raith turned and walked backward just as the man entered the shop. He fired and Raith fired back. The man ducked. People screamed and scattered, taking cover behind display cases and the checkout counter. Autumn took Raith's free hand and ran. The gunman fired again.

Pushing through the back door, they ran into an alley. Raith hauled Autumn into an inset back entrance back door to another shop. Leaving her in the corner, he eased to the edge of the brick building and peered into the alley.

The man walked toward them. Now Raith could see he was smaller than Garvin. He could shoot the person right now. Something stopped him. Autumn. The baby. He was going to be a father.

What was the matter with him? Where before he wouldn't hesitate, now he was full of reluctance.

Giving Autumn the keys to the rental in case she needed to get away, he moved into the man's sight. The man froze, and when he saw that Raith had a clear shot, he dived for cover behind a car. Raith stepped out into the alley. The man ran in the opposite direction, no longer the predator.

Raith ran after him.

Autumn's scream stopped him. He turned and dread sickened him as he saw Garvin standing at the door where he'd left her. Raith aimed.

Garvin started running. Raith looked back at where the other man disappeared around the corner at the end of the alley, then went after Garvin. Out into the street, Raith dodged people on the sidewalk and jumped over a dog someone walked at an intersection.

The driver of a Jeep Wrangler slammed on his brakes as Garvin ran across the street. Raith ran behind the Jeep and closed the distance between them. He was taller and faster. Down the street, Garvin veered into a park and that's where Raith tackled him.

They rolled and Raith bent Garvin's arm up behind his back. Garvin cried out in pain.

"Why are you here?" Raith demanded. "Let me go."

"Tell me now. Why are you here?" He had to have been following the man who'd fired at them. "Who was that back there?"

"I don't have to tell you anything!"

Raith hefted him up and flipped him over onto his back, putting his pistol against his forehead.

"No?"

"You killed my best friend," Garvin hissed.

"Your best friend was a murderer. He killed an innocent woman I rescued. That's how I know your *friend*."

"Go ahead and shoot me. I'm not helping you."

"Did Nash Ralston hire him to kill Kai Whittaker?" Raith asked.

Garvin smiled and then chuckled. That's all Raith got out of him. He didn't put the bomb on his and Autumn's rental car. He didn't hire an assassin. But he knew who did.

"You there!" a man shouted.

Raith looked up to see a policeman standing at the edge of the park, gun raised.

"Drop your weapon!"

Raith rolled into a summersault and got to his feet behind the trunk of a tree. Using playground equipment as cover, he ran across the park and made it to the street. A quick glance confirmed the officer had initiated a foot chase.

Raith avoided a car turning on the street and cut across another. Sprinting down the sidewalk, weaving his way around people, he heard a horn and Autumn shouting, "Raith!"

She had gotten the rental and now drove along the street. Raith could have kissed her. He ran around to the passenger side, jumped into the car and she raced away. Twisting, he saw the policeman had stopped, watching them get away. Raith never rented cars in his real name. Even if the policeman tracked the car, he wouldn't be able to track him. In the distance, he could see the park and Garvin turning to jog away.

After returning the car and walking a few blocks away before finding a cab, Autumn marveled at how talented

Raith was at anonymity. The cab dropped them off at their hotel and Raith arranged for a new rental using a different ID. Once they had that, they checked in on his dad and then headed back to the hotel. By then it was late.

Raith went to the window and stuffed his hands into his jean pockets, thinking.

Picking up the remote, Autumn turned on the TV and plopped down on the sofa to wait for him to come to whatever conclusion he was working toward. The channel was set to the last one Leonardo had chosen. And since he was obsessed with movie stars, it was tuned in to a loud and obnoxious entertainment program. He'd told her he read about stars, did crossword puzzles with movie-star themes, watched movies at home and in theaters. She didn't hold it against him, however. Not once did he treat her like a celebrity. Sure, he'd been curious, but in a get-to-know-her sort of way.

Autumn was about to change the channel, when a picture of her and Raith kissing in front of the hotel appeared. They'd expertly dodged the media every time they returned to the hotel. Or Raith had for them both. He was very good at picking out the photographers and finding a way to avoid them.

"Looks like our second oldest of the Ivy offspring has found herself a mystery man who just might have what it takes to keep her around," the loud host of the show said with a wily smile. His teeth were too straight and too white and he wore a lavender button-up shirt with a dark vest and pants, his blond hair impeccably combed.

Raith turned from the window.

"No baby bump yet, but we have it from a reliable source that Autumn Ivy is pregnant, and this is the father. Who is he? It's a mystery many would *love* to solve."

The co-host was a beautiful brunette with long, thick

and shiny hair, magnetizing blue eyes and a figure-hugging blue dress. She fanned her face with her hand. "He's a real hottie. Whoa, what a man. She always attracts the good-looking ones, but this one tops the charts. I guess we'll have to wait and see if she'll hang on to him."

"What's with her, anyway? Why does she go through so many men?" the woman's co-host asked.

The woman in the blue dress shook her head in befuddlement. "She's not a committer. We'll see if a baby changes that."

Autumn clicked the off button on the remote, disgusted and sick to her stomach. Dropping the remote onto the ottoman, she put her elbow on the armrest of the soft black leather sofa and rubbed the side of her forehead. The media would never leave her alone until they exposed Raith.

The photo of them fueled the imagination. He did look hot. Sexy. Big and tall and a sculpture of fit and trim muscle. The way his eyes were closed. His thick hair messy. Stubbly jaw. All of it. He radiated sexual attraction. For her.

And she, putty in his arms, slender and beautiful and yearning for the man who held her. A princess straight out of a fairy tale. The media had done it again, portrayed her as someone she wasn't. Lofty. Magical. Iconic.

Turning to look at Raith, she saw his eyes shift to her, hard and accusatory. He'd removed his hands from his pockets and now they hung at his sides, his body tense.

Getting up from the sofa, she went to the menu. They'd eaten dinner early and she was hungry again.

"Anything for you?" She hoped the diversion would take his mind off what they'd seen on TV.

"No."

She called for cookies and milk and a side of regular potato chips. Sweet and salty sounded good right now.

Raith came over to sit at the dining table with her. "Cookies and potato chips?"

She was surprised by his playfulness. And then maybe he'd rather not dwell on it. There was nothing either of them could do about what the media said or the fact that there was a steamy picture of them out there.

"There's nothing better than chocolate and chips together. I normally have them with a glass of wine."

He smiled without showing any teeth, the softness not reaching his eyes. Clearly, he was still burdened by whatever thoughts plagued him ever since talking to his dad.

"Are you sure it isn't cravings?"

"It could be." This was the first time he'd ever broached any type of talk about their baby. "I'm hungrier than usual."

"No morning sickness?"

"No." Maybe she'd be one of the lucky moms.

"Are you tired?"

"No. I actually feel really good."

"Pregnancy agrees with you."

Now she smiled, beaming. She felt an in explicable bond with the unborn baby, one she'd blocked from blooming into something she couldn't ignore. But Raith's acknowledgment of the new life opened that door.

"It'll most likely have green eyes," he said.

They both had green eyes. Hers were dark and his were light and radiant. She watched him look at her, how the weight left him and warmth took over.

"He or she."

"He." His soft smile grew.

Folding her arms on the table, she leaned toward him. "You want a boy?"

His grin faded and he only met her look.

That was too close to accepting fatherhood.

"I don't have a preference," she said.

"I suppose I don't, either. A boy would be easier for me to handle."

She hadn't expected him to respond. "You handle girls just fine." Keeping things light might help him.

That grin returned. "You liked the way I handled you?"

"Yes." And she'd like him to handle her again.

A knock at the door interrupted. Raith stood and went to open it. Tipping the server, Raith brought the tray to Autumn.

She ate a cookie and watched Raith drift off into more deep thought.

"What are you thinking about?"

He turned to her. "Nothing."

She couldn't stop herself from digging anymore. "You and your dad had a long conversation."

He didn't respond, only looked unresolved on the matter. Autumn could guess what Leonardo had said to him. She'd gotten to know him pretty well in the short time he'd been here.

"What would you have done with your life if your dad hadn't drunk and your mother hadn't died?"

"Autumn…"

"Would you have still chosen politics?" she asked.

He leaned back in his chair and thought a moment. "Yeah. I think I would have."

"You could have still been a tough guy, you just would have been a tough senator or something. A Charlie Wilson. He made a difference and some could argue that he never followed the rules." He didn't have to work outside of politics to be a rebel.

"Maybe. Why is that important to you?"

She ate a bite of cookie and then a potato chip followed by a sip of milk. "Charlie Wilson had a legitimate, law-abiding job."

After a moment, Raith responded. "My dad says I should give up what I do, that I do it because of the way I was raised."

"Do you agree with him?"

"He also pushed me to be with you and raise a family."

"Oh." That was bold of Leonardo. "How do you feel about that?" And that was bold of her to ask....

She ate another bite of cookie and chip.

"It's a lot to take in."

She seconded that. He still seemed reluctant to embrace that he'd be a father soon.

"But I think my dad was right about one thing," he said.

She looked up from dipping the last of her cookie into the milk.

"I did like superheroes when I was a kid."

What did he mean? Something that put mischief in him, playful mischief. Her heart did a ticklish flop just before he sat forward and reached over to wipe milk off the corner of her mouth. Then he took the cookie she still held and bit off the part she'd dunked in the milk. Chewing and swallowing, he put down the cookie and then kissed her, sharing a sweet taste.

What began as fun and games ignited that mystical passion they had. He opened his eyes and she melted inside just looking into them, watching desire flare and trigger a deeper kiss. Putting her hands on each side of his face, she kissed him and moved off the chair and over to his.

He pushed his chair back and she sat on his lap, uncertainty over how far this would go lingering. He didn't seem as uncertain. He brushed her hair back and trailed warm kisses along her jaw and neck, pushing the soft black material of her shirt out of the way to continue on to her shoulder.

When he lifted the shirt over her head, she didn't protest. As he kissed his way down to her breasts, plumped within her front-clip bra, his hands glided along her bare back to her waist. Her uncertainty began to drown in the pleasure he elicited. None remained when his fingers released her bra and his eyes met hers as he pushed the straps off her shoulders and the bra dropped to the floor.

He toyed with her breasts awhile, kissing her nipples and wetting them with his tongue, puckering them into hard, sensitive raspberries. His breath cooled what his tongue warmed. Autumn stood up and began to remove her pants, watching Raith lift off his shirt, kick off his shoes and slide his pants down his hips and legs. Having left her panties on, she let Raith do the honors of removing them.

His fingers left a trail of fire on her skin as he pulled them slowly down her body, until they dropped around her feet. Stepping out of them, she moved closer.

Raith put his hands on her hips and parted her with his tongue. She raked her fingers through his hair while he found her hard nub that yearned for his attention and worked his magic there. Autumn tipped her head back, eyes closed to sheer ecstasy. She gripped her fingers in his hair as sensation drove her wild. He stopped just before she burst.

Lowering her head, she straddled the chair, loving how he took in her body from her legs to her breasts and finally her face. She bent to kiss him. His hand held the back of her neck and head and the other went to her rear.

She lowered herself down on top of him. He guided her until he entered her. It was the same as the first time. Three, two, one, liftoff.

Holding on with her hands anchored to his neck, she began to move on him. He grunted and helped her with his hands on her hips. The ride lasted several reverent moments before Autumn lost control and gave in to a powerful release. Only as she came down from the high did she realize he'd climaxed with her.

She kissed him softly, basking in the afterglow. He returned the caress. Then she looked into his eyes, still warm but fading in intensity. She needed to ask him what he was thinking. What did this all mean? Were they satisfying lust or was there more to it? It meant something to her.

Holding her, Raith stood and carried her into the bedroom. He lay her down. Getting in with her, he opened his arm for her and she snuggled next to him.

He didn't say anything. Autumn wondered where this would leave her in the morning. She had just fallen deeper toward love with him and didn't think he felt the same. He was too withdrawn right now. He held her, but she sensed it was because he felt he had to.

He was undecided. Still. After what had just happened. How could he not embrace what they had together?

A familiar trapped feeling came over her, only different than anything she'd ever experienced. She had invested her heart in him and he wouldn't invest his.

Men before him had zealously tried to possess her for her wealth and name. Others had genuine feelings for her. Either instinct had led her to run the other way. Instinct led her to do the same now, but she'd do it to protect her heart, not her independence. No. Her individuality.

A need for individuality had driven her before. Pregnant and falling in love, she didn't need individuality. She needed unity. Family. Raith might not be able to give her that, and she had to protect herself. The baby. She wouldn't raise a child if she had to lie about what his or her father did for a living. And if she left now, she could spare herself a worse heartbreak.

She waited for him to fall asleep then eased away from him. When she was sure he was sound asleep, she got off the bed and quietly packed.

Chapter 18

Autumn called the Ivy travel coordinator. The woman was in California, so at least it wasn't too terribly late there, only two hours behind Houston time. She looked around for anything or anyone suspicious before waving for a cab. One pulled out from a parking space and stopped in front of her. She climbed in after the driver put her luggage in the back.

Just as she closed the door and the driver got behind the wheel, she heard a shout. A man ran toward them yelling, "Stop!"

The cab driver pulled away from the hotel, driving fast and swerving onto the street.

"Hey!" Autumn exclaimed.

The driver didn't acknowledge her. At that moment she noticed the hat and mustache and bulky sweatshirt. It was the same man who'd chased her after meeting Kai.

"Stop this car." Autumn dug into her purse for her cell phone.

The driver turned a corner so sharply that Autumn had to hang on to the back of the front passenger seat. Racing down the road, the driver lifted a gun and aimed it into the backseat, glancing from the road to her repeatedly.

"Give me the phone."

That voice…

Autumn looked closer at the man. His eyes were feminine and familiar. Not a man. This was a woman dressed up as a man, and Autumn had met her before.

India Whittaker.

While she recovered from her shock, India pulled into the parking lot of an office building.

"Phone. Give it to me."

Autumn looked at the steady barrel of the gun and decided to comply. She handed over the phone.

"Now get out."

Her chances of escape were better outside this car. Autumn got out and searched for possible routes. The parking lot was vacant except for three cars, one of them parked next to the cab.

"Get in that car," India ordered.

"Why did you try to kill Kai?" Autumn asked. "Did you kill him yourself?"

"Stop talking and get in or I'll kill you right now."

Right now? So, she planned to kill her at some point. Believing she'd pull the trigger, seeing it in the crazed gleam of her eyes, Autumn got into the car.

Autumn started the car while India kept the gun aimed at her as she walked around the rear of the car. Autumn contemplated driving off. But India opened the passenger door and it was too late.

"Drive."

Autumn didn't move. She listened for sirens. That man who'd run after them must have been the real driver of the taxi. He'd call the police and they'd start searching. The more time that passed—

"I said drive!" India shouted in a high-pitched tone. "I've had all I can take of you two. You've caused me too much trouble."

"Why are you doing this?"

India hit her alongside the head with the gun. "Drive, damn it! I won't ask again."

Smothering a cry of pain, Autumn put her hand on her head and checked for blood. Finding nothing but a sore spot with a lump forming, she put the car into gear and drove as slowly as she could out of the parking lot.

India kept the gun low and pointed at her. Autumn drove out onto the main street. India wouldn't shoot her in such a public setting, would she?

A police car went racing by in the opposite direction, toward the hotel, followed by two more. Of course, they weren't looking for this car. Only a cab may have stood out, or not. Maybe they'd go to the scene and question people first. No one would know where she was taken, or by whom.

Raith thought it was Nash Ralston who'd hired Leaman. And although India's costume didn't resemble Ralston, he wouldn't know it was Kai's wife behind everything. The only uncertainty Autumn had now was how Garvin was involved.

"Turn here. Go left," India said.

The road led into the neighborhood where India lived. She was actually taking her to her own home?

"Why are you doing this?" Autumn tried again. "Is it because of your husband's affair?" She'd acted as though she was shocked to learn of his betrayal, but maybe she was just a good actress. In the rearview mirror, Autumn saw her face turn into a scowl.

"That imbecile thought I was too stupid to figure out what he was doing," she hissed. "I followed him many times."

"So you hired a hit man?"

"He was going to keep it from me forever. He never planned to tell me."

The betrayal had built up in India. And Kai deciding not to confess his sin had hurt her more.

"And so you went to Garvin Reeves and asked him to help you. Isn't that how you found Leaman Marshall?"

"How do you know Garvin?"

"We questioned him trying to find out who hired Leaman. Leaman's sister told us about him."

"I've known Garvin since we were kids. He and Leaman were close friends of mine. We grew up in the same neighborhood in run-down houses with low-life parents."

That explained why Leaman had agreed to do a drive-by shooting. He may have even done it free or for a discounted fee.

"Was it Garvin who put the bomb in our car?" Autumn asked.

"Stop asking questions."

Autumn drove into the long driveway and up to India's house.

"Get out."

Autumn didn't see any other way out of doing what India asked. Not yet.

She got out of the car and India jabbed the gun into her back as they began walking toward the door.

"How did you know I'd come out of the hotel so late?" Autumn asked.

"I didn't. I was about to leave when you showed up."

"Must be your lucky day."

India opened the front door and shoved her. Autumn stumbled inside and faced her.

"Go through that door." India gestured to a door in the hallway that must lead to the garage.

"You should think about what you're doing. Murder is a serious crime. You'll spend the rest of your life in prison."

"I have thought of this. Go through that door."

Autumn opened the door. Wide stairs lowered into a finished basement.

"Down." India jabbed her again.

Autumn stepped down the stairs. At the bottom, she saw a man tied to a chair.

It was Ralston…

Raith woke to his ringing cell phone. Groggily he sat up, looked beside him and immediately felt a chill. Where was Autumn? Reaching for his phone, he recognized her number.

"Autumn? Where are you?" Why had she left?

And once again, he'd slept through her getting out of bed. He'd fallen into such a relaxed sleep.

"Mr. De Matteis," a female voice said. It wasn't Autumn.

"Who is this?" And what had she done with Autumn? She hadn't taken her from their room. Autumn must have left on her own. The woman's voice sounded familiar.

"I have something you want," the woman said.

India.

"Mrs. Whittaker?" he asked, incredulous.

"Raith?" Autumn's voice came onto the line.

"Autumn…"

"Come to my house outside the city." India came back

on the phone. "Come alone, and be here within thirty minutes or she dies."

The call ended.

Cursing, Raith jumped off the bed and dressed in black jeans and a black T-shirt. He ran out the door and onto the elevator, the ride down excruciatingly slow.

Out in front of the hotel, he spotted police cars and an officer questioning a cabdriver.

There was a throng of onlookers. He stopped next to one.

"What happened?"

"Someone stole a cab and took off with a woman in the back."

India had disguised herself in a cab this time. She'd also disguised herself as a man. She'd set everything up. It hadn't been Ralston who'd hired Leaman. It had been India. But she and Ralston were lovers. Were they working together?

Kai was worth a lot of money. How much would she have gotten if Kai had died?

Morbidly he realized Kai was probably already dead. Where was Ralston? Had she killed him, too?

When he thought of all the clues that pointed to Ralston, he answered his own questions. India had set Ralston up. She'd known about the blackmail. She must have also known about the affair long before she'd overheard Rylie at the coffee shop. That had been a show to cover her guilt. But if she'd set the bomb in his and Autumn's rental car, why had Garvin been there?

As a valet driver brought his car, he called Mayo. Mayo answered as Raith got into the vehicle.

"I need you to look something up for me and I need you to do it now."

"Is it that urgent? It's the middle of the night."

"It's more than urgent. It's life or death. I don't have much time."

With a sigh, Mayo said, "Hang on."

Raith heard him getting out of bed. A few seconds later, he must have reached his office. "All right, what have you got?"

"I need to look up everything you can find about India Whittaker."

"India Whittaker…"

Raith heard him typing on his computer. One of the reasons Raith had chosen this man was that he wasn't shy about tapping into government networks.

"Married to Kai Whittaker, who seems to have disappeared."

"Yeah, yeah, go deeper."

More typing…

"Here's something. Grew up in a bad part of Dallas. Her FaceShare page shows her with Leaman Marshall and another guy."

"Garvin Reeves?"

Mayo did some more searching. "Yeah, looks like he shared the photo."

Mayo did more typing. "No police record."

"Have you seen the news this morning?" Mayo asked.

"No."

"Kai Whittaker's body was found in a remote area under an overpass about halfway to Galveston."

The news didn't surprise Raith, but it was never easy hearing about the murder of an acquaintance.

"He was shot six times in the chest," Mayo said.

"Crime of passion."

"Poor son of a bitch."

A sense of foreboding kept him from joining in on that comment. All he could see was Autumn lying dead under an overpass and it made him sick. And then it made him furious.

Raith drove up to the Whittaker's second home outside Houston but didn't park in the open. He turned off the headlights and parked on the side of the road, out of sight of any security cameras. Getting out of the car, he opened the back door and retrieved a combat vest from his duffel bag. He'd stocked it full of ammunition as soon as they'd arrived in Houston. Luckily, he hadn't had it in the car that exploded. But he'd moved it to this one after that so he could be prepared for exactly this type of situation.

Checking his gun, he slid the clip back in and inserted it into his holster. Next, he dug out the thigh straps he'd also packed and fastened them to his legs. They held knives and more ammo. He had another knife strapped to his ankle, hidden by his pant leg. Then he retrieved a powerful infrared laser pointer. Last came the small night-vision goggles attached to a durable headband. Marveling at the irony of using a night-vision device, he positioned the single optics component over his left eye.

Closing the car door, he took out his pistol and kept the weapon ready in his hand as he jogged into the trees in the direction of the house. He stopped where the trees cleared and searched for any surprises, closing his right eye to see in the darkness. He spotted two cameras, one on each opposing corner of the roofline.

Lifting the laser pointer, he turned it on and held it steady as he aimed at the camera. When he was sure the sensor was burned out, he advanced and made his way to the side of the house. Disabling another camera, he crept up onto a large stone deck with a built-in grill. Crouching low and using the stone construction of the grill to block him from sight, he came around that and then took two steps to the wall beside the double glass doors. The glass was broken and the door partially ajar. Someone else had broken into the house.

Peering inside with only his night-vision device, he caught movement. There were no lights on, but he could see someone moving toward him. Pulling back, he ran and ducked behind the built-in grill, listening as the person's feet crunched over broken glass, discovering as he had that the door had been breached.

Sneaking a peek around the stone, Raith saw that the person, probably India, had retreated. He went back to the door, staying out of sight. She hadn't touched the door. India may be a killer but she was no professional. Silently, he avoided the broken glass as he entered a large kitchen with two islands and moved to the other side of the room. His soft-soled shoes were soundless as he moved to the interior kitchen entrance and spotted the form of a woman standing with her back to him on the other side of the living room. She was searching out the front window. For him? Who did she think had broken into the house? Who had broken into the house?

He'd take care of her later. Right now he had to find Autumn. If there was someone else in the house, he had to reach her fast.

There were two wide stairways, one leading up and the other leading down. He heard something fall over downstairs. India may have heard it, as well. He hurried down the stairs before she reached them. At the bottom, the landing turned in the opposite direction. There was light on down here, so he switched off his optics and moved the device out of the way of his eye. As soon as he followed the landing and faced the open space of the basement, he saw Garvin untying Autumn. India had put her on a dining chair on the other side of a seating area. A man was in a chair beside her. Both of their backs were turned.

Assured Autumn was all right and that Garvin, at least for now, was on their side, he waited for India. She came down the stairs slowly. Raith hung back in the shadows of a bedroom door.

As soon as she appeared on the landing and headed for the others, she raised a small handgun.

Raith stepped behind her and put his pistol to her head. "Drop it."

India froze.

"Drop it now or I'll shoot." She had to know he would.

She dropped the gun.

"Now walk forward nice and easy." Ahead, he saw Garvin move back from Autumn, and the other man turn his head. Raith saw that it was Ralston.

Autumn finished untying herself and then hurried to untie Ralston, who ushered her to the side of the room, away from Garvin and Raith and India.

Raith watched Garvin closely. The man was too unpredictable.

Garvin lifted the chair Autumn had vacated and faced it toward Raith and India. Raith would have done it, anyway, so he pushed India to the chair.

"Have a seat," Garvin said.

She looked back at Raith, whose aim hadn't altered, and then at Garvin, who opened his palm and gestured in invitation over the chair.

In defeat, she sat, glaring up at Raith while Garvin tied her wrists behind her and her ankles to the legs of the chair. When she was secured, Raith put his gun away.

Garvin moved so that he stood in front of India, but far enough away from Raith to indicate his distrust. Autumn stood beside Ralston, he with his arm around her.

It was an uncharacteristically protective gesture on his part and Raith wondered if this ordeal would humble him.

"I thought you were on my side," India said to Garvin. "I thought we were friends."

"We were up until the point that you asked Leaman to kill your husband."

"I don't see why you'd have an issue with that. It's what he did for a living."

"He would have done anything for you. You took advantage of him. You made him love you and then you married another man."

While Raith picked up on that telling detail, India's face showed no empathy; she was so beautiful and yet so evil. "Leaman and I were good together and we remained friends even after I married Kai."

"You married Kai for his money." All of Garvin's pent-up resentment poured out of him.

"I didn't see a way to live a normal life with Leaman. I did love him, Garvin, I just couldn't marry him."

"He must have jumped at the opportunity to kill the man who stole you from him. Did you pay him?"

Garvin hadn't known India had hired Leaman until after he was killed.

"I insisted. He wasn't going to take any money."

"Did he know you were setting me up?" Ralston moved away from Autumn a few steps.

India smiled wickedly. "That's why he drove by the house instead of sniping him."

"You slept with me to make it look like I wanted to get rid of him so I could have you?"

"You had motive, Nash. Didn't you think Kai talked about your exports to Singapore?" She gave a quick laugh. "Don't look so injured. A man like you doesn't give much respect to women. You were perfect for what

I needed. Easily manipulated because you made the mistake of thinking I was stupid."

Ralston didn't respect certain women. Not women like her. Smart or not, she was still a trophy. And what she needed was revenge. All of this was because Kai had cheated on her. Probably there was more that drove her, like her upbringing. Raith saw Autumn watching India in an assessing way and wondered if she thought the same.

Ralston knelt and picked up the gun Raith had made India drop. "And this?" As he straightened, he gestured with the gun and his free hand to the rest of them in the room. "Was I supposed to be the one who killed Autumn and Raith?"

India didn't say anything, only wore a smug grin.

"Put the gun down, Nash," Raith said.

"She was setting me up. And she would have succeeded if Garvin hadn't intervened." He turned to that man. "Why didn't you tell me?"

"You were sleeping with her," Garvin said.

"I wouldn't have if I'd have known she was setting me up. I should kill you now." He aimed the gun at India, who stared at the barrel, some of her smugness fading.

"If you do that, you'll be charged with murder," Raith said. "Don't take the law into your own hands."

Raith caught the way Autumn looked at him after that last comment. Raith always took the law into his own hands. Was that why she'd left him at the hotel?

"I called the police before I came down here," Garvin said to him, and then to India he continued, "I told them everything, including that I thought you are the one who killed Kai."

Ralston hadn't lowered the gun.

"They would have figured that out on their own,"

Raith said. "She shot him six times." He looked at her sobering face.

"Why did you do it, India?" Garvin asked, a longtime friend struggling to come to terms with how corrupt she'd become. "Because of you, Leaman is dead."

All of her bravado gone, India's eyes began to tear up. "No one ever loved me. All I ever wanted was for someone to hold me dearer than all else in their life. I thought I had that with Kai."

Raith used India's emotional exchange with Garvin to move closer to Ralston.

"You had it with Leaman."

She shook her head. "No. He was incapable of loving anyone."

Leaman was an assassin. It would be difficult to kill for a living with a soft heart.

Raith stopped beside Ralston, who looked from him to India.

"We all had a rough childhood," Garvin said, regret and disappointment in his tone, "but I never thought you'd go to this extreme. Now, instead of losing one of my closest friends, I've lost both of them."

Reaching over, Raith gripped Ralston's wrist with one hand and took the gun with the other. Ralston met his eyes and didn't fight him.

Looking back at Garvin, he said, "I'm overdressed for police."

Garvin took in his vest and the straps around his thighs before meeting his eyes again. "I won't lie for you."

What did Garvin know about him? Not much. Not enough. And he couldn't reveal too much about Leaman's involvement without attracting attention to his illegal gun sales.

"I wouldn't ask you to." Raith went to Autumn and

reached for her hand. "You have to come with me or this doesn't work."

"Do you mean taking the law into your own hands?"

She was mad about last night. Mad because she'd let it happen? Or mad because she felt too much?

"We can talk about that on the way to the car."

Chapter 19

This was the kind of life she'd have with Raith. Sneaking through the woods with an armed man while police cars with flashing lights rushed up to Kai and India's second home. Big and all in black, decked out in all his gear, he strode ahead of her, unknowingly taunting her with his fit rear, keeping a vigilant eye on their surroundings to make sure they weren't followed and irritating her more because he felt the need to.

"Why did you leave?" Raith asked, looking back at her.

"I thought I was doing you a favor." Leaving just the way he'd left the last time they'd had sex.

He faced forward. "That was different than the first time."

"I don't see how."

"I wasn't going to leave you in the morning."

"Probably not, but now that India is being arrested,

there's nothing to stop you." If they'd have had sex tonight instead of last night, he'd have disappeared again.

He didn't respond right away, which only confirmed her assumption.

"We do have a lot to work out," he finally said.

"We can do that over the phone." Autumn felt a lump grow in her throat.

He stopped abruptly and turned.

She nearly ran into him.

"I'm not going to leave you."

He wasn't? She fought the flare of hope and it died all on its own with his next announcement.

"We have to figure out what we're going to do. How we're going to handle…"

The baby. How they were going to *handle* their baby. He still wasn't sure. Oh, that hurt so much more than it would have if she'd have just kept her pants on last night.

"Are you saying you intend to be part of this baby's life?" she asked, forcing detachment. She'd used *this* instead of *our*.

He hesitated. "Yes."

Because he felt obligated? She so hadn't pictured her life taking this direction. She looked away from his beautiful green eyes. It hurt looking at him.

"We haven't known each other long, Autumn. If you're expecting me to ask you to marry me, I can't. Not yet. But I can promise to be there for you and the child."

She became embarrassed over the realization that she had, on some level, expected that. Maybe she even felt enough for him to wish for that.

"Is that what you meant by liking superheroes when you were a kid?" she asked.

And he actually grinned. She was crumbling on the inside and he thought that was funny.

"Yes."

He thought he was being a superhero by standing by her with no other promises other than to be there for her and the baby? He could end up marrying someone else and still be there for them.

That went against her will in such a strong, potent way that she had to start walking again. They had to get out of here, anyway. Why was it so important that Raith give her more than that? She wanted his heart, that's why. And he wasn't giving it.

They had met recently. They didn't know each other enough to get married. That made sense to her brain, but her heart had other ideas. She was falling in love with him and he hadn't even mentioned his feelings to her once. Not once. What did the baby mean to him? What did she mean to him? She contemplated asking him but refused to appear needy and desperate. She felt desperate. Never had she felt this way. A baby would change her life so much, she was lost.

She had to get away from here. But more importantly, she had to get away from him.

Raith took her to the cab, which miraculously was still there and unlocked, and retrieved her luggage. The sun was beginning to come up. After removing all of his gear in the vacant parking lot, he drove back to the hotel and handed the keys to a valet driver.

She hadn't spoken all the way back here.

"What's wrong?" he asked for the fourth time.

And for the fourth time he received the same stiff answer. "Nothing."

Had her hormones already started to go wild? He was aware that wasn't the cause of her mood. What had she expected him to say back there in the trees? That he loved her? *Let's get married?*

While a deeper part of him urged for exactly that, he hesitated. He could love her. Maybe he already did on some level. But how much would it cost him? What he hadn't said to her was what he'd been thinking when he'd made that superhero remark. He'd been thinking he could grow into marriage with her. He hadn't quite jumped off the fence. He was still so mixed up over what to do with his life. Would he change his profession? And if so, for whom? For himself or for Autumn?

She lifted her arm as a taxi approached. The car slowed to a stop in front of her.

"Where are you going?"

"Milan," she said.

Before he had a chance to react, a reporter started taking pictures of them. Raith found himself looking right at the camera as Autumn got into the back to the cab.

She looked at the photographer and then him, unconcerned regarding what this could do to him. Conflict churned in him. A powerful instinct to get into the cab with her clashed with anger over being caught—again—on camera.

His feet stayed where they were as the taxi drove away. Autumn stopped looking at him, but he watched the taxi vanish down the street. After a moment, he turned to the photographer and the man bombarding him with questions. Had Autumn just broken up with him? He felt like responding with "Had she?"

Raith went to the hospital that afternoon and berated himself for looking for Autumn. As if she'd change her mind and rush back into his arms.

What was the matter with him? Entering his dad's room, he noticed how much better the older man looked.

"Tough night?" his dad asked, lifting his attention from a magazine. It was an entertainment magazine.

"Why do you read that stuff?" he asked as he sat down on the chair.

"It's better than regular news. Where's Autumn?"

"She left."

"For Dallas?"

"Actually, she said she was going to Milan." A sure sign that she was getting rid of him. They'd have to see each other because of the baby. How would she manage that? Drop the child off with him every time she decided to fly off somewhere?

As he imagined having such a dysfunctional relationship with her, something gouged him through the heart. He couldn't shake the feeling that he'd made a mistake letting Autumn go.

"She left you?"

Raith just looked at his dad.

"Why? What did you say to her?"

"Nothing."

"Did you ask her to marry you?"

"No," he retorted, indignant.

"Why not? I mean, you don't have a gentleman's job, but I thought you were a gentleman at heart."

"This isn't the fifties, Dad. People don't marry because of pregnancy. They marry for love."

"You don't love her?"

Again, Raith just looked at his dad.

"At all? Not even a flicker of emotion toward her?"

Still, he couldn't find any words to say.

"What did you tell her, that you'd give her child support?" His dad sure did have a lot of energy today. He was clearly appalled by his son's behavior.

"No…not like that." But in retrospect, he may as well have said it like that. Something began to shift in him. He felt bad for the way he'd spoken to Autumn. There was more he should have said.

"Why are you running away from her?"

He gave his dad the standard answer. "She has reporters following her around all the time."

"Is it really the media that you're so afraid of?" His dad asked derisively.

"Well…yeah."

"You don't think you'd find a way to keep them away? And would they camp out in your driveway the rest of your life? Isn't it just Autumn's skittishness with men that captures their interest?" When Raith remained silent, his dad went on. "She is incapable of commitment and yet she would have committed to you."

Raith felt his entire body recoil. His hands tightened on the arm of the chair. His legs went rigid. He stopped breathing for a second. She would commit to him. He'd felt it last night. And instinctively he'd avoided acknowledging it.

"Son," his dad said, much more gently. "It isn't the media. It's the way your mother died. You have abandonment issues. Don't let a good woman get away because of that. Build a life with her that's better than the one I gave your mother. It wouldn't be only the baby that would bring the two of you together. I've seen you with her. You both are falling in love. You already have a good foundation, a good head start. It doesn't matter how fast it happened. The important thing is that it has."

Everything his dad said was true. He hadn't seen it until now, but he did have abandonment issues. That's why his job appealed to him so much. He could be alone. He could be left alone. He didn't have to risk not being alone.

All of the sudden he no longer wanted that. He wanted to be with someone. Autumn. Their baby. He wanted them to be his family.

His dad chuckled, sounding healthier than Raith had ever seen him. "I can see you've finally come around." He sighed with a long ah as he rested his head back on the pillow, content and happy and...

"What kind of drugs do they have you on today?" Raith asked.

His dad's grin widened and he turned his head to see Raith. "The new one. I had a test this morning and they said the cancer cells are beginning to die. My immune system is fighting back."

"It's working?"

"The doctors are being cautious, but yes, I think so."

"You're going into remission?"

"I might be or at the very least, I've got more time."

If it worked...if his dad survived...

"Dad..." Raith couldn't remember if he'd ever been so choked up in his life. When his mother died, of course, but any other time? No. And now he swallowed back a traitorous tear. "That's the best news I've had since..."

"Since the doctor told you Autumn was pregnant?" his dad asked.

"Not right then, but soon after." Raith stood and went over to the bed where his dad laughed softly. "I have to go after her." He kissed his father's forehead.

"You do that."

"I'll be back to get you."

"Not if I walk out of here on my own a healing man."

"Deal." Raith smiled all the way out of the hospital.

Chapter 20

Autumn reclined on an outdoor lounge chair, staring up at the blue sky, listening to birds and her dad's movement in the pool. He was swimming laps. Mom had gone to answer a phone call.

Savanna lay on the chair beside her. Her boyfriend had just broken up with her. They were an entertaining pair.

"I can't believe he was seeing her the whole time we were together."

The fancy attorney's ex-wife wouldn't be his ex-wife for much longer. They were getting remarried.

"Let's keep the TV off for a few days," Autumn said.

"Okay."

Autumn looked over at her sister. Savanna had opened her heart to a man for the first time since the first one she'd loved broke her heart and now she was heartbroken yet again.

"Do you want to go to Milan?" Autumn asked.

"No. I want to stay here."

Autumn looked up at the sky again. "I don't, either."

"Go to Milan? That's new for you. Why not?"

"This is my first heartbreak, Savanna. I'm too depressed to go shopping."

"Shopping normally cheers you up."

"Not this time."

"You're going to see him again, aren't you? The pictures of you made it seem like he wouldn't have it any other way."

"Unfortunately." She patted her tummy.

"He'd really abandon his own child?"

"Not entirely. He'll *support* us. Which means that for the rest of my life I'll be tortured with seeing him on a scheduled basis."

After a long contemplative silence, Savanna said, "Men are weird."

"Well, it looks like your schedule starts today."

Autumn turned her head to see her mother standing beside her chair.

"What?"

"Raith is here. He brought his armored vehicle and a platoon of men, but he's here."

"How did he know I was here?"

"I told him."

"Mother!" Autumn sat up on the lounge chair.

"He called yesterday. I said I'd keep it a secret. He didn't want you jumping on a plane for Milan."

"No fair. You get your man and I don't get mine."

Savanna kept levity in her tone, but Autumn wasn't fooled. She was hurting. Bad.

But Autumn would have to tend to her later. Raith was here. He'd come for her!

No attempt to tame her rapidly beating heart worked.

She slipped into her sheer swimsuit cover-up and walked through the mansion to the front entry. Outside, three big black SUVs were parked and running in the circular driveway.

She opened the heavy door and stepped outside. A maid deposited her suitcase beside her on the stone porch. Autumn looked back at her as she timidly retreated into the house.

"Just following orders, ma'am," she said.

Her mother had told her to do that. The door shut before she could say anything. Not that she would.

She faced the SUVs as Raith climbed out. He wore a suit and tie and his dark hair was smoother than it had been lately.

Walking toward her, he stole what little breath she had left in her. He was so handsome.

He stepped up the stone stairs and removed his sunglasses as he came to a stop before her, his eyes mesmerizing her as they lowered down and back up, touching her body through the sheer cover.

"Did everything go okay with India and Garvin?" she asked while her heart pounded a hole through her chest.

"As far as I know."

"What happened with Nash?"

"His assistant turned over evidence of the illegal exports to the Department of State. There will be an investigation."

Maybe not entirely what Nash deserved, but something he should and did expect.

They continued to stare at each other.

"What brings you here?" she asked.

"I have two questions for you," he said.

She smiled. "The first?"

"Can you ever forgive me?" he asked.

"If that's the first question, the second one must be a whopper."

"Can you?"

Forgive him. She'd forgiven him the instant her mother had told her he was here. "For what?"

"For being such an idiot."

"*Idiot* might be too strong a word. *Insensitive* might be better."

"Okay, insensitive. Can you forgive me?"

"That depends on what your second question is."

He grinned, sending sparks showering all over her core and not improving her breathing.

From his suit pocket, he took out a ring box and opened it to reveal a giant round diamond with two smaller diamonds on either side of it.

Autumn gasped and covered her mouth.

"Will you marry me?"

When she recovered, she lowered her hand. "Are you serious?"

"Never been more serious in my life. I'm not traveling anymore. I'm going to take a sabbatical for a while and figure out what I want to do next. But I need a wife first, and a baby. I can't do it without them."

"Raith…" Was he sure? "If you're doing this because—"

"I'm not doing this because of the baby. The timing is because of that, but I know you're the one I want, Autumn. I've been falling in love with you ever since I saw you in Iceland."

"Raith…" Her thoughts raced with possibilities, the pros and cons, the utter thrill of him coming here and asking her to marry him.

Taking her hand, he took the ring out of the box and

slipped it onto her finger. "Marry me, Autumn. Will you?"

Autumn looked from the stunning ring up to his face. There was no doubt in her mind. "Yes! I'll marry you!" She flung her arms around his shoulders and he lifted her as he kissed her.

Over his shoulder, she saw the SUVs again. "I see you brought something to protect us from the media."

"Plenty of it."

"They'll never get by that."

"I don't care if they do. I only did it to be funny." He extended his hand while one of the men took her suitcase to the middle SUV. "And to make a point."

"That you should have never played the media card?"

"Nothing's going to keep me away from you."

She gave him her hand. "My dreams couldn't beat this. You've made me the happiest woman alive, Raith."

"Then let me take you home where I can continue to do that."

She walked with him toward the SUV, where the driver opened the back for them.

"No Milan, huh?" Raith asked in a teasing tone.

"Nope. For some reason I didn't feel like running."

He grinned at her as the reason became clear to him. She didn't run because she loved him.

* * * * *

REQUEST YOUR FREE BOOKS!
2 FREE NOVELS PLUS 2 FREE GIFTS!

H HARLEQUIN®

ROMANTIC suspense

Sparked by danger, fueled by passion

YES! Please send me 2 FREE Harlequin® Romantic Suspense novels and my 2 FREE gifts (gifts are worth about $10). After receiving them, if I don't wish to receive any more books, I can return the shipping statement marked "cancel." If I don't cancel, I will receive 4 brand-new novels every month and be billed just $4.74 per book in the U.S. or $5.24 per book in Canada. That's a savings of at least 14% off the cover price! It's quite a bargain! Shipping and handling is just 50¢ per book in the U.S. and 75¢ per book in Canada.* I understand that accepting the 2 free books and gifts places me under no obligation to buy anything. I can always return a shipment and cancel at any time. Even if I never buy another book, the two free books and gifts are mine to keep forever.

240/340 HDN F45N

Name _____ (PLEASE PRINT)

Address _____ Apt. #

City _____ State/Prov. _____ Zip/Postal Code

Signature (if under 18, a parent or guardian must sign)

Mail to the **Harlequin® Reader Service:**

IN U.S.A.: P.O. Box 1867, Buffalo, NY 14240-1867
IN CANADA: P.O. Box 609, Fort Erie, Ontario L2A 5X3

Want to try two free books from another line?
Call 1-800-873-8635 or visit www.ReaderService.com.

* Terms and prices subject to change without notice. Prices do not include applicable taxes. Sales tax applicable in N.Y. Canadian residents will be charged applicable taxes. Offer not valid in Quebec. This offer is limited to one order per household. Not valid for current subscribers to Harlequin Romantic Suspense books. All orders subject to credit approval. Credit or debit balances in a customer's account(s) may be offset by any other outstanding balance owed by or to the customer. Please allow 4 to 6 weeks for delivery. Offer available while quantities last.

Your Privacy—The Harlequin® Reader Service is committed to protecting your privacy. Our Privacy Policy is available online at www.ReaderService.com or upon request from the Harlequin Reader Service.

We make a portion of our mailing list available to reputable third parties that offer products we believe may interest you. If you prefer that we not exchange your name with third parties, or if you wish to clarify or modify your communication preferences, please visit us at www.ReaderService.com/consumerchoice or write to us at Harlequin Reader Service Preference Service, P.O. Box 9062, Buffalo, NY 14269. Include your complete name and address.

HRS13R

SPECIAL EXCERPT FROM

H HARLEQUIN®

ROMANTIC suspense

Discovering he's a father of a newborn, rodeo cowboy
Theo Colton turns to his new cook, Ellie, to help out as
nanny. But when Ellie's past returns to haunt her,
Theo's determined to protect her and the baby…
but who will protect his heart?

Read on for a sneak peek at

A SECRET COLTON BABY

by Karen Whiddon, the first novel in
The Coltons: Return to Wyoming miniseries.

"A man," Ellie gasped, pointing past where he stood, his
broad-shouldered body filling the doorway. "Dressed in
black, wearing a ski mask. He was trying to hurt Amelia."

And then the trembling started. She couldn't help it, despite the tiny infant she clutched close to her chest. Somehow, Theo seemed to sense this, as he gently took her arm
and steered her toward her bed.

"Sit," he ordered, taking the baby from her.

Reluctantly releasing Amelia, Ellie covered her face with
her hands. It had been a strange day, ever since the baby's
mother—a beautiful, elegant woman named Mimi Rand—
had shown up that morning insisting Theo was the father
and then collapsing. Mimi had been taken to the Dead River
clinic with a high fever and flulike symptoms. Theo had Ellie
looking after Amelia until everything could be sorted out.

But Theo had no way of knowing about Ellie's past, or the danger that seemed to follow her like a malicious shadow. "I need to leave," she told him. "Right now, for Amelia's sake."

Theo stared at her, holding Amelia to his shoulder and bouncing her gently, so that her sobs died away to whimpers and then silence. The sight of the big cowboy and the tiny baby struck a kernel of warmth in Ellie's frozen heart.

"Leave?" Theo asked. "You just started work here a week ago. If it's because I asked you to take care of this baby until her mama recovers, I'll double your pay."

"It's not about the money." Though she could certainly use every penny she could earn. "I...I thought I was safe here. Clearly, that's not the case."

He frowned. "I can assure you..." Stopping, he handed her back the baby, holding her as gingerly as fragile china. "How about I check everything out? Is anything missing?"

And then Theo went into her bathroom. He cursed, and she knew. Her stalker had somehow found her.

Don't miss
A SECRET COLTON BABY
by Karen Whiddon,
available October 2014.

Available wherever

✦HARLEQUIN®

ROMANTIC suspense
books and ebooks are sold.

Heart-racing romance, high-stakes suspense!

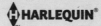

ROMANTIC suspense

THE AGENT'S SURRENDER
by **Kimberly Van Meter**

Rival agents uncover a monstrous conspiracy

From the moment they met, sparks had flown...and not
the good kind. Agent Jane Fallon would rather chew nails
than work with arrogant—and much too good-looking—
Holden Archangelo. But, convinced his brother was no
traitor, Holden had Jane's investigation reopened.
And now Jane is forced to partner with him.

As new leads come to light, Jane's certainty about the
case is shaken. But the assassin's bullet whizzing past
her head convinces her they are onto something. Jane's
determined to keep things professional, but as the danger
around them intensifies, so does the fierce attraction they
try so hard to deny....

Look for *THE AGENT'S SURRENDER*
by Kimberly Van Meter
in October 2014.

ROMANTIC suspense

Heart-racing romance, high-stakes suspense!

SNOWSTORM CONFESSIONS
by *New York Times* bestselling author
Rachel Lee

Available October 2014

*Return to Conard County...where reunited
spouses face a dangerous obsession*

The last man that Nurse Brianna Cole expects to bring home
is the one she remembers all too well—her ex-husband,
Luke Masters. But when he needs to recuperate from serious
injury, her Wyoming cabin becomes his refuge. Though
concussed and hazy, Luke is convinced someone pushed him
off the snowy mountain he was evaluating for a ski resort.
And though he can't remember why, he knows Bri is next.

Snowed in with her ex, Bri is blinded by old feelings, an
attraction that never died. But the closer she gets to Luke,
the closer she gets to murder. Because someone is watching
her...stalking her...and if he can't have her, *no one* can!

Available wherever books and ebooks are sold.

Love the Harlequin book you just read?

Your opinion matters.

Review this book on your favorite
book site, review site, blog or your own
social media properties and share
your opinion with other readers!

HARLEQUIN®

A Romance FOR EVERY MOOD™

Stay up-to-date on all your
romance-reading news with the
Harlequin Shopping Guide,
featuring bestselling authors, exciting new
miniseries, books to watch and more!

The newest issue will be delivered right to you
with our compliments! There are 4 each year.

Signing up is easy.

EMAIL

ShoppingGuide@Harlequin.ca

WRITE TO US

HARLEQUIN BOOKS
Attention: Customer Service Department
P.O. Box 9057, Buffalo, NY 14269-9057

OR PHONE

1-800-873-8635 in the United States
1-888-343-9777 in Canada

Please allow 4-6 weeks for delivery of the first issue by mail.